3, 21. 22 2 23 40 24

SKELMERSDALE

FICTION RESERVE STOCK

EXIT

EXIT

Duncan Kyle

HarperCollins*Publishers*

05587522

HarperCollins*Publishers*
77–85 Fulham Palace Road
Hammersmith, London W6 8JB

Published by HarperCollins*Publishers* 1993

1 3 5 7 9 8 6 4 2

A catalogue record for this book
is available from the British Library

ISBN 0 00 224041 6

Photoset in Linotron Trump Mediaeval by
Rowland Phototypesetting Ltd, Bury St Edmunds, Suffolk

Printed in Great Britain by
HarperCollinsManufacturing Glasgow

For Alison, of course

1

The Doctor was blowing cool and boisterous in the late afternoon; that's the Fremantle Doctor, the breeze off the sea that knocks down the Perth area's heat. We had a fair old lop bouncing us on the Indian Ocean; the water hissed and bumped, and shrapnel flew as Bob Collis cut his toenails with one of those Japanese gadgets. You could cut bolts with them. Beautiful afternoon, it was. We were full of grilled crayfish fresh off the Rottnest reefs, of Chardonnay and of good temper. The western sky stood streaked turquoise and salmon pink as the sun began to fall into the water, and Bob used his unoccupied foot to steer us neatly south of Rous Head and into the harbour. Bob's sixty plus now, and he got himself a mooring young, with the freehold to go with it. Parking a boat in the metropolitan area's three times harder than parking a car; but not for Bob. In a trice, as we sailors say, the *Sundown Marauder* (which I contend is a name for a drink, not a boat) was out of the water being hosed down. Five minutes later I was in my old Range Rover en route for South Perth and my apartment.

I walked in, drank a glass of cold water, and switched on the answering machine. When you're a youngish lawyer with a smallish office and a newish brass plate on the door you need all the work that may be offered. I hate answering machines and was just a bit ashamed of having one. But I listened. Only one call: a voice I didn't immediately identify said, 'Jim here, John. Got news for you. Give me a call back.' Click. Why do people dislike telling you who they are? There are thousands of them, and they drive me nuts. Combine that habit with Australia's other habit of dispensing entirely with surnames and confusion breeds faster than laboratory mice. How many Jims do you know – or Peters or Marys or

Craigs or Lees of either sex or both? So I sat down and played the tape again several times and hunted through mental sound archives for timbre, pitch and age group.

Three possibilities. I mean, this wasn't a serious problem or anything approaching it – merely one of modern living's multiplying irritations. Tonight, or maybe tomorrow, Jim was bound to call again.

But inside me some restless demon demanded to know *now*! I began dialling. But five Jims later the mystery remained. Then, while I was trying to find further Jims in my address book, the phone rang and there he was. I'd never have thought of McQueen in a century of effort; he's a doctor down in Albany, as far south as you can get and still be in Western Australia, and among his patients are fairly desperate criminals locked up in the maximum security prison there. I know him well enough to say, 'G'day, Jim', and that's about all.

'Sorry to bother you Sunday night,' he said.

'My pleasure, Jim.' I waited. He might be buying a house, divorcing a wife, making a will, any of them useful business for me.

'It's Peterkin,' McQueen said.

'What about him?'

'He's dead.'

I felt that thud in the abdomen you get with bad news. You believe a doctor when he says things like that, but my mind found it hard to accept. We were talking here about a man who had always looked like the life force incarnate.

'How?'

'Inquest in the morning. We'll know then for certain. It looks like he fell down some stairs.'

'The way people often do in prisons?' I inquired. 'Assisted by others.'

'Don't think so – not this time. I thought you'd want to know. He was your client.'

'Who's doing the postmortem?'

'Government pathologist. Will you be at the inquest?'

I thought a moment. Albany's four hundred kilometres from my little burrow and it was now eight o'clock. Sitting there with the phone in my hand, I pictured five hours on the dark, quiet Albany Highway with big kangaroos on the edges of the road, and sometimes in the middle of it, standing petrified in your lights. Hit a big bull and he's likely to come crashing in through your windscreen and rip you to bits in his death throes. Dangerous. Anyway I hate random killing.

'I'll try to make it. What time?'

'Ten, but I may be able to get a delay.'

'Okay. If you can, I'll leave early. Let me know, will you, Jim?'

After all that I made myself a Scotch and water and sat myself in an easy chair, and soon found I was thinking about Peterkin . . .

Hell of a name for a start, isn't it? Until him I'd only ever met a Peterkin in *Coral Island* when I was a boy. But this Peterkin was nothing like R. M. Ballantyne's juvenile lead. No boy, this. My Peterkin was – correction: had been – a real giant. Six feet three or so, and with all the clichés applying – hard as nails, tough as teak, broad as a barn door – and a good wide grin that made friends any time he cared to make them, which wasn't all that often, because Peterkin was private.

I don't mean he was private in the sense of being modest, as many of us are: we people who switch on the TV and close the door and don't want to open it again; who keep ourselves to ourselves etc, etc.

No – Peterkin's privacy went down very deep. It amounted, often, to silence, to distance. Not that he was rude – but if people invaded his space, Peterkin excused himself and went away, usually about a hundred miles.

I'd defended him twice. Bob Collis had given him my card. Bob's a retired superintendent of police and a relative of sorts, and he hands out my cards like confetti whenever he goes visiting old mates at their HQ down the far end of Hay Street.

The first time, Peterkin had been in a street fight. Three beery larrikins had jumped him, looking for money for more beer, and Peterkin had fought them off. Trouble was one of them had died and the charge against Peterkin was manslaughter.

9

'Defendant could just have knocked the bloke,' the prosecutor said to me, 'but what he chose to do was turn the neck through three hundred and sixty degrees.'

'Accident,' I said. 'Didn't mean to do it.'

'Just look at him. Knows exactly what he's doing, that bloke.'

And you couldn't deny it. There was a special stillness about the big man, an air of hard, contained competence. I'd spent quite a bit of time talking to him by then, and all through it the impression grew: inside Peterkin's skin there was indeed a man who knew what he was doing. You'd have to be very drunk indeed to think of taking him on.

He got three months. When he came out he went away; I don't know where, specifically, but he'd earned his living in the hard jobs all his life: pearling in the heat up in Broome, loading ore in Hedland, tree-felling in the hardwood forests of the south-west. All the jobs where big men earn good money. But always I wondered why. He was not dim. or reliant on strength alone. You only had to meet his glance to see the intelligence.

Perhaps he'd been unlucky to go to prison that first time. Perhaps my defence could have been better. The second time was another matter. To begin with – well, I'd have thought he was honest.

'I tire of the work,' he'd told me. There was an accent he'd never lost. 'I want to see my country again.'

'Where's that – what country?'

'Montenegro.'

So he was Jugoslav. Lots of New Australians are and were.

'That's why you did it – to pay the fare?'

He nodded politely, smiling at me.

'Tell me.'

'I meet a man in prison first time. He tell me if I need money, there is a way.'

'Go on.'

Peterkin was amused. He faced a year or three in prison, but this had been fun.

'Gold,' he said, smiling. 'You know about gold?'

'All West Australians know about gold, Peterkin. You know that.'

'Okay. An ounce is maybe three-fifty dollars US. But how much for nugget one ounce?'

'Bit more.'

'Can be two times. Three times. This man tell me.'

What this man had also told him was how to make a furnace. It's a trick with long white whiskers on it, this one. What you do is you buy some gold, an ounce or two will do. Then you set up a furnace somewhere quiet, and while the heat builds up to the thousand degrees or so necessary to melt the magic metal, you scrape a little hole in the dirt and you pop into it a couple of little bits of quartz and maybe a bit off the handle of Auntie's silver salt spoon to give a trace of silver for authenticity's sake. Then when the gold has melted in its little crucible, you take the tongs and pick up the crucible and you pour the liquid gold into the hole in the ground and drop some more rubbish in with it so the shape is nice and irregular.

You then sit and smoke and wait until it's cool enough to handle and when it is you hoick it out of the ground and go looking for a sucker.

Peterkin argued with the police, and with me, that it wasn't dishonest. Mother Nature's own *natural* gold nuggets were made the same way, he said. If you bought a nugget from Peterkin you bought a real gold nugget, he said. What was the difference?

The difference, said the judge, was called intent to defraud, so off Peterkin went for three years in Albany, still grinning. He'd sold a twenty-ounce nugget to a rich American tourist for fifty thousand. The tourist was thrilled and all would have been well except that Peterkin had been careless in his manufacturing and the head of a rusty nail was faintly visible among the rubbish in the nugget. Only faintly, but the American had a wife who carried a jeweller's loupe in her handbag as a matter of course, and off to the cop shop she sprinted.

11

By that time, though, Peterkin was airborne, Jugoslavia-bound. They arrested him only on his return.

But, though pretty well everything was tidied up, one question did remain. Had Peterkin actually succeeded in spending fifty thousand US dollars during a fairly short holiday trip to Montenegro? It seemed unlikely, but Peterkin was very silent on the matter.

So it was thought the balance might still be around somewhere. And it seemed to me there would be people, especially in a maximum-security prison, who would wish to learn where.

2

Technically I had neither obligations nor responsibilities in the matter of Peterkin, and certainly I had no standing in the coroner's court. I sat there as a spectator, and in ten minutes the whole thing was wrapped up. Peterkin had indeed fallen down a flight of steel stairs; no one had been near him at the time; his heart was sound. The pathologist suspected a stroke, given age and size and slightly raised blood pressure.

A bit of a mystery, then. And Peterkin bound for a pauper's grave, his affairs bound for a lawyer appointed by the state; no last will and testament anybody knew about.

Afterwards, outside the court, I talked to McQueen.

'I do a Sunday locum while the prison doctor has the day off,' he told me. 'So when he fell, they called me out, and I remembered he was a client of yours.'

'Had you examined him before?'

'Yair.'

'Was he healthy?'

'Youser. Strokes are funny things though. They can chop a bloke down any time.'

'You think that's what happened?'

He shrugged. 'Who knows? Something happened. There was some occurrence within the physical envelope – goodbye Peterkin.'

'Was it really a stroke, or is that a convenient hook to hang it on?'

He shrugged again. 'Maybe he just over-balanced. Everybody does sometimes. He'd have struck his head bouncing down the steel stairs, there'd be a bit of haemorrhaging maybe. What's the difference?'

'The difference between natural causes and accidental death,' I said, and told McQueen about the money.

13

McQueen said, 'Ah,' in a thoughtful way. After a moment or two, he said, 'I was with the assistant governor when his possessions were brought in. There was four dollars in bits and pieces, his uniform, a tape player, and a postcard. Nothing else.'

'Nothing?'

'A handkerchief in his pocket. Peterkin travelled light.'

'Who'd sent the postcard. Did you look?'

'Yes. Picture postcard of Singapore Harbour and the message said, "I'll come and see you quite soon." Signature Nik, spelled N-I-K.'

The Christian name thing again. 'Man or woman?'

'The writing? Quite bold. Upright. I'd guess a man.'

It was an odd sensation to nibble away at Peterkin's carapace of privacy. There'd have been women in the life of such a man, but I'd never seen or heard of any of them. Nor had anybody visited him in prison; I knew that because I'd asked. I said, 'Well, his privacy is total now,' and was shaking McQueen's hand when the assistant governor of Albany prison came out and said there was to be a funeral at Geraldton according to Peterkin's wishes, as expressed on entry to the prison. Money had been deposited. By whom? By him.

'Geraldton,' I said, 'is a bloody long way.'

'He bought a grave plot there.'

I remember sighing an audible sigh and saying, 'I wonder if there'll be anyone else there.'

Three days later, five hundred miles away, I stood in the baking sun as the service was said over Peterkin, and he was laid in the ground by four strong mutes.

And I wasn't alone. I had been at first, in the church. Then clicking footsteps sounded behind me and I turned my head and saw a woman entering a rear pew. She was in black, complete with veil, so at that time I couldn't see anything of her face. Later, though, with Peterkin buried, as she hurried off to a car, I had a glimpse of eyes that looked a little aslant and high cheekbones to match. Asian, probably somewhere in her late twenties, and attractive.

As she went by me, I asked, 'Are you Nik?', and was ignored. In seconds she was gone – inside a metallic blue Holden of which there are thousands. The priest came over. 'In a hurry,' he said.

'Know who she is?'

He shook his head.

'You were pretty close to his character in your oration,' I said. 'Did you know him well?'

'Never met him in my life. He got the grave thirty years ago. Don't know why he chose Geraldton. I know of no connections here.'

'Strange.'

'I'm new, of course. Perhaps he lived here once.'

I said I believed Peterkin had once been a cray-fisherman, and the priest nodded absently.

'Certainly had things prepared. The bloke had bought the grave. He'd even got his own tombstone ready.'

'How long ago was that?'

'Dunno. Fair old while, I think. It's in the store.'

'I'd like to look at it.'

'No worries. Over here.'

As we walked off together I saw a bloke in a dark Akubra hat looking our way. He stood a hundred metres away, and had been there a while.

The tombstone leaned against the wall of the asbestos shack, wrapped in corrugated paper and tied round with baler twine. 'Not often,' the priest went on conversationally, 'that people have 'em cut beforehand. They don't know the date, you see. Don't want to, either, I expect.'

He cut the string with a penknife and pulled off the paper, and we stood back to look. Most people's gravestones are pretty wordy. Dearly beloved husband of Elizabeth Mary and father of Albert and Henry and Jane and Eliza and so on, plus years of birth and death. This one bore a single word:

Peterkin

There was also a design. A leaf, as crudely chiselled as was the lettering.

Plainly he'd done it all himself.

15

Minutes later I was on the road south.

That was it. My car had a lot more kilometres on the clock by the time I was back in Perth, and there wasn't a thing to show for it.

Not until morning, when the post arrived.

Among the junk about computer printers and filing cabinets and life assurance schemes, there was an A4 envelope *sealed and taped*. All very secure. So secure it took knives and scissor blades to break in. Even then there was another envelope inside: a white one this time, also heavily taped. When I'd found my way inside *that*, I discovered a pile of dollars lay in my hands.

A lot of money – that much was immediately obvious. For quite a long time I just sat and stared at it, probably with my mouth hanging open. I counted it, though, eventually.

The notes were American: fifty-six of them, fifty-five of one thousand dollars. The remaining piece of paper was a one-dollar bill: perfectly ordinary, except that a design had been drawn on it.

In the pattern of a leaf.

Right, I thought, mind like a steel trap. No problem and no mystery. This money came from Peterkin. Plainly he hadn't posted it himself, being dead at the time when it went into the slow-but-moderately-sure grip of Australia Post.

But the cogs meshed and the thought-engine ran readily enough: here was missing money returned to an officer of the court (which, like all solicitors, I am). And not hard to arrange. 'Listen, mate, keep this for me and if I die suddenly, bung it in the mail, okay?' Peterkin had been honest in the end, despite earlier and minor deviations. There was almost something pleasant about it: the sense that a circle had finally been closed with decent propriety.

I found myself thinking about Peterkin, then about his American victim and that hard, hard lady, the tourist's wife (Lord preserve *me* from one like that!) and the fifty thousand they'd both sworn they'd given Peterkin.

Fifty thousand. Having got it, our boy set joyfully off to his Montenegro homeland, there to holiday and meet old

16

friends and drink much slivowitz. I'd wondered before how much he'd spent on his nice vacation. Now the answer seemed to be that he'd spent almost nothing, had even made a profit of five thousand.

That's clever operating.

The notes sat there, smiling at me, as my steely mind sauntered along. Bit of profit, yes, but he could comfortably have made that in a building society: only ten per cent, after all, and there'd been a pile of shares on the Perth Exchange that had done a lot better than ten per cent since Peterkin heard the door go slam. Maybe he wanted the money to be returned to the tourist – and the lady with the loupe. Okay, but if so, why post it to yours truly, John Close, formerly a prosperous young partner in a highly successful Perth firm, now a solo player in the great game of law, a fact Peterkin knew very well. John Close might very well pocket the lot, a thought which was going temptingly through John Close's mind. Nobody'd know, Satan whispered, that it was sent to you; there's *no* record. Little notions like that.

I don't *think* I'd have pinched it, left to myself. But what stopped these fledgling criminal impulses in their tracks was a new realization that all this had been recently engineered! By somebody, presumably Peterkin, who'd carved one leaf and drawn another so that only I knew the various connections. I thought: if he was scheming complex schemes, he'd include something somewhere to prevent a rascally lawyer pocketing a capital sum.

Why scheme at all, though? He could hardly be sending *me* a message, by way of all these flounces and curlicues. Any message could easily have been written out and sent with the dollars. Perhaps it had been. I went through the thousand-dollar notes one by one, examining each and every piece of paper on both sides, holding them up to the light. There was just the drawing of a leaf on the one-dollar bill, nothing else.

I looked at the ruins of the white envelope. Nothing. The manila envelope showed the previous day's Perth postmark and my name and address – inscribed in a hand that in an odd sort of way looked faintly familiar. The letters were all *too* square or too rounded to be natural, in a way I'd seen before. After a moment it came to me – whoever had addressed the envelope had used one of those plastic lettering stencils that come in drawing sets.

I remembered a splendid phrase of Churchill's about the riddle wrapped in a mystery inside an enigma. Somebody *must* be playing games, but you don't play silly games at fifty-five thousand dollars a throw!

Try it another way – what *had* Peterkin set out to achieve? He couldn't have known I'd be at his funeral, and I'd been only a few months in my little office. But the leaf design had to be important, or he wouldn't have repeated it.

Above all, the money was for a purpose; I knew that. Peterkin had not been a man who did things idly. But what *could* the purpose be?

I was due in court, and to court I went. In my position at that time you're glad of any work you get, and you try to do it well so there'll be more. I had one case and got appointed to another, and won one and lost one and afterwards as I sipped some hot coffee, Austin Steere tapped me on the shoulder.

'I see you've lost a client.'

I turned. 'You see what?'

'Bloke with a funny name. Made gold nuggets. I prosecuted. What *was* –'

'Peterkin,' I said.

'Manslaughter, then manufacturing naughty nuggets,' Steere said. 'That was it, I seem to –'

'He was a good bloke. Shouldn't have gone to gaol.'

Steere held up a restraining hand. 'Tell it to the judge,' he said. 'I just state the facts. But I was wondering – did you go?'

'Go where?'

'His funeral.'

'Why d'you ask?'

'Ah, you *had* forgotten. Knew you would. It was in his

18

statement to the police, remember?' He looked at me inquiringly, waiting, and in that moment I did.

'Yes,' I said, 'the business with flowers . . .'

'On graves,' Steere said. 'That was the first case, the manslaughter. Your bloke Peterkin said, "We have a saying in my country"' – Steere was smiling, putting on an accent – '"that a friend is a man who brings flowers to your grave and my lawyer is my friend."'

I smiled and said, 'I remember now.'

'Did you take the flowers?'

'No – but I will.'

'Do you suppose,' Steere said reflectively, 'that it's a good thing to have your lawyer as your friend?'

'Depends who your lawyer is.'

That confirms that, I told myself, walking away from the court. Peterkin's first court appearance had been five years earlier, and even *then* he'd been preparing the way. Planting thoughts in my head. As long ago as *that* he'd been out to ensure I attended his funeral.

Funny. It really was. Why had he been thinking morbid thoughts of wreaths and death when at that time he'd been a strapping bloke in rude health? Why me, anyway – apart from the fact that I'd defended him without fee? Messages in the form of leaves, large sums of money – yes, it was funny all right. But not funny-comic – funny-strange.

Back in my office, I opened my safe and took out the banknotes again. One at a time, carefully now, I went through them again, holding each one up to the light. Fifty-five one-thousand-dollar bills had nothing to contribute. The one-dollar bill now seemed to have an extra watermark. Or a grease mark. I couldn't make it out, in spite of turning the paper round and round and over and over. After a bit I decided this wasn't properly a do-it-yourself activity. Expert advice, fortunately, ought to be at hand.

I rang Bob Collis, who said he was busy on his Shiraz vines and would I mind being brief because it was delicate and important work. 'Tell me about watermarks,' I said.

'Defensive measure,' he said. 'No other purpose. They go in during paper manufacture. Used by governments, banks, insurance companies and other friends of the common man, by paper-makers and stationers. Very difficult to counterfeit convincingly, though it can be done, I seem to remember, with certain oils or greases.'

'Thanks,' I said.

'No worries, son.'

'Aren't you going to ask?'

'Why you need to know? No.'

'Okay.'

He said, 'Last time I got involved with you, it turned unpleasant.'

'So it did.'

'And I'm elderly now and happiest at gentle, outdoor tasks.'

'Goodbye, Bob.'

'But I do still have a friend or two in the police lab, if you have a sample.'

'Thank you.'

'I'll make the call, you deliver the goods, okay?'

There is, it seems, a fine, powdery chemical substance which adheres to oil or grease and not to paper. A quiet, balding police sergeant wearing a white coat sprinkled some of the stuff over my one-dollar bill, shook it about a bit, then blew. A small cloud of powder flew into the air. Some, however, remained attached. 'Best take yourself a photocopy,' said the sergeant.

I thanked him and he nodded. 'We keep a charity box over by the door,' he said.

So I paid and made my photocopy – I believe that, technically speaking, I was committing a serious offence by making photocopies of US banknotes – setting the copier to dark for contrast's sake.

There were four letters in the mark and they were set out – though not rudely – in a small design. They didn't constitute a word, or not one I could recognize. They would mean something to someone, no doubt; and indeed must have meant quite a lot to Peterkin, or he wouldn't have inscribed them so secretly and with such care on the dollar bill.

But how could he have known I'd actually *find* his phoney watermark? Or set out to discover what it was?

Because he knew me. Had taken care to know about me. Seemed to know me at least as well as I knew myself, and *that* wasn't an altogether comfortable thought.

3

'Lettering's clear enough, as you can see,' I said to the girl at the counter in the State Reference Library.

She gave me a nice, just-a-little-vacant smile. She was fair and tanned and shining with health and she had a straight nose that was much more accustomed to wearing barrier creams and Ray-Bans than pointing at books. She said, 'Er, well, I'm not sure,' and then smiled again hopefully.

'Perhaps there's somebody here who'd have that kind of knowledge?'

'There will be, no worries. Won't be long.'

I watched her walk away, tall and graceful. Perth grows them like that, almost as a crop, and like a crop a lot of them are exported – to chorus lines in places like Paris and Las Vegas, where the tallest in the row are the West Australians. She might not have a PhD but she had everything else, including manners.

'Mr Forrest can help you, sir,' she said, 'if you'll come this way.'

Mr Forrest's nose was very much of the books-and-beer-glass pattern. It hooked a little and pointed downward, and there was a small smile visible on either side of it.

I said, 'We're winning, are we?'

''Bout even. I haven't any Dutch.'

I said, 'Dutch?' And thought: where did Peterkin from Montenegro get tangled with Dutch?

'What you've got is the identifying mark,' Mr Forrest said, 'of the Dutch East India Company. Stands for several long, polysyllabic words, all middling hard to say. I can find 'em if you want 'em.'

'I'd be grateful.'

He nodded and smiled and walked off. The girl came towards me after a moment. 'You all right now?'

'Yes, I am. Thanks for your help.'

'Well, right,' she said, and she left me, to go and smile at a newcomer.

Perth's big new library really is a place where people smile, I thought as I saw Mr Forrest returning. He was carrying a piece of paper, which he placed on the counter in front of me.

And I frowned.

DE VEREENIGHDE OOST-INDISCHE COMPAGNIE

Those were the words on the paper. 'Reckon you may be right,' I said.

'We try to help.' He coughed discreetly. He was English, that was plain, and he said, 'You'll forgive me if I –' which is hardly Perth-speak, and went on '– I mean it really isn't my business *why* you want to know, but –' then stopped.

'I'd appreciate any help,' I said. 'Anything at all.'

'Well, you could visit the *Batavia* exhibition at the WA Maritime Museum in Fremantle. I believe I've seen this mark there.'

I said, 'There's one thing left unexplained.'

'I know. The letter A.'

'Could it be Amsterdam?'

Mr Forrest said, 'Oh, I'm sure it could, but I'm not sure if it is. If they can't tell you at the museum, I'll go into it for you with pleasure.'

There had been no need for him to explain *Batavia*; nor any need for me to ask. It's one of those things everybody knows about in the west. *Batavia* was a ship, wrecked on the coastal islands in the early seventeenth century, and a nasty, gory story it was. The wreck had been found in the 1960s, and, thanks to a lot of expert underwater archaeological work, many of *Batavia*'s timbers had been recovered and treated and reassembled. I ought to have been to see them long ago, but as a London friend (who passes St Paul's Cathedral every day yet has never been inside) once said to me, 'You don't, do you, when it's so easy?'

The exhibition, in the old Commissariat built by convict labour at Fremantle, is pretty beguiling. They brought tons of the *Batavia*'s oak timbers up after three hundred and fifty years on the reefs, and some of the skeletons, too. *Batavia*'s destruction on the rocks came about because a nasty piece of piracy went wrong. A lot of people were murdered. It gets to you as you stand looking, and it got to me to the point where I entirely forgot to inquire about the letter A, because I was looking too closely at some of the other stuff. And brooding.

Peterkin was pointing me in one direction or another; that was perfectly clear. My mind, alongside Forrest's at the reference library, made an immediate connection between the Dutch East India Co's logo and the wreck of *Batavia*. But it wasn't making any new connections now, as I moved through the cool, stone building, looking at the great sandstone gate, which, intended for a castle in Java, had ended up on the reefs; I simply had no idea what I was being pointed at.

I came to an exhibit showing a scuba diver looking down at the grinning skull and bones of one of the *Batavia*'s victims: dramatic to look at and the more impressive because everything was real. Yet *nothing* was real for me. What could Peterkin be trying to point me towards in this place? Some sign, some relic? A place, perhaps?

Some days I'm worse than others, really I am, but still, after a while, the light bulb did come on over my head as it does in the children's comics. Where, I asked myself, did *Batavia* actually sink? Because it didn't sink there in the museum.

Answer: the Abrolhos Islands.

And where are the Abrolhos?

Indian Ocean, off Geraldton.

And what is the industry there?

Answer: cray-fishing.

Everything depends on how you look at a thing, doesn't it? I'd already read the display card, earlier in my circuit of the exhibition, and it had meant nothing very much.

Now I read the words again. They said roughly this: 'In darkness, on 4 June 1629, *Batavia* ran aground on Morning Reef in the Wallabi group of the HOUTMAN ABROLHOS. Of the 360 people aboard, all but forty survived to struggle ashore on the little, barren island known today as Beacon Island.'

I stood back and thought for a bit about the links. About Geraldton, where Peterkin had chosen to be buried and whence the cray-boats sail to the rich Abrolhos fishing grounds; about the East Indies logo on the money; about the leaf design. Conceivably it *could* all have been coincidence, but the money and the careful directing of the clues at *me* pretty well ruled that out.

Peterkin's wishes could not, I thought, now be clearer. He'd laid a trail, and he'd wanted me to follow it once he'd gone; the money was to pay my way. Up to now, it hadn't involved me in anything more than a few hours at the wheel. But from here on . . . well, the 55,000 dollars seemed to indicate that something more than a bit of motoring was in prospect. So what about my job, my (ever-so-slowly) burgeoning legal practice? In other words, was I going to do as directed – or was I going to say to hell with it, and see what new work I could rake together? Last time I'd gone rushing off with a legal riddle, it had cost me a partnership. I tried to make all this into a rational-seeming decision, but there was no way that could be achieved. Truth was – I was intrigued.

The law, happy, as always, to wait, could therefore wait a little longer.

This thought brought a perceptible lift of the spirits. On leaving the museum, I glanced in the window of a bank and did a quick exchange calculation in my head. Changing my US dollars into Aussie dollars would give me nearly 65,000 dollars, so whatever my expenses might be, there'd be enough left for a decent fee. I spent twenty dollars on some first-class sea-food and a bottle of a West Australian white wine so crystal clear it gleamed, then went off to pack a grip with un-lawyer-like clobber, to fill the fuel and water tanks of the Range Rover, and to leave a note for my part-time secretary.

I felt as if I were going off on holiday, which, in view of what was to come, was the wrong sensation altogether. But the sun glittered invitingly on the carpet of broken beer bottles that line the roadside; the road itself was quiet, a tape Bob Collis had given me (of Shostakovich's 'Gadfly') buzzed along on the stereo as I went northward once again, heading for the weird world of the Abrolhos, about which I knew a little, but not enough.

Distant lights in the wide, encircling dark gave a first sight of the town. Geraldton isn't big, but it's busy. In three months a year it deals with thirty million dollars' worth of crays, which is a lot of lobster dinners. Then comes the wheat: there's a wheat belt a few hundred miles long in Western Australia, and much of the crop is exported through Geraldton. Then there are tourists, and winter-dwellers. Geraldton is a place where the sun shines all the time. Perth has cool, wettish winters, but Geraldton doesn't. It has a cathedral and an opera house and an air of contentment which attracts a lot of city dwellers to move themselves north for the winter. One of these days the world is going to wake up to Geraldton, and after that, in ten years it'll be the size of Tokyo.

I checked myself into a motel, went out looking for food and found fresh, fried schnapper down by the harbour. Strolling back amiably afterwards through the balmy evening, with the Southern Cross like platinum points in a velvet sky, I was passing a little line of shops –

'Close. Mr Close!' A deep doorway and, as I stopped and peered, a dark shape.

'Who –?' I began.

'Shhh. Pretend to look in the window, and then listen.'

I looked. The window was full of fishing tackle and cross-bows and nasty-looking knives. I waited.

'You are being followed,' hissed the voice. It all seemed impossibly melodramatic in the languorous warmth of the Geraldton night.

'By whom?'

'I think,' the voice continued sibilantly, 'that he's Russian. Be careful. Now go.'

'Who are you?' I muttered. I could see little in the deep doorway. The dark shape was a pile of plastic rubbish sacks.

'Go. I will be in touch again.'

I had alternatives. Go obediently on my way, or plunge into the doorway and get to grips – perhaps with a big cray-fisherman with a bale-hook in his hand. So I strolled off, now looking with care in all reflecting surfaces which might show anyone behind me. But either I was a poor spotter or no one was there. I passed two middle-aged ladies discussing grandchildren, and that was all.

Staring at the ceiling in my motel room, I brooded, as the wine wore off, on this strange occurrence, which seemed to come direct from one of those 1940s movies with Joel McCrea or Paul Muni. Questions bred questions. *Had* somebody been following me? Well, somebody else not only thought so but was making a drama out of it. Russians, indeed, scoffed what passes for my intellect – I'd never met a Russian in my life, or even had distant contact with embassies or consulates. Anyway, who *was* my informant, that lurker-in-the-shadows who must have spent an hour waiting for me to finish my plate of schnapper and emerge from the restaurant? I had the impression the hoarse whisper had come from a woman's throat, but it was no more than an impression, and when, in the darkness, I experimented with a whisper or two of my own, nothing was proved.

But the word 'Russians' was the one that echoed most loudly in my mind as the minutes passed, and after a while I found I was sitting up in bed with the light on, and wearing a heavy frown. Russians, I kept thinking, and following *me*!

I soothed myself down at about one-thirty, put the light out, and just about jumped out of my skin when the taps came at the window. Could this be the bloody Russians? You read about people being awakened in the small hours, terrified out of their wits. It's all true.

I got up, found the window latch and opened it, hoping a million sabre-toothed mosquitoes wouldn't swarm in. When I peered outside, there was stillness and there was silence. And after a moment I realized there was also a small piece of paper taped to the window glass. 'Go to No. 23, caravan park, Separation Point, at first light,' it instructed me, in English.

When I went to knock on the door of the trailer with '23' on it, having risen in the dark and walked a kilometre or so through a darkling world, the door opened before I managed to touch it. Trustingly I stepped inside.

The last and only time I'd seen her, she'd been veiled and dressed in black, hurrying towards a waiting taxi, and I'd had a quick impression of the high cheekbones and narrow eyes of an Asian face. Now she was jeans-clad. The face was still Asian.

'Who are you?' I demanded. 'And what's this about?'

'His daughter.' She was whispering.

'Peterkin?'

'Don't say it. And talk softly!'

'Why not?'

'Later,' she said. 'I'll explain later. Why are you here, in this town?'

I shook my head. 'My business.'

She frowned. In a face less harmoniously constructed the frown would have been a full-blown scowl. She was evidently displeased.

I said, 'What's your name?'

'Alex. You must believe in –'

'He didn't have a daughter,' I said. 'Or a wife. Not if we're talking about Pe . . . about *him*.'

'They never married.' She gave a toss of the head. 'But he was my father.'

'Okay. Now – why did you bring me here – and what's all this about Russians?'

'They are here. You saw the man at the funeral, did you – in the stupid hat?'

'It may be stupid,' I said, 'but the Akubra hat is Australian.'

She exhaled noisily through both nostrils. In most people it would have been a snort. 'I have a boat,' she said. 'She's tied up by the jetty at Fisherman's Wharf. Go there now. Go aboard. Wait for me.'

'Yes, miss,' I said. 'And the name?'

'I told you. Alex.'

'Of the boat, if you don't mind.'

'*Abrolhos Lady.*'

I said, 'Well, it's appropriate. Any way of making coffee on board?'

She snorted once more, then shoved me out, and I sneaked off through a kilometre more of the dawn streets, trying to look inconspicuous, and feeling all the time as though a pair of binoculars or – such was my idiot state of mind – a sniper's rifle was trained on the small of my back.

There's always bustle about a harbour in the early morning. Fishing boats were in with the overnight catch; men were fixing nets and pots, stringing things together, all those things fishing people do and lawyers don't. I looked for *Abrolhos Lady* and found her after a minute or two: white letters on a black stern, and the boat tied up alongside the jetty. A ladder with its iron rungs set into the stone of the jetty led a few feet down to the deck: not hard to negotiate. I tapped on the wood-and-glass hatch that led below and, getting no answer, opened it and clambered inside, and it swung to behind me. I was still fumbling for a light switch when there was a soft thud on the after-decking outside as somebody jumped aboard. There followed the sharp click of a lock.

4

'Hey,' I yelled.

But answer came there none. Instead a moment later I heard the sound of the engine turning over and firing, and I stopped shouting because the chatterky-chatterky of the diesel would comfortably drown my voice. I was in darkness – the utterly unfamiliar darkness of a strange boat, and the prisoner, at least temporarily, of Peterkin's supposed daughter, who, it struck me, watched too many episodes of too many TV series.

I didn't believe in the Russians for a moment. The Russian bear is all goodwill these days, isn't it? If I had, I'd have been terrified. Miss Alex, with her veils and waiting taxis and darkened doorways and nocturnal window-tapping, was an over-gilded lily. Accordingly I was concerned, but not exactly scared stiff. The boat would pull away shortly, I thought; it would then run for a while, then the hatch would open, and framed in it would be a pretty Eurasian face. So I felt around me in the darkness until I had worked out which bits of the boat I could sit on. I then sat and waited.

My forecast came true, more or less, except that the face framed in the hatchway turned out to be not Miss Alex's, but that of Popeye's old rival – the big, strong brute with the toothy snarl and the black whiskers.

'Stay there,' he rasped. 'Don't come out. I mean it. Okay?'

I nodded and he moved away. Now a new face appeared in the square of daylight. I said, 'Alex, this is ridiculous!'

She looked at me thoughtfully for a moment, then gave a sudden wide grin. 'I can see that you would think so. Okay, go on below. You can have your coffee and we'll settle things.'

'I'm not sure about settling,' I said, and I certainly wasn't. For one thing, if she was Peterkin's daughter, then all the dollars were hers. Whether she was born in or out of wedlock didn't matter, except for bits of legal process; she inherited, and I, as the lawyer, was now engaged in misuse and misappropriation of a client's funds! I'd be following the late Peterkin into Albany Gaol if I wasn't careful. For the moment, though, I didn't actually *know* she was who she said she was, and her physical appearance, I might plead, strongly suggested otherwise.

She bustled about. Ports were uncovered and light streamed in. She was plainly accustomed to what she was doing, automatically switching on a fan to clear gas from the bilges, before putting water on to heat.

I sat in silence at the galley table until the mug of hot coffee was in front of me. She plonked herself down opposite and looked at me through steam.

'If you could identify yourself,' I said, 'we'd be off to a useful start.'

'Can *you*?'

'Driving licence,' I said, taking out the leather case, 'Medicare, business card, Diner's and Visa.'

She opened a cupboard door. Inside, pinned to the wood, was a photograph of me. 'I believe you *are* actually you,' she said.

'And now it's your turn.'

She shrugged. 'I am the registered captain of this boat, licensed to fish here in the season.'

'Which isn't now.'

'No.'

'And your name is –'

She passed a certificate across the table. Ms Alex Tashita was entitled . . . etc. There was a photograph of her.

'Tashita?'

'My mother was Japanese. From Broome.'

'She's –?'

'Dead, Mr Close.'

'I'm sorry.'

'It's three years ago.'

31

All this had taken me nowhere. I said, 'Have you proof you're Peterkin's daughter?'

'There's a letter my mother wrote to me. That's all. She confirms that he was my father.'

'Was it sworn and witnessed?'

'No.'

All the same, I reflected, it had weight. 'Did he acknowledge you in public?'

She shook her head and the blue-black hair swung, gleaming in a spotlight from the port. 'You knew him, Mr Close. He was a very secret man. When I saw that little piece in the newspaper that he had died, I felt a part of me went with him.'

'Secret' struck me as an odd choice of word. This girl was articulate and intelligent. I said, 'I'm not correcting your syntax for fun. You mean he was secretive?'

'He was secret. Everything about him. A walking secret, that was my father. You never saw him with people, I'm sure.'

'I saw him either alone, as his lawyer, or in court where there are always people. But I know what you mean.'

She nodded. 'His whole life was what I said – a concealment. He lived in shacks, or old trailers out in the bush. There were lots of them, Mr Close, more than I can count. When I was a kid, Mother and I used to go to live with him in one of those places for a few weeks, or a month or two. He didn't come to us in Broome, except once or twice, and always at night, just to bring money.'

'Where'd he get the money?'

She said, 'He'd get jobs. Then move. He'd send money. Always sent money. Never missed more than once or twice. He'd work cattle or timber or shell, you know the kind of job – away from crowds of any kind. Hard work in the sun, big hat over his eyes. Usually a beard and dark glasses.'

'Any idea why?'

'You won't believe me,' she said. She looked down at the coffee in her cup, swirling it thoughtfully.

'I already don't, if you're talking about the Russians. Have you proof "the Russians" wanted him?'

The slant eyes glittered. 'Proof? You mean a certificate like that one – signed and officially stamped? Of course I haven't! But I have a lifetime of knowing my father, seeing him always in hiding, wanting to be with us, with his family, but not daring to *live* with us, except in the remotest places he could find.' She paused. 'You knew him. Would you say he was a coward?'

I pictured Peterkin in my mind, and felt myself smile. 'It's not the first word I'd choose.'

'You see!' she said, almost triumphantly. 'He was incredibly strong, too. But I have seen him sneak off into the bush and hide when a child came near.'

'Seems simple enough,' I said. 'He must have been A Man with a Past. Somewhere, some time, he'd done something he shouldn't, and it put him permanently on the run.'

'Like what?'

I shrugged. 'There are plenty of things. Murder, for one. He killed one man for certain. That much we know.'

'An accident,' Alex said dismissively.

'Court didn't agree. Have you any clues to his past – whereabouts in Montenegro he came from?'

'He wouldn't say. Wouldn't tell me, wouldn't tell my mother. Past is past, he told her; it is over, I not want to remember.' She was mimicking him, but fondly.

'When he took that holiday there, didn't he even send a postcard?'

'One.'

'From?'

'London,' she said. 'From London.'

'Why was he in London?'

She spread her hands, palms upward, in the universal gesture meaning: who knows?

'You still haven't told me,' I said, 'about several things that seem relevant. This belief of yours that the Russians wanted him – what's it based on?'

'I told you – I have nothing more than impressions. I've heard him talk in his sleep in a strange language –'

'I expect that Montenegran, or Serbo-Croat or whatever it is, sounds fairly damn strange.'

Alex said impatiently, 'He would often scratch with a stick in the dust – letters he obliterated instantly if anyone went near, even my mother or me.'

'Russian letters, were they?'

'I don't know – didn't see them.'

I said, 'Russian must be doubtful. Tell me about your mother.'

She gave me an angry glance. The Russian notion in her was deep and long-lasting, almost bred in the bone. She thought better of the irritation, though, and said, 'She was Japanese, a girl from one of the old pearling families.'

'Where'd she meet him?'

'Broome in the early fifties. He stayed nearly a year, that first time.'

'She was content, was she? With all this secrecy with a man who'd never live at home, who didn't marry her, who was forever in hiding – what did *she* think?'

'It may surprise you, but she was happy, Mr Close. She was a product of the Japanese tradition and her man's behaviour was not questioned. Remember he always did his best for us. There was a house and money. She never had to work. For me he was buying this boat. We were never poor.'

'You're going to be even better off,' I said.

I told Alex about the money and she wasn't much surprised because it was she who'd posted the manila envelope, although she didn't know it contained money. Peterkin had once given her a packet to be opened only after his death. The other thing in the packet was her mother's declaration that Alex was his daughter. She showed me that, too.

'Why didn't *he* confirm it?' I asked.

'He never would, that's all.'

'You asked him?'

'A hundred times.'

'Did he give you a reason?'

'It was important nobody knew he had a daughter – or a child of any kind. That's what he said; it's all he ever would say.'

34

I sipped the coffee and looked at her. 'What is it that *you* want?'

She said simply, 'To find out. What do *you*, Mr Close? Why are you here a second time?'

'To find out, like you. He set me a riddle. I want to find the answer.'

'What's the riddle?'

'All right, but I need some assurances. Who's your cabin boy – and where am I being taken?'

'He's Joe Hag, he's a kind of uncle or something, and he works with me.'

'With or for?'

'With. Half-shares on catches, running costs, the whole thing. Except she's my boat, and you're not being taken anywhere. We are standing offshore so you and I can talk privately.'

We wrangled around it, then. Did she know why Geraldton was so important to Peterkin? She didn't, and why was I there? Well, I'd been pointed at the place. Pointed – how?

And so on.

I didn't even mention to her the leaf pattern and its recurrence, even though it was the real reason I was there. But to pass it on to someone else, even to Peterkin's own daughter (if she was) and sole surviving relative, still seemed something of a betrayal.

We got on to the man himself, and what he was like. She told me how he always loved water all his life: how a few times when she was smaller, he took her to visit the dolphins at Monkey Mia, to touch them and swim with them. 'That was his idea of paradise,' Alex said. 'In the water at Shark Bay with those beautiful creatures. Have you been? Do you know what I'm talking about?'

'Yes, I know,' I said. And it's true – until you've shaken hands with a wild dolphin you haven't lived. 'I always wonder what lunatic called it Shark Bay!'

'When I was bigger, when I could begin to steer a boat, we used to go together out there' – she pointed a finger westward – 'to the Abrolhos. It's where I learned. You have to learn fast among the rocks. It's not just a matter of catching crays, you know, you've got your life at risk every time you go in to pick up your pots.'

'But you like it, and *he* liked it.'

Alex said, 'He could be by himself there. If I say it's another world, you'll think that's just a cliché – yet you couldn't duplicate it anywhere on earth. But what made the islands for *him* was the privacy. We had a little shack on an island in the Easter group and we were alone there, him and me, and sometimes Joe Hag, too.' She grinned reminiscently, and that grin, occasional as it was, seemed to change her personality. Usually she was serious, almost grave; but grinning gave her an air of mischief. 'Mostly the islands don't rise more than a few feet out of the water. If the ocean gets up it'll wash clear over. When it happened to us, Dad used to laugh and start building another shack.'

'Was he good with a boat?'

'I'm better; so's Joe Hag. But Dad could manoeuvre pretty well.'

'Did he,' I asked innocently, 'have favourite places to fish, favourite islands and reefs?'

'The one we always lived on in the season,' Alex said. 'I don't think it has a name – it's only half an acre – but he said he was making me a present of it and we always called it Alex Island.' Then she looked at me, head cocked in inquiry. 'Would you like to see it?'

We were nearly three hours getting there. The water was bouncy, the way it often is off the coast of WA. You get a seven- or eight-foot swell, and it looks okay because there's not much white on it, but what you have to remember is that it's had six thousand miles from the Cape of Good Hope to gather its strength and even on a good day it'll fling you about.

I talked to Joe Hag as he stood at the helm, his big feet just hanging on to his 'thongs' by means of massive, almost prehensile, great toes. The 'thongs', in turn, hung on to the decking. I hung on to the rail and cross-questioned him. Yes, Peterkin had been his friend. Yes, Alex was Peterkin's daughter. No, he knew nothing of Peterkin's origins, Peterkin's holiday in Europe, etc, etc. I liked Joe Hag: a good, straight, loyal man. Alex, meanwhile, had busied herself in the galley, and up came bacon sandwiches with fried eggs tucked inside, and mugs of coffee. There was a breeze of sorts, and any amount of flying spray. As mornings go, that one was a beauty, full of the exhilaration only nature can give. It was full of optimism, too, for a while. Peterkin's spirit messages had indicated the Abrolhos, and to the Abrolhos I was bound.

I was close to singing shanties. But then Joe Hag nudged me and gave a nod of his head, and when I looked there was a great black dorsal fin about thirty yards away; its tip must have stood a good four feet clear of the water, and the brute's back wasn't even breaking the surface; Heaven alone knows how big it was.

'White pointer,' Joe said conversationally. The rest of the world calls them Great Whites, but a rose by any other name smells as sweet, I suppose, and that was a death machine out there. It stayed with us, sniffing, for a few minutes, and we never saw anything but the fin, nor wanted to, and then suddenly it was gone, and the earlier sense of bright hope was gone with it.

Alex Island wasn't your usual landfall: we didn't catch sight of it in the far distance and sail slowly closer; one moment there was an empty sea and the next we were in among a scatter of rock and reef and white eddies and Joe Hag was busy with gear, throttle and rudder like a man playing an organ in a pub Friday night. At the highest point the little patch of rock couldn't have been more than ten feet out of the ocean. Yet, miraculously a couple of wooden shacks, that looked as though they'd been banged together out of packing cases, stood up there.

'Home!' Alex yelled in my ear.

By now we were in a still little pool in the lee of the rock – a freakish place where *Abrolhos Lady* rode in flat water, rising and falling no more than a few inches with the passing swells.

Alex stood up at the rail and jumped confidently ashore. I stood there too, hesitated, then hesitated again. It wasn't much more than a metre I had to jump, but there were saw-toothed rocks down there, and falling between boat and rocks wouldn't make for much amusement.

My cowardice did, though. Alex appeared before me, laughing, hand outstretched, yelling 'Jump!' And I did so, and of course there was nothing to it, was there?

'Come and I'll show you,' she said merrily, marching off. But not marching far: the little island was perhaps sixty yards long by fifty wide at its widest and longest points. We went first to where one of the huts stood. It was bare and empty and the wood looked damp.

'You could actually live in that?' I said.

'Very comfy – you'd be surprised.'

But it didn't seem comfy to me. The flimsy woodwork had about it the white look of bleached bones, as though for a long time the water had been at it, and then the sun, and then the water again.

'Three-month season?'

'Right,' she said. 'And nice when it's over and you're counting the money.'

I stepped inside, looking around me: looking for anything, I didn't know what.

Behind me she said, 'Don't worry yourself. I've been over both shacks with a hell of a lot of care. There's not a message, not an artefact, not a sausage.'

Then she led me round the perimeter, the shore, the rock edge of Alex Island, pointing to places where, in good weather, she had swum, places for fishing, and other places where, as she said, 'You stay wide awake or the ocean lifts you off the rock and never puts you back!'

But the talk, ostensibly about fish or rock or wave or boat, was always really about Peterkin and his attendant mysteries. He strode with us every step we took, and he was, in death as in life, uncommunicative. The hour or so we spent there told us nothing that might remotely help to solve his puzzle. Apart from the two flimsy huts there was nothing of men on the island. Once there had been a layer of guano on top of the rock, as on many of the Abrolhos, but commercial mining had stripped it for the phosphates, and the profits, of course, and now there was just rock.

'No messages here,' I said finally, more than a bit disappointed. Peterkin had sent me up there and I'd just walked end-to-end and side-to-side of his favourite island. There was a feeling of futility.

'You thought he'd leave something here?'

'There's *something* from him in these islands. Has to be.' I turned to her. 'Look, apart from this island, what's the place you'd associate with him most strongly?'

She didn't hesitate a moment. 'Beacon Island.'

'That's where the *Batavia* was actually wrecked.'

'It's where the violence was. The story of it fascinated my father. He'd go ashore there sometimes and try to work out exactly where the horrors occurred. He made drawings showing –'

'Have you got these drawings?' I asked sharply.

She blinked. 'One of them, yes. Just one.' Then she gave me her grin. 'Reckon it's a map of pirate treasure, do you?'

'Where is it?'

'On the *Lady*.'

5

I knew the *Batavia* story, but only in the usual general terms.
What happened was this: a Dutch East India Company convoy, of half a dozen ships, sailed in 1628 from Holland for
Java. *Batavia* was the flagship – a big new vessel of twenty-
eight guns and the pride of the entire Indies fleet. Nevertheless, *Batavia* was in trouble from the start: there was a
conspiracy aboard; mutineers determined to take the ship
and steal her considerable treasure. All this a century and a
half before James Cook even discovered Australia.

Well, the convoy, having rounded the Cape of Good Hope,
was scattered by storms in the southern seas, and *Batavia*
finally found herself alone. She also soon found herself running aground on miles of dangerous reefs where no land was
thought to exist.

There was no getting the big vessel off and she duly sank,
but most of the people aboard got ashore on what's now
known as Beacon Island. The captain, a man named Pelsaert,
sailed for Java in the ship's boat to get help, and during the
four months he was away, more than a hundred of the sur-
vivors were murdered by the small group of mutineers. When
Pelsaert returned, the guilty men were captured and sum-
marily tried. Some had their hands cut off, some were
hanged, some both. In the tale of the *Batavia* wreck, all the
horrors happened exactly as you'd imagine, once you knew
that treasure, booze, women and children, and a criminal
conspiracy, were all put down together on an island the size
of a football field.

There were a few records, of course: Pelsaert's own, for a
start, plus details of court hearings and investigations in Java.
But records get dusty and dull after a century or two and
nobody took too much notice until the marine archaeologists

got to work in the early seventies and began bringing up bronze cannon, silver coins, and skeletons bearing the signs of violent death. At that point a lot of people became interested; here was *Treasure Island* brought to life.

Alex pulled a big sheet out from the rack beneath the chart table. We were heading northward now, away from the little island in the Easter group; with Joe Hag at the wheel, *Abrolhos Lady* was making for the so-called Houtman Abrolhos.

As she smoothed the paper on the table, I said, 'Who was Houtman?'

'Another Dutch sailor. They'd get blown south as they crossed the Southern Ocean, and finish up somewhere here. Know what Abrolhos means?'

'No.'

'It's a corruption of Portuguese. Means "open your eyes".'

'Portuguese were here, too?'

She shook her head. 'Not that anybody knows. But it's still good advice!'

The big piece of paper was part map, part diagram. Peterkin hadn't been much of a draughtsman, but he'd undoubtedly been meticulous. Each known incident was marked by a small black circle on its location, and a carefully drawn line leading to the margins, where a neat panel contained an explanation, the names of the people involved, and so on.

'How long did all this take?' I asked Alex.

'Two or three years, on and off,' she said. 'He'd read a new article, then bring it up to date – but not till he'd been to Beacon Island to walk over the ground and check.'

'Didn't go diving for coin?'

She looked offended. 'He'd never have done that! This was his hobby. He was absorbed in it. After he came back from Europe – when he was arrested – he was working on this map when the police came.'

'Were you there when they came?'

She nodded.

'What happened?'

'He was at the table –'

'Where was this?'

'A trailer near Carnarvon. He was going to go to work at the fruit.'

'And when the police came?'

'He just stood up and went with them. I never saw him again.' Her eyes glistened.

'You didn't visit him?'

'You must already know I didn't. Nobody did.'

'Why not?'

She said bitterly, 'The usual bloody reason, Mr Close – because nobody must bloody well know. If you'll forgive the unladylike speech.'

'Afterwards,' I said, 'after the arrest – what happened to his things?'

'I cleared out his trailer, that's all. There wasn't much to clear, either, just some work clothes and a few tools.'

'Papers?'

'His passport.'

'What was his first name?'

She smiled. 'Jack is what it says.'

'And the place of birth?'

'Yair,' she said. 'I looked at that too. Skopje.'

'Is that in Montenegro?'

'Funny thing, I didn't bring an atlas.'

A double stamp of Joe Hag's foot on the decking above our heads interrupted us and Alex scurried obediently up on deck. When I followed, a shade more slowly, having paused to take another hopeful look at the diagram, this time from slightly longer range, they were standing together, staring open-mouthed at something.

'Come look at this!' Alex said.

I turned and then gasped. No more than half a mile away the black shape of a submarine was passing us on the surface. I know nothing of such things, and on the rare occasions I'd seen one near the naval base at Garden Island, it had always looked long and flat and low in the water. This one didn't. It was a monster, and rounded.

'That, mister,' Alex said, in quiet awe, 'is a nuke.'

Several men stood atop her sail. We scrambled for the

binoculars to get a better look, and they were laughing and waving. They wore dark trousers and white sweaters and no hats. When my turn with the binoculars came and I got a better look, I could see no markings anywhere: not on the men and not on the ship.

By then she'd passed us, making no sound.

'Russian,' Alex said.

'More likely Brits,' I said. 'Or the Americans. Remember the Pacific Defence Treaty.'

'Russian,' Alex repeated. 'There's not a paint mark on her. But there'll be other marks unless she's careful of the rocks.'

The sub was turning as she spoke, the bow going round to point westward where the water was deeper and safer. We stood watching as the silhouette narrowed and thinned.

'Reckon we should report that?' Joe Hag asked.

'Why bother – they'll know all about her by now on Garden Island.'

He said stubbornly, 'How can they when the sea's so big? Nobody can watch the whole sea.'

'Oh, but they can, Joe. They've got more cables on the ocean bottom than you'd believe. When one of those fellers goes by, the monitors pick up its sounds. They can even identify individual subs by their engine sounds, so I read somewhere.'

Minutes later the sub was gone from view, and while we speculated about her nationality, *Abrolhos Lady* forged steadily north, and at last the ocean surface began to be marked in white as the swells began to find stone outcrops and break over them.

Careful navigation was needed now. With the cray-fishing season over, the sea here was empty of shipping. 'Mid-season,' Alex said, 'you'd see cray-boats everywhere. Get into trouble, you fire flares and its fair odds somebody'll see 'em. Maybe not in time to save your bacon, mind. Not now though!'

We came to Beacon Island from relatively calm water to the east. On the other side the Indian Ocean flexed its

43

muscles more evidently, but we could stand off and take a good look before venturing ashore.

There were a number of huts – one of them solid-looking and probably prefabricated, and presumably the property of the Maritime Museum and its archaeology team. The others were wooden and battered-looking, like the one Peterkin had put up on Alex Island. 'As a matter of interest,' I asked, 'what do the fishermen do out of season?'

'Tell him, Joe.'

Joe held up a big hand. 'One – you get your engine over-hauled. Two, you scrape your bottom.'

Alex giggled. 'The boat's bottom, he means.'

'Three,' Joe said, 'you make sure your cray pots are in good order. Four, you paint your boat.'

'And five,' Alex said, laughing, 'you go to Perth and take a suite at the Hyatt or the Parmelia , if they'll have you. And you stay drunk for a month, right, Joe?'

Joe gave a grim smile. 'Me, I build my house.'

'He's been building it twenty years, haven't you, Joe? When it's finished it'll be like the Bond building in Perth, only on a bigger scale.'

'You going ashore soon, Alex,' he asked, 'or do we talk all day?'

We went ashore.

'The size of a football field' – that's the phrase that's used for Beacon Island, and it sounds small put in those terms. But it's still a good-sized area to search with only two people to do it – Joe Hag having necessarily to remain on board.

We quartered it, Alex and I, then quartered the quarters, then consulted Peterkin's map and walked over the ground, heads down and side by side, and all we saw was rock and sand and traces of sea birds. Whatever else the island was, it was no territory for hiding things. From any one part of it you could see every other part. True, there were fissures in the rock, but they'd been well scraped out, either by treasure hunters or by archaeologists; after forty minutes or so, I began to get the impression that what we were doing was wrong.

Then Alex halted. 'Right on this spot,' she said, holding

up Peterkin's drawing to check, 'was where the boy was murdered. Know about that, do you?'

'In a sort of a way.'

'Andries de Vries, his name was,' Alex said. 'The mutineers made him cut the throats of the sick. Eleven the first time, or they'd kill him. Then he had to do it a second time. Then they killed *him* for talking to one of their women. Here – they did it on this spot.' She was hanging on to the map with one hand, and pointing with the other at one of Peterkin's panels, and now a sudden small flick of the wind had it out of her fingers and skittering, as paper does, off across the ground. I grabbed at it, missed and gave chase. Grabbed and missed again and then realized that a few more feet would see both paper and me in the sea. I dived full-length, pinning it down with my body, tearing the sheet and scraping skin off my knees in the process, and up comes Miss Alex saying crossly, 'You've ruined it!'

'It wasn't me,' I said, 'who let it go.'

'All the same, my father –'

'Would have understood.' I was gathering it together with care, putting edge to edge and keeping the folds straight. 'I hope you have some sticky tape on the boat!'

And then my eye fell on something. It was upside down, but only a few letters and easy to make out: what had happened was that the tail end of the word GALE and the front end of the word AFTER, each tinged by dark panel lines in Indian ink, were juxtaposed, the two bits making a word, as is common in crossword puzzles. The word, obviously, was LEAF.

Too simple, I thought; and looked again, turning the paper right way up. The word was 'leaf' all right, yet in some curious fashion one barely saw it with the paper held correctly. I reversed it again –

'What are you doing?' Alex demanded.

'I may have seen something,' I muttered, hurrying off, working out on-the-run the relationship between Peterkin's penmanship and God's outline of the coast.

'What have you seen?' Alex was trotting behind, asking and asking. 'Is there something on the diagram? *Tell* me!'

45

By that time I was almost at the spot. Nothing visible . . . not yet. In a moment, then . . . no, still nothing. Then I was there and the little rock space where island and ocean meet was quite bare.

I halted, blinking. It couldn't be, surely! This was exactly as . . . No, damn it – it wasn't *here*, it was *there*, yes, where the rock turned . . .

Yes, *there*!

Carved is maybe the wrong word, since it carries connotations of precision, but certainly the design of a leaf had been chipped into the solid rock sufficiently well to be recognized and deeply enough to endure.

Alex's footsteps pattered up beside me. 'What have you found?' She was panting a little, and so was I. I remembered I hadn't told her about the significance of the leaf pattern. I could hardly avoid doing so now. I pointed. 'There.'

'What's – ?' Then, 'Is it a leaf?'

'Yes,' I said. 'And it ought to be the X that marks the spot.'

The leaf didn't move, wouldn't move, couldn't *be* moved! I walked round it, shoved at it, did everything but jump on it. While I did all these futile things, I told Alex about her father and his leaves, and she said in response, quite angrily and with perfect truth, that while she'd been straight with me, I hadn't been straight with her and I was a drongo of deepest dye, and in among all the vituperation she said that to the best of her knowledge leaves had never figured in any way in Peterkin's life.

And then she said, 'If you're so sure you're on to something, whatever it is isn't on land, is it? So try the water!'

The leaf was chiselled into a rock no more than three feet from the sea's edge. I stood there, peering down into water which was not obligingly still and limpid, but moving and impenetrable.

'Anything there, you drongo?' Alex demanded alongside me.

'I can't see anything.'

'Should do. It's shallow here.' Then, 'Maybe it's not, though, not here. Can you swim?'

'At Scarborough Beach I can.'

'Then you'll be okay here, unless there's a moray eel backed into his hole down there. Or that shark we saw.'

'What about the Russian sub – he could be down there!'

'Just go look and see. I'll turn my back if you're the modest type!'

A minute or so later, dressed in the cute little crimson undershorts a smirking sister-in-law had given me last Christmas, I was in water up to my waist, hunting with my hands in the sand below the leaf rock. The sand was compacted and had to be scraped at, but it moved easily enough, and soon I found myself excavating a kind of hole. There was hard rock all around it, but the little fault – it was a bit like pushing your arm down a drain-pipe – was filled with sand. I pulled it out by the handful, and, as is the way with sand, half a handful immediately seeped back. Alex crouched, urging and asking. 'Dig harder!' she'd say. 'What's that – what have you found?'

'A pebble.'

'Dig some more!'

I dug all right, fingers sifting sand as I scooped handfuls out.

'Well?'

'I've reached the bottom. There's nothing.'

She said, 'Don't be ridiculous!'

I could actually feel the smooth, almost sand-free base of this natural hole in the rock. It was, I thought, very smooth . . . too smooth . . . I felt round it with my fingertips and found suddenly a little loop of some kind of fine wire . . . I pulled once, then again, and found myself lifting up, out of the ocean, a pale piece of what seemed to be pottery.

And, indeed, when it and I were on shore, and I was looking at it carefully, pottery is what it proved to be. A lump of clay, shaped into a rough, thick, leaf-like form, and then fired: that's what it was. 'Very crude,' I said, 'but it's undoubtedly –'

'It's a leaf,' Alex said. 'You wanted a leaf, you got a leaf. What do you mean, crude!'

'His defence was *my* job,' I said.

47

'Yes, and he went to gaol. That's not a bad leaf, when you think who made it! But what's it for?'

'And think,' I said, 'what he used for glaze, because it's glazed, and where he got the use of a kiln to fire it, because it *is* fired. And ask why.'

'Let me hold it.'

I passed it over. She rubbed it with her thumb on the underside, then leaned over to rinse the object in water. 'There are marks,' she said. 'Look.'

I looked and she was right. Letters had been scraped into the clay before it was fired.

'It says R & I Gtn.'

'Well, that's simple enough.'

She said, 'It means what I think it means, right?'

'Well, what it says to me is Rural and Industries Bank at Geraldton.'

'Me, too.' Alex grinned at me. 'What do you think, Mr Close – could we raise a loan on it?'

6

And we did, but not that day, because that bank, like every other bank on earth, is unfailingly and tightly closed when you need it most. The following morning we did find doors open for business, placed the leaf on the counter, and the girl looked down at it, then up at us, smiled, and said, 'Good morning. How may I help you?'

'This is a crudely made leaf, in pottery,' I said, and Alex booted my ankle for saying it. 'I have reason to believe that this bank holds something that relates to it, probably papers. Can you check your safe?'

She brought a manager. Whether he was *the* manager I don't know: he wore a frown and cream shorts and long socks and a yellow short-sleeved shirt plus tie, as bank staff do in Western Australia, at any rate when it's hot. Visitors from overseas are often surprised. He wanted to know who we were, did we have some form of ID, and so on, and what made us suppose, etc.

I showed him everything. The underside of the leaf, my Law Society card, and so on. He said to sit and wait, and came back a few minutes later with his frown gone and the words, 'No worries' on his lips. 'Trifle unusual,' he went on, 'some of these arrangements. This envelope to be handed over upon presentation of a leaf made of pottery, photographs attached.' Now he smiled. 'If you'd just sign here.'

The next few minutes saw us scuttling back to *Abrolhos Lady*, Alex chattering excitedly and me using the breath I wasn't wasting to take longer, faster strides. Solution at hand – that was what I was thinking, confident that the envelope's contents would tell us what the hell Peterkin's elaborate trail was all about, and why it had been laid.

I sat at the galley table, the envelope in my hands, looking

49

at it greedily. Somewhat disappointingly it was unmarked, though it *was* sealed several times round with sticky tape. I was about to start prising it open when Alex sat down opposite and, with a neat, swift flick of her hand, snatched the envelope from me.

'Ladies first,' she said.

I lunged to get it back. 'Property of the estate,' I said, missing. 'I'm his lawyer,' I insisted, not entirely accurately, 'and I have the right. You, until declared to be Peterkin's daughter, have no standing in the matter. Hand it over.'

So of course she didn't. We negotiated: we tossed for who read it first. She won, and having done so, deservedly broke two fingernails trying to get it open. Scissors were then employed on envelope and on fingernails.

There were a number of pages, all covered in bold script. 'Father's handwriting,' Alex said at once.

Here is what he wrote:

My name does not matter, unless it could be used to trace me. This is ever in my mind, for they do not forget, not ever, even after very many years.

First as to my age. I was born in 1923, in Ukraine, 1940 join the Red Army, 1941 fight German invaders, was wounded, was given medal, was in hospital near Moscow.

Stalin himself came to visit, to see us, mostly to be photographed with us is my thoughts.

A big thing happens on this visit he make. In my ward was man wounded in head. I do not say he was mad, probably he was very sane. But he have pistol, from where I do not know, but nobody know he has it.

There is photograph taken. Stalin sits among us; beds, chairs, all are so. And so. Stalin in the middle and I am next to him, on the left. My bandages cover chest and shoulder. They are new, very white.

So we sit. Then I see moving, in the corner where head wound was, see him rise from bed, move towards us. Stalin himself saw nothing. For photographer position mean men could not move.

I saw pistol, this man creeps behind the photographer, steps out with pistol raised, will now shoot at Stalin. I throw my body across Stalin's body and pistol shot hits me. Guards shoot man dead. Shoot me also. Think I am part of plan. Three wounds, but I live. I am taken to prisons, Lefortovo, Lubyanka. Am interrogated by MVD, have injections. I tell truth. In several weeks I am well again. Am to return to the front, every soldier needed as Nazi army approach Moscow.

Comes officer to my cell. He has blue shoulder boards. I did not then know these signal Kremlin Guard, Special Regiment. Officer say I will be transferred, if I agree.

I am surprised. In Red Army private soldier never asked to agree. When I say this, officer smile and say Stalin Guard all volunteers – heroic volunteers, he say. I say agree. Officer say everybody must hope it not necessary to save Generalissimo again. I must be proud to have saved him once. I am proud.

So I wear blue shoulder board, and am taught many things about combat, about defence of the self, about security. One day I am taken to special office where Stalin pin my medal on me and shake my hand. Soon after I am chosen as soldier-servant in white coat. Two on duty every minute, every day, every night, all of us young. We taste his food for poisons. We open his special sealed bottles of vodka. We open new tube every day of American toothpaste, clean our teeth before him. Stalin is careful man. Very careful.

We are careful, too, we soldier-servants. They tell us one time such a servant is shot for carelessness. They tell us he fail to stop important man at entrance to Stalin's apartments. Man was Beria, head of MVD secret police. Beria had him shot for this.

After one year I become evening servant with my partner Yuri Anastasovich Gusenko. Our duty from 6 P.M. to 2 A.M. includes Stalin in bath, we outside door ready if needed. Includes tasting food and drink when he eat dinner, in room if Stalin alone, outside if

51

he have guests. We bring tobacco and pipes, also brandy from Georgia in bottle made for medical products. When he leave table we follow to take position outside office suite or bedroom suite. We are armed, always, except when Stalin eat. All doors are steel, are locked by Stalin when he enter room. Always we and all others are on other side of door.

Many such things I remember but not important now. Important is period of 1943 after surrender German VI army group Stalingrad. Then five/six weeks Stalin use other apartments. Work under control of Engineer-General Chentessky. Twice I hear Stalin talk to Chentessky, ask when work done, if plans for disposal ready. I am invisible in white coat, nobody see servant. I hear things, little things, put little pieces together in my head. Men working on Stalin's apartment are prisoners, Germans, elite engineers from Sixth Army of Von Paulus.

All is finished. I return to duty in old apartments, in so-called Palace of Amusements, look round for new things. No new things, everything is same in same place. Soon we hear Chentessky is shot, Chentessky traitor, hear this from sergeant of soldier-servants as example of need for always perfect conduct. I am shocked that traitor can be so near Stalin. Gusenko, my partner, is cold man, not shocked, not anything. Be alert, he tell me, always alert. Duty is first, always first.

There comes a night, this is late 1943, when Gusenko is in dunny (lavatory) for third time. He has eaten something or has virus and we ask ourselves: has Stalin eaten this? But Stalin has seemed in health.

Then buzzes the intercom at my position, Stalin say, 'Quickly.' Has unlocked door. I enter.

He drunk. Deep drunk, now is vomiting. His greatcoat half on, half off. He sick on floor, self, on desk of papers. I hold his head, talk softly, take off greatcoat, feel there is water on cloth.

I help Stalin stand. He is weak, balance gone, says

52

bed, must sleep. I help him to couch, he fall on it, groan, is asleep. He is snoring.

I must clean him and his room. This a room I never in before. I look for bathroom, can see open door. Go to it, it is not bathroom. My heart in terror. Open door lead to steps; steps go far down.

I now very fearful. Stories say many secret passages in Kremlin. Say Napoleon even leave Kremlin by one. This is secret passage. I look at door; on room side it is panels of wood and shelves of books. It is secret door. I remember Stalin's coat is wet with snow. He has been outside drunk.

Only I know. And Stalin. Also I know tomorrow he will remember and I will be shot. There is no doubt of this. None. If I stay I die. I take his coat, rip off rank badges, same with cap. He is small man, I am big. It does not matter, this is all I have.

I close secret door behind me and go down steps by electric light. At foot is steel door, on it diagram of door's mechanisms. I read carefully. I stand listening, hear only quiet, then operate mechanism. Door opens, all lights go out. I step through. I am on outside of Kremlin wall by tower. It is black night, no moon, no light permitted in case of bomber raid.

Door is closed now. I walk away. I am smart soldier. I march smartly. Good boots are on my feet and this is good for I have very far to go. Very far. It is necessary I try to leave my country even though I know it not possible to do.

If you imagine Alex and I read all this in silence and without comment, you'd be wrong. I remember saying 'German engineers!' and Alex, 'Imagine *him* as anybody's servant!' And so on.

And silly things ran through my own mind, which is, at all times, a ragbag of useless facts, particularly about people. I know the middle names of long-dead cricketers and the date of Hitler's birthday, that kind of junk, and I knew Stalin was about five foot five and Peterkin a burly six feet three, and I tried to picture the one in the other's overcoat. Maybe Stalin liked a loose fit, or Peterkin was skinnier in his youth. But you'd think it would be a real giveaway for a man on the run in a police state.

Must have worked though, and the coat must have been a beauty, because it held him together and kept him alive on the most hellish journey I've ever seen described. Peterkin recounted it at considerable length, and with justifiable pride; but it's a book in itself, that trip of his, so if I may I'll summarize the tale we read that day.

There was a stroke of luck to begin with: Peterkin found skis and the poles to go with them stuck in the snow outside a block of flats. He thought it probable somebody out visiting a lady had temporarily forgotten their existence. At any rate, he strapped them on and slid quietly away. The snow that had originally moistened the greatcoat was falling still, quite heavily, so his tracks were covered, more or less as he made them. It was after midnight as he ghosted away into the outskirts of the city and then into the birch woods.

'I went always east,' he wrote, 'for they would believe I would go west, towards front to reach the Germans.'

He reckoned he had a few hours' start as Stalin would sleep until seven at least, eight perhaps, and wouldn't be thinking any too clearly when he *did* awaken. But after that . . .

And there was always Gusenko, he thought fearfully, as he skied through the dark night. Gusenko would find Peterkin gone. Gusenko was always a stickler for duty, and Be Alert was his watchword. But Gusenko would be faced with the thought that Peterkin might, just might, have been summoned by the great man to pour coffee or fasten buttons, or one of the little duties Stalin sometimes required. Gusenko, however alert he might be, would hesitate at least for a while.

So until morning his special Kremlin Guard pass could be used. The idea gave him confidence.

He got out of the city. Something in the greatcoat, chafing at his armpit, turned out to be a silver flask containing about half a pint of Georgian cognac, off which he breakfasted not

54

too heftily. He then paused, got his breath back a bit, and began to think, in the calm of the birch forest.

Peterkin now decided that the further east he went, the safer he would be. Siberia was not only big and empty, it was a place where many people had gone, or been exiled, for all sorts of reasons. If he could reach the open spaces, the taiga or the great steppes, his chances would improve. Best, as a long-term ambition, to reach China if he could. He would have preferred India, but knew the mountain barriers were enormous and could not be attempted by one man alone.

He made other decisions at this time. The first was that he would not kill in order to escape. But he did, and soon after, at that. He emerged unexpectedly from the forest into a clearing at dawn. Two soldiers squatted by a fire whose light had been masked from him by a bright, low sun. He was sliding straight up to them before he knew it, and they were on him immediately, not pausing to ask for papers, presumably knowing a fugitive when they saw one. They were no match for him; smallish men in some pioneer unit, facing a highly trained and very powerful expert in hand-to-hand combat, do not normally triumph. But they fought and he had to kill.

He gained from it. They had a small store of tinned food, plus haversacks and rifles. Peterkin stuffed the tucker in one of the haversacks along with a water bottle, and took one rifle and the bayonet that went with it. Everything else he buried with the bodies.

His theory was that if he could reach the Trans-Siberian rail line, and find the right spot for boarding, he might, just *might*, be able to ride a long way.

And eventually he did. But that was only a beginning! The first train he rode was packed with prisoners bound for an arctic labour camp. One way and another he was bundled in with them. He suffered in that camp, and knew he'd die if he didn't get out.

And he *did* get out. Killed three hungry guard dogs and tore down a barbed wire fence.

He walked, then. Something of the order of two thousand miles he walked: eventually right down to and then along the frozen shores of Lake Baikal, then on and on southward. He'd managed, somehow, to hang on to the coat, just as he managed to hang on to his sanity; what he couldn't maintain was his determination to go east. South was just as impossible, but far shorter. He knew death lay either way, but still he struggled on south, starving, living day after day on a handful of snow. He struggled into mountains, probably the Hindu Kush, and climbed, now frostbitten, in the remaining rags of his boots.

He met a bear, a smallish black one. That was some battle, with the bear, because Peterkin says they were both starving; and the fight went on for hours. He killed it by breaking its neck, and ate the flesh raw, day after day, tearing at the carcass with his teeth in a patch of blood-stained snow in a little gully. The meat did strengthen him and he began to climb again. And climb, and climb.

He walked right into India, in the finish. Never knew *where* he'd walked, what the route was, but it must have been into and through Afghanistan or more likely Bhutan.

India was still British then; the Raj had a few years to go and a war still to win. Peterkin presented himself to a corporal on the gate of a barracks, said he was a Pole and wished to join the Polish forces, having escaped from Russia.

They didn't exactly welcome him, the old Pommy bastards. He was interviewed repeatedly after first being clapped in the guardroom cell. There were two officers. One of them wanted to hand Peterkin straight back to the brave Soviet ally, and the other to have him shot as a spy. Peterkin kept talking Polish at them, which he could do with fair fluency because his home area of the Ukraine was the bit bordering Poland on the Bug River, northwest of Lvov. Eventually – it took weeks, but *eventually* – the Brits discovered they were short of driver/mechanics, sat him in a Bedford three-tonner and put him in a convoy of lorries heading to the Mediterranean via Persia. Once he reached the Middle East he found there were plenty of Poles, and was graciously permitted to join them by the Brits, and to fight his gracious way through the nasty bits of Italy and then through northern Europe.

With the war over, Peterkin was given the same choice

offered to most other Poles: be repatriated or stay. Naturally, having no alternative, he chose to stay in the West and – another 'eventually' – he turned into what was then known as a DP, or Displaced Person, and found himself in Britain, learning to be a textile worker in the shoddy factories of Dewsbury and Batley in Yorkshire.

It may not sound much of a job, but Peterkin loved it – for a while, anyway. He had a room of his own, money in his pocket, food in his belly. He made a friend or two, and the refugee Poles, all of whom had been through several tough and bruising years, understood the need to respect a man's privacy. He went to cinemas and markets and football matches. Filled with wonder, he saw the English conduct a local election, with speakers slanging each other. Yes, he enjoyed it *all*. Here was a community and he was part of it. He decided he must join the Catholic Church. Every Pole he knew was Catholic; all of them attended Mass regularly every Sunday. He should go too: it was a matter less of religion than of proper conduct, and loyalty to friends.

Peterkin therefore began to take instruction in the faith. His tutor was Father Bodinski, a former chaplain in the Polish forces, holder of the Military Cross for gallantry, a man of powerful good sense, who asked Peterkin one evening whether he had yet been approached by agents.

'By agents?' I ask him. 'You tell me what agents are these?'

He say, 'Peterkin, the new Polish Communist Government want Polish men in Poland, not in England. They send agents here. Some men in England are already agents. They ask we Poles to return. If they not return, agents try to learn names of families in Poland, then force return with threats to family.'

I have never been approached, but then one day I am. I say no. Man try to ask me questions. I say no, no, no. We are in street in back of pub. I have drunk beer. I argue, he listen. Then he say, 'I hear you speak. You speak British like Ukrainian.'

I stare at him. He say, 'You are Ukrainian!' I say no.

He say, 'If you are Ukrainian you are Soviet citizen. You must go back to Soviet Union. You are traitor. You should be shot!'

I hit him and run. He not know my name but to learn it will be easy for him.

I go to Father Bodinski. He live for few weeks now in Bradford. I tell him about this agent. The Father say it is difficult for me now. Always. My name will be entered on list, all agents will look for me, and they report also to MVD.

Then he say we must proceed with religious instruction and he make me kneel. He teach that night the need of confession, which is much for me to think about. Then he send me to bed in room in his house. Next day he telephone mill where I work and say I am sick. Then we talk.

Bodinski soon know I have secret. Big secret I discover when escape through secret passage. I not tell him this, but he clever man who know. He ask is it important? I say, yes. How important? I say is one of big secrets in world. Is dangerous? Is most dangerous. Who else know? Only me.

He say this is bad. If I die, secret die. Advise I write it down. Say this take burden from me. I look at him. I pray. I think. At last I write it down. Next day Father Bodinski take writing away. He promise safe hiding for paper. Secret safe – I write in Ukrainian. The Father cannot read it. He give papers to head of English school for priests who swear to pass on to successor. I am given name of church, number of pew. Is special code. My secret comes back to me this way if I want one day to have it.

All is so far good. I take other man's place on immigrant ship to New Zealand, this Father Bodinski has fix for me. I stay two years. This I have to do. Then go to Australia, to far west where not many people. I live here always. I move from one place, find another. Always good places. Always sunshine, good food.

Each year I send postcard to Father Bodinski, each

year he send postcard to his priest-friend in Perth. I telephone priest-friend. Is okay? Okay, he say. This until 1953. In this year I telephone. Is okay? Listen, he say, Father Bodinski, he disappear. In England is great mystery. Father Bodinski one night he go out to telephone at phone box, is hundred fifty yards. He not return, not seen again, not ever. Police, priest say, believe Father Bodinski kidnap by secret police, Russian or maybe Polish, for reason he great enemy of Communists. Think he taken in Polish ship to Gdynia. No proof, no anything.

After this I keep moving. One month only I live in every place, then move. I am strong, there is plenty work. Also I begin to feel safe.

One day, in same year, I hear Stalin die, Malenkov to be new Stalin. I saw Malenkov many times when he Stalin's secretary, do not think he can do Stalin's work, think him not strong man. For a while, also, I think Stalin's death make me more safe, my secret not important now. Two men knew, but only one man know this thing now.

But then I think in Kremlin is battle. I read newspapers; in my head I see men I saw come to Stalin, and all are cold, brutal, greedy, full of ambition. I remember eyes of Kaganovich, remember Beria, remember Molotov, Khrushchev, Mikoyan. I think Malenkov soon go, and soon he go.

Now Cold War continues. I have my secret. There are many who would give all for my secret, all they have, men in East, men in West. It is great weight on me. If I give it to others, what will happen? It will be used. If only Peterkin have it, it cannot be used. That is my decision, and now Stalin is dead, I do not have to hide always.

I go to Broome, live there with woman. She Japanese Australian, very kind, very pretty. We have child, name Alexandra, also pretty. We say we marry soon.

Then I see newspaper. It is chance I see, this is American newspaper, left on hire boat I have to clean in my

*job. In it is story. There is protest at United Nations
that USSR appoint Yuri Gusenko to UN staff. It say
Gusenko at right hand of Andropov in Hungarian
bloodshed. It say Gusenko was man sent to Prague to
drag Dubchek in chains to Moscow. It say Gusenko
high official in KGB. I ask myself – is this man Yuri
Gusenko my partner in Kremlin Guard? Many
Gusenkos in Soviet Union. Then in same paper find
second article by former journalist, about Gusenko in
time of revolution in Budapest. This man give patronymic. He write that Yuri Anastasovich Gusenko was
man who shot General Maleter in head after promise
of safe conduct.*

*So this was end of my freedom. Gusenko is powerful
man now, high in State Security Committee, also
United Nations. I wonder always, from this day, what
Gusenko knows. Does he know I am in Australia? No,
I think. He cannot know. If he did, I would be like
Father Bodinski, and be taken away. I am now Peterkin, how could he know about Peterkin? After these
years, these thirty and five years. I am forgotten. But in
my heart I know Yuri Anastasovich Gusenko does not
forget that his partner Pyotr Ivanovich Kinsky disappear in night from Stalin's apartment. Such a man
wish always to know how Pyotr Ivanovich did this
thing.*

I whistled and said, admiringly, 'What a man Peterkin was
– I'd no idea!'

Alex had a funny look. Her face was shiny with pride and
at the same time her eyes were streaming tears. She kept
blinking, and muttered, 'Why didn't I know – why didn't I
know!'

'Because this was *his* secret.'

'But I'm his daughter!'

'A fact,' I said, 'which he acknowledges, at least in part.'
She brightened a bit. 'He does, doesn't he!'

'That he has a daughter, yes; and your name!'

She said sharply, 'There's more – look. Writing on the back of the last sheet there!'

I turned the page over quickly. There was one word and a number.

'What's it say?' Alex demanded.

I handed it to her.

She said, 'What on earth does that mean?'

'CH.AD.11,' it said. Like that – punctuation, capitals and all.

7

'Peterkin's already told us what it means. There's a church and a pew number.'

'Okay, so CH stands for church, and the eleven is the pew number. Is that right?'

'Dunno if it's correct, but it's the way I'm thinking.'

'What's AD, then?'

'Could be something like Adrian or anno Domini, I suppose.'

'Or Adam?'

'Tell you the truth, I've never heard of either a Church of Adrian, or a St Adrian's, and as far as I know Adam was never sanctified or canonized or whatever they do. Also, 11 A.D. was a while ago.'

She grinned, excited now that the trail was warm again. 'How do we find out?'

'Reference books, I imagine.'

'Because I want to know Dad's secret. He was *my* father. When you prove it and I inherit, I get his secret, too.'

I said, meaning it: 'Do you want it? Peterkin was scared of it all his life.'

'You don't know much about women, do you, Mr Close?'

'Never claimed I did.'

'If there's one thing no woman can resist, it's a secret.' She was laughing, proud of it, as she spoke, and I smiled too though my heart wasn't in it. Alex was a happy girl by nature: the kind that can forget troubles, or live with them. I'm the kind of bloke who broods darkly in corners, and even the dazzling sunlight of Geraldton couldn't disperse the pall of fear that old Peterkin's knowledge carried around with it, any more than a cheery wave from men aboard a nuclear sub disperses awareness of the sub's unimaginable power to destroy. Alex and Joe Hag both plainly believed the sub's presence off the Abrolhos had been merest coincidence. Alex *had* believed earlier in a Russian involvement with her father, and the belief had now been borne out, but the possibility that somebody might even have despatched a nuclear sub several thousand miles because of Peterkin had plainly not entered her head.

But the same possibility thudded through *my* mind like a heartbeat. Boom-boom-boom it went, threat-threat-threat, kill-kill-kill. For none of these was an idle matter. Perhaps, if the knowledge, whatever it was, had existed only in Peterkin's head, then his death would have been the end of the affair.

But it didn't. Peterkin had not only *written it down*, he'd left the writings *with a third party*! Furthermore, fourth or fifth parties, in the shape of Alex and me, were also in this thing up to our necks. .

Also a sixth. Not just a possibility, not even a probability. Peterkin himself *knew* that Yuri Anastasovich Gusenko, his long-ago opposite number in Stalin's time, was in it. He also knew the kind of man Gusenko was. The young, hard, stern Gusenko had grown into a truly terrible man; one who did not give up. Ever.

So what was to be done? The thing could not be abandoned here. We could not walk away. Peterkin, all his life, had believed himself in danger and, given the mysterious circumstances of his final, fatal fall, had perhaps been proved horribly correct. Now Alex was in peril, not because she *knew* Peterkin's secret, but simply because the chance existed that she *might*!

Likewise me . . . !

So the pursuit of knowledge had to continue. An end to proceedings could come only when there was nothing to be hidden any more.

'We'll have to go to England,' I said at last. 'Find what Peterkin hid.'

Alex shook her head. 'I'm not going. You must go.'

'Why me?'

Her face, as she looked at me, was very sober. A small shiver rippled across her shoulders. She said, 'I've been thinking, too. Here I can hide, like my father, and I realize now that I *have* to hide. So look at me: how could I hide in England, a Japanese girl with an Australian accent!'

'I've got the same accent.'

'Not you, sport. You're half Pom – listen to yourself some time. You can go – there's sixty million just like you over there. It must be why my father provided the money. Remember it was to you he gave it, not to me – and it must have been so you could go to England.'

'Okay,' I said equably. I like England. And Jane's there.

Well, there was nothing to delay me. Alex had Joe Hag and the cray-fishing community to protect her there in Geraldton, and to get her out. After that, well, she'd a lifetime's experience of finding shacks in the bush to tuck herself away in.

She wrote a letter To Whom It May Concern, appointing me her attorney and representative, for all *that* was worth.

As for me, I didn't even bother going home for suits and ties and the trappings of formality. I'd stop and buy in Hong Kong. But first I'd have to catch a plane to Perth.

We left *Abrolhos Lady*, the three of us, and walked side by side along the Geraldton mole. We hadn't gone far when a figure stepped out of shadow into sunshine, a man who wore a dark coat and an Akubra hat; he stood leaning against a wall, watching us come nearer.

Joe Hag muttered that he 'could take that bloke any day, and how about it?'

I said, 'Only if he tries to stop us, Joe.'

And Alex said, 'If he has a gun – no!'

We walked towards him; he looked at us. He wore sunglasses with blue lenses, as before. He was about five-ten, squat build, powerful. He simply watched us pass.

I said goodbye quickly, went off in the Range Rover to Geraldton's small airport, parked there, and just scraped on to a Perth flight in the kind of little twin-engine plane that scares the hell out of me. They waggle and weave on take-off and landing, and this one was Brazilian-made, which didn't do a lot for my confidence.

But it got me there in a few minutes over the hour, which is efficient, and everybody was helpful, and the pilot radioed ahead to try to find me a seat on something outbound. That's the problem with Perth; there aren't too many flights, and they're usually booked up well in advance. The answer was no. Everything had gone for that day, the BA and the Cathay and a Philippine Airlines jumbo and . . .

Except . . . hold on . . . Yair, well, there was the Qantas from Sydney for Hong Kong via Perth . . . been delayed by engine trouble and was just now on its approach to Perth International, and just this second Qantas had a cancellation in business class. I'd have to wait twenty-four hours in Hong Kong, but then there was a seat on an overnight to London. All very simple, really.

But.

My passport was at home. I thought for a while. Then I said could Qantas call Bob Collis. Bob could easily break into my flat, grab my passport, and bring it to the airport, couldn't he?

He could and he did. Easily.

Something about me gets up the nostrils of girls on airline check-in desks. I wish I knew what, because I'd do something about it, damn quick. They take one look at me, then they look at the seat plan and they find one seat empty in the rows where the mothers with five young kids are distributed. And that's what I get. And while check-in girls may not like me, kids do. The kids also take one look, and confuse me with daddy and crawl towards me, and the more they're covered with sticky sweets and half-digested food the faster they crawl. Appeal to the cabin staff and they say there's not another seat, and add things like, 'Aren't you glad you're not a mother?'

This time, though, was different. Business class. Peace at a thousand a throw. There may have been babies aboard, but they were far away from me in cattle class. The movie was beginning, the grub not bad, the booze fine. Seven hours to Hong Kong whispered by.

Next day, in my new twenty-four-hour tailored suit, and twenty-four-hour bespoke shoes and my eight-hour made-to-measure shirt, I was on Qantas for London, feeling very dandified. There were four more shirts in a pilot bag, and some pants and socks, and I was stuffing it under my seat when a man appeared beside me and remained beside me, waiting politely for me to finish, meanwhile putting his shoulder bag in the overhead locker. I looked up and smiled and said, 'Okay, now,' and watched a black Akubra hat go into the locker, too.

He kept the blue-lens glasses on as he took his seat: not the aisle seat, the one next to me. He filled it, too: lots of shoulder and chest, meaty thighs in a navy-blue suit. He gave me an affable nod, and said, 'Good to see you again.'

'Clever of you to get that seat,' I said with irony.

'As you Australians unfailingly say, no worries.'

'We Australians, eh? And what about you?'

'A friend, I hope.'

'Ah, but a friend from –?'

'From an unexpected direction.' He smiled. 'I'm going to have a can of Swan Export, I think, after the wheels leave the ground. What about you?'

'Vodka.'

He laughed, and I said, 'I've been listening to your accent, and it sounds –'

'My accent,' he said, 'was acquired at The Queen's College, University of Oxford. To match liquor to it, you should order a decent claret.'

'Let's stop this, shall we? What do you *want*?'

'I want to talk to you for a while, when we're in the air and unlikely to be overheard or disturbed.'

'There's an empty seat next to you. Somebody may take it.'

He frowned. 'This obsession with aircraft seats! They're all exactly alike, and everything is pre-arranged. No one will take it. Ah, we're moving.' He sat perfectly placidly through the take-off run and rotation, and almost as soon as the wheels thunked into their housings, said, 'To clear the matter up, I was an exchange student a long time ago. Your first guess was correct. I am as Russian as your friend Pyotr Ivanovich Kinsky, known, in recent years, as Peterkin.'

'Not my *friend*. I'm a lawyer, and he was my client. What's *your* name?'

'Sergei.'

'Well, Sergei, I know nothing of any value to you at all.'

He nodded equably. 'Not entirely true. What you know has some value. The point is that you are likely to learn more, far more likely than, for instance, I. And when you do, it's my hope that you will be on the right side.'

Considering what, by his own admission, this man was, and considering even more what he looked like, this display of easy urbanity was surprising, not to say startling. Here I am, I thought rather wildly, in the next seat to an agent of the great, if weakening, Marxist-Leninist conspiracy, a genuine Russian spy! And am I afraid? Not at the moment, I'm not. In my time I've been more afraid of motor-car salesmen and certainly of traffic cops.

Beside me he said, 'You're right, of course. Things have changed quite a bit. Nothing to be afraid of at all.'

'You mean you're not hung about with lethal cigarette lighters and poisoned umbrellas?'

'Not even with ancient intellectual baggage,' said Sergei, complacently. He examined his nails, which were well maintained, and then added, 'If I am an agent, as I am, I am probably only an agent of change, one way or the other.'

'*Perestroika*, you mean – or is it *glasnost*?'

'A moment,' he said. 'First things first.' The girl had arrived with the trolley. 'Swan Export, thank you.' And when she handed him the can he examined the small print, and handed it back. 'Made in Sydney,' he said to her, 'and we are Perth people. It really won't do.'

'So what'll you have?'

'Vodka,' he said contentedly. 'Just ice. And the same for my friend.'

'Plus orange juice,' I said. When she'd moved on, he said, '*Perestroika* means reconstruction.'

'So it does.'

'Of practically everything in the state.'

'If you say so.' He was so bland, so at ease, so unruffled, that I'd almost given up, even so soon, thinking about what he was. 'Does that include, for instance, the KGB?'

'It does. All Komitet directorates –' Then he grinned broadly and said, 'Well, almost all. It includes the GRU, the army's intelligence service. Everything is up for reform. You must have noticed we have new presidents. Very energetic, very determined. And you know the second law of thermo-dynamics, I'm sure.'

'I learned it in school.'

'Would you be kind enough to repeat it now?'

I parroted, '"Every action produces an equal and opposite reaction." Principle of the jet engine. So there are people who don't like change.'

'The difficulty is,' he said, 'that some such people have access to rockets, nuclear missiles, warships, tank armies, and the jets of which you spoke. Some of them are marshals of the Soviet Union, some are navy, some are air force, some are members of the Supreme Soviet, though fewer than there were.'

'What are you?'

He laughed. 'A humble functionary, that's all, John. I may call you John, may I, after the Australian fashion?'

'Yes, Sergei, you may.'

He poured the vodka down his throat in a sudden move-ment. 'You can see the problem, *my* problem.'

I thought about it for a moment. 'A single brain,' I said, 'with a bullet in it, would be the answer to many people's problems?'

'If you like. You can't really blame these people, you see. Anybody under seventy has spent a lifetime absorbing a single view of the world he lives in. It may not be an especially comfortable world, and there may be a shortage of beet for the borscht, but the rules are clear, and people do *like* the rules to be clear. Now along come the chaps with all the reforming zeal, and suddenly the peasants on the collectives are no longer free to spend their days leaning against a broken-down tractor and working on their private plots in the evenings. Now they are expected to *work*! I tell you, the man with the hoe in his hand is at least as disgruntled as the man with the baton in his.'

'So you're on Gorb—'

He interrupted me. 'Not so fast. It is not a matter of taking sides. Not so simple.'

'But you've just finished lining up the sides for me!'

'There are no battle lines, *yet*. That's the point. Now, I invite you to consider this: here are two groups, opposed to each other ten times as implacably as Liberals and Labour in Australia, where you have no tradition of political violence. But this is in Russia, where such a tradition is endemic. One side is led by Mr A and the other by General B. How easy is it for one to get rid of the other – by assassination of one form or another? It is not easy at all. Each is surrounded by every kind of safety measure yet devised. Barriers of every kind – electronic, physical and so on.'

'Didn't save Julius Caesar,' I said.

'The leader is always vulnerable – to his friends. There's nothing anybody can do about the lifelong friend and colleague who turns homicidal, says "Morning, George," then plunges a paper knife in the boss's belly.'

'Where's all this leading?'

Sergei sighed softly. 'We've imported management education, you know. Charming, apparently civilized people, people from Harvard and MIT who speak of symphonic music as "product". No article, definite or indefinite. My "job description" speaks of "outer ring". I have to prevent a strike by the enemy.'

'Would I be right about whose side you're on?'

Another sigh. 'There, you see, is the difficulty. I could say one thing and be another. But you will have to find out, because sooner or later you will have to trust *somebody*. Another drink?'

Well, we went on talking. The plane landed at Delhi, then flew north, first over Afghanistan and then Russia, and when the captain said we were over Russia, Sergei pointed downward with a forefinger, smiled, and said, 'That's where it's all happening!'

But he was an enigma. Even when the jumbo was on its finals nearing London, I still hadn't made up my mind which side he represented in Russia's internal struggles.

At one point I closed my eyes and pretended to sleep, principally in order to think, and decided after a while that among all the uncertainties and speculation, only a small number of certainties existed, and *then* only if . . .

But, no, it wasn't like that. This world doesn't provide too many certainties, apart, as the wise man said, from death and taxes. But it was extremely likely that Peterkin had been telling the truth. Extremely likely, too, that Sergei must be part of Gusenko's apparatus. I said, as the green fields of Old England flashed by beneath our wings, 'Which side is Gusenko on?'

Sergei beamed at me. 'Gusenko is on Gusenko's side, so what's new?'

I thought: that was a mistake. Be careful. 'Will I be seeing you elsewhere?'

'Depends where you're going,' Sergei said. 'But in your shoes I'd consider it a possibility.'

I said, 'Till then, then. Tell me this – when you get to immigration, which channel do you go through?'

'UK and EEC citizens, of course.'

'What if I tell them you're a Russian agent?'

'They won't turn a hair. Might ask you to prove it. Can you? Whereas' – he held up the blue British passport – 'this is entirely valid. One other thing.'

'Go on.'

'There's a good deal of interest in you, I suspect. And not just from me.'

'Who, then?'

He yawned. 'I'd say the interest appears to be general.'

8

I lay in my Heathrow hotel trying – and failing – to sleep, and waiting for the jet-lag to relinquish its absurd control over me, and thinking absurdly confused thoughts. Hours passed. I dozed, woke, dozed, and thought a lot. It was essentially simple, so I eventually concluded. Thirty-five years ago Peterkin escaped from a Kremlin that was locked, bolted, barred and guarded. This should have been completely impossible; nonetheless, he did it. His partner, Gusenko, wrestling in the lavatory at the time with some kind of gut-crunch microbe, was probably thought to be in on it, and must accordingly have gone through a number of investigatory mangles of assorted size and severity. In the process he must also have been brought face to face with every aspect, and every *possible* aspect, of Peterkin's disappearance. He must have thought, in the end, like Sherlock Holmes that when every other possibility has been examined and excluded, then what remains, *no matter how unlikely*, must be the truth. Therefore if Peterkin had left the Kremlin fortress *without* passing security desks, guarded gates and the rest, then he must have left by some other exit; an exit, what's more, that was *entirely unknown* to the security authorities.

The problem of all this for Yuri Gusenko, thirty-five years ago, was a Stalin very much alive and far more than merely kicking, who might very well have a secret exit, *could* have sent Peterkin through it for reasons unknown, and would certainly frown on the matter being even suspected, let alone discussed.

History then happens. Stalin dies, and all the rest. And still there's a secret exit. Peterkin knows there is and Gusenko suspects it.

71

Meanwhile, where's Gusenko? Well, if Peterkin's old newspaper is correct, by 1956 – i.e. a mere three years after Stalin's death – Master Gusenko is at the right hand of Andropov in the throttling of the Hungarian uprising. So *he's* made a quite startling rise, from humble Kremlin guard under suspicion to upper-rank MVD/KGB man in a situation of trust and responsibility. How was *that* achieved? Well, if nothing else, it showed Gusenko to be a man of resource *and*, if he did shoot General Maleter in Budapest, of very considerable ruthlessness.

I got that far, and tumbled abruptly into sleep. The Australia–London run is the equivalent of being belted over the head with a cricket bat and not just once; what has been scrambled in there stays scrambled for a long time and when I tried to force my mind on to logical tracks it said: not now, not now.

So I busied myself with the little tasks of travel: showering and shaving and dressing, and wondering which reference book would identify CH.AD.11 for me, and then acknowledging, as the water ran over me, that I couldn't find out by telephone from a hotel room at Heathrow. No – what I wanted lay somewhere in an unknown church in West Yorkshire, and really I should go there forthwith.

I picked up the phone, asked about flights, and flew two and a half hours later into the Leeds/Bradford airport at Yeadon.

I am getting older and wiser and longer in the tooth. Once upon a time I would have rented a car and then driven to a library, and tried to park in a zone where nobody is ever allowed to park. I would have been moved on, and fined, and found myself pounding long streets between the periphery, where the quieter car parks may perhaps be, and my destination.

I took a taxi (having looked at the map given me by Hertz) to Bradford. Batley and Dewsbury, where Peterkin had lived, were not far away; and there was a large reference library. First, though, I needed certain facts to be confirmed, and asked the driver to drop me off at the editorial offices of the local newspaper, where I asked for the librarian. It took a little time. The librarian would like to know my business before he could authorize my admission. I explained that I was a lawyer from Australia, badly in need of assistance and willing to pay reasonable fees.

He was a nice man, a Mr Holdsworth, and when I reached his office finally, he smiled at me. 'How can I help?'

'What I want,' I said, 'is to see the file on the disappearance of a man named Father Bodinski. Dunno if you remember?'

'Remember! I worked on the story,' he said. 'I'll get you the file.'

It was a fat file, but not especially informative. I read each cutting minutely for a while, before I realized all of them said the same things. When I looked up, Holdsworth said, 'He vanished. He was there one minute and gone the next. Not a word of explanation. Not a shred of evidence.'

'Any idea why?'

'Police always believed – well, Bodinski was boldly anti-communist both in and out of the pulpit, and they thought he'd been shifted for that reason. There was a lot of mucking about at that time, you know, with the Poles trying to get their people to go back home.'

'You believe – what?'

'It's hard to know. He wasn't the only turbulent priest, you know. There were a lot of angry clerics about, but I never heard of another being kidnapped. Did you?'

'Me?' I said, a little taken aback at being asked. 'No, I never have.'

'What's your interest anyway?' Holdsworth was looking at me a little aslant.

I'd prepared a little story; now I told it. How I had a client, a Pole in Australia, who'd asked me to find out anything I could because he was thinking of making a bequest to Father Bodinski's old church in the Father's memory.

Holdsworth nodded when I'd finished. 'It's a funny thing,' he said. 'That file's an old one. But you're the second one to ask about it this week.'

'Who's the other?'

He laughed. 'Well, this one pulled the other leg, Mr Close.

Didn't come in. Rang up and asked if we had a file on Bodinski.'

'You said you had?'

''Course I did. Maybe they'll be in this afternoon.'

'If they are, will you let me know?'

'Where'll you be?'

'Tell you what – I'll ring you.'

I needed a room. I'm aware that people have run advertising agencies and even been bookies with nothing to lean on except the shelf in a phone booth. But I can't. Round me, paper spreads. The Victoria Hotel being just across a cobbled yard from the newspaper, I checked in, left my shirts on the bed, and went out again. A small piece of paper in my pocket bore the names Holdsworth's cuttings had given me of the two churches to which Bodinski had been appointed. They were St Cuthbert's at Dewsbury and St Mary-the-Virgin in Horton, a mile or so away.

Walking that mile convinced me of the difficulty of the task I'd blithely taken on. I became increasingly certain that Father Bodinski, had he been miraculously returned on this day, would barely have recognized this place. In this area, anyway, one face in two was Asian; the shops were Asian. I passed two churches, Victorian, sturdily built of local stone, which were now cinemas showing exclusively Asian films. I'm not disapproving; no modern-day Australian can complain about people seeking to better themselves by moving. But the sensation was strange – like going to, say, Bali, and finding it full of Africans. I began to have the feeling that perhaps I was wasting my time tramping up the hill to Horton, because when I got there, St Mary-the-Virgin would have become a Pakistani drapery full of shimmering saris.

But, no, it was there still: a bit sooty on the outside, very peaceful inside. I looked to see if the pews were numbered. They were not. I counted eleven from the front, sat in the row on the left and looked about me with care. The pews were wooden and plain and smelled of furniture polish; the hassocks, covered in some kind of carpet, had been worn to near-smoothness by many knees. This was plainly not a rich church, but its congregation looked after it. So far as I could tell, all the pews were like the one I sat in, and none offered any kind of hiding place. A hassock might have been opened, perhaps, and had something tucked inside it, but that didn't seem likely. Hassocks would be moved wholesale every time the church was cleaned, which was often. No, I thought, anybody looking for a long-term and stable hiding place wouldn't choose a hassock.

I crossed the aisle and looked some more, then sat down, tilted back my head, and saw the fine, high roof, with its blue heaven filled with stars, and nearly jumped up there myself when a voice beside me said, 'Can I help you, my son?'

'Rubber soles and heels,' he said a moment later, smiling. 'They're a bit more reverential when you're in my line of business. I'm Father Franklin.'

I introduced myself, and explained, and asked about Bodinski. The priest crossed himself and said it had been a terrible thing, all those years ago. 'A wave of fear went through this parish, so I'm told,' Father Franklin said. 'Everybody wondering if he was next. And not just here, either.'

'There were a lot of Poles?'

'Still are,' he said. 'The wartime Poles are getting old now, of course, starting to die off, but their children and grandchildren still wear costume and go to the clubs and do the songs and dances. All these old refugee groups are very tenacious – very.'

In churches it's always footsteps that distract. There were some behind us now. Father Franklin turned his head, murmured, 'More visitors,' and went off silently to greet them. I rose a moment later. There was nothing here for me. He was murmuring to a man and a woman in a rear pew, but as I passed he fell in beside me, and once we were outside the building said, 'You've come a long way. Would you like me to show you where he was seen last?'

'Thanks. At the risk of seeming morbid, I'd be fascinated.' We walked down the hill a little way, and he showed me a house. 'Father Bodinski lived there,' he said. It was unremarkable: a plain, stone terraced house, of a type which, as I'd already seen, existed nearby in hundreds.

I nodded. Peterkin had stayed in that house, too, a man already much hunted, even so long ago. And while both men had left it only to disappear, Peterkin had merely disappeared into the welcoming warmth of West Australia; poor Bodinski had been translated into eternal mystery.

'Said he had to make a phone call,' Father Franklin murmured beside me. 'As you see, there's a phone box just up there.' It was only a hundred and fifty yards.

I asked, 'Whom did he tell?'

'The housekeeper. Elderly lady.' He laughed. 'In a presbytery, you know, the ladies are always elderly. She's been dead a lot of years, now. Anyway, he closed the door behind him, and off he walked.'

'Did he make his call?'

Father Franklin shrugged. 'Who knows if he even reached the box.'

'Nobody saw anything? A priest's a distinctive figure.'

He shook his head. 'It was night-time – evening, anyway – but it's a busy street and there are lamps and buses. Nothing seen, no clues. Whoever took him away, Mr Close, was remarkably efficient.'

We were standing, by now, beside the phone box. I turned and looked back towards the church and the presbytery beyond. The man and woman were just coming out of the church and getting into a car.

'Americans,' he said. 'A pretty little contribution of fifty dollars.'

I said, 'Are any of his friends still around here?'

'Father Bodinski's? Indeed, oh, indeed.'

'I'd like to talk to someone who knew him.'

He said, 'Well, let me see . . .'

'One of his real friends.'

'There's Pavel, of course. Great pal of the Father. Pavel played football for Poland, you know, before the war, and the Father was an enthusiast. He's no longer a parishioner, unfortunately, since he moved. Yes, you could go to Pavel. Pavel Blanck.'

He knew the address. Pavel lived in Heaton – 'in the road beside that old Baptist chapel which has been turned into flats.' Number 11.

'I'll need a taxi.'

'No. Hop on this bus. Get off at Southfield Lane. Get another bus there – number 74. It'll drop you off at his door.' I must have looked doubtful because he said, with a laugh, 'Good bus service, hereabouts. You *must* have faith, my son!'

Number 11, he'd said. The same eleven, could it be – the eleven of CH.AD.11? Damn good chance, I thought. Plus, Pavel Blanck, the old friend. I was gloating a bit. Too soon, it turned out.

On the second of the two buses I had climbed to the empty top deck and was sitting in the seat at the back, looking out at a Victorian city beginning to fight its way out of a long depression. This had been the wool capital of the world, its links with Perth and Fremantle strong. From my rear seat I could look in all directions, and I did, and I realized, after a time, that while a procession of cars overtook my bus whenever it stopped, one did not. A Ford. It contained a man and a woman. She was driving. Sunlight reflecting off the Ford's windscreen made it hard to be sure, but they *could* be the pair who'd given Father Franklin his fifty dollars. If so, or, indeed, if *not*, why were they following this bus – *my* bus? Was this part of the 'good deal of interest' in me that Sergei had talked about?

Or was I simply being stupid? There are innocent reasons for following a bus in a car – I've done it myself, to pick up somebody who's going to get off – and I was by no means sure the car's occupants were the 'Americans'. All the same, when the conductor called me and I went downstairs, and he said, 'That used to be the chapel,' the car was still right behind.

I looked at it doubtfully. At this range the faces were clear, but in church the woman had been wearing a hat. Now she wasn't, but the man was. I'd taken no notice whatsoever of the faces. Silly, I thought, when I was so near to Pavel Blanck, to be scared off in broad daylight by flights of fancy.

I got off the bus. The car remained stationary. Just across the road I could see the nameplate for the short street in which Pavel Blanck lived. No, I thought. The occupants of the car may be innocent, or they may not. And if they're not, I'll be damned if I'll take them straight to Blanck's door!

There was a steep road behind me, down into a valley, houses on the far slope perhaps a mile away. I'd go that way. I turned to start down the hill. As I passed the car, the passenger-side window glided electrically down, and the man said, 'You – into the car!' He was holding what looked like, what *was*, a gun!

But it wasn't levelled, not yet. The barrel still pointed upward: he'd bring it down level in a moment, but in the second we were then living through he couldn't fire it at me.

I was off in one bloody big bound like a great bull 'roo. Came down about twenty feet away and running. No shot was fired, not that I heard, but there was engine-revving and tyres squealed several times; the woman must have been struggling to turn the car on what was a dangerous and busy bend.

Meanwhile, I was plunging into God knows where – down one of those hills that starts at one in ten, or so, and turns into one in four on the first bend, the kind of hill that takes instant control of the runner: speed and gravity mean you can't stop, your toes jam painfully in the toes of your shoes and you wonder, as the hill gets steeper, how this can possibly end with you still on your feet.

I hadn't run like that since I was a boy. It had been frightening then and it was frightening now: guns are guns, but steep roads with loose granite chippings all over them also make for memorable injury if you tumble.

Well behind me I heard tyres squeal again. It wouldn't be long before the Ford came roaring after me, faster and safer than I on this almost lethal road surface. At that second I heard an exhaust rasp, higher on the hill, and found myself trying to cope with a road that bent gradually round to the right. The sheer pace of my flight was terrific; I hadn't run so fast in a decade, and I knew, as my feet flew ever more erratically on the treacherous granite-chipped surface, that in a second or two I'd be down. Nothing without four legs

78

could cope with that breakneck descent and stay upright,

I heard the vroom of one gear-change, then another. And on the bend before me, I saw the road levelled briefly, before a further plunge into the valley. To my left was a hill, rising upward from where I was – all newish houses and roads and no use whatever to me. To my right – trees and a big stone gateway with a signboard.

Now I could hear the skitter of small stones as the Ford dropped down the hill after me. Ahead was another steep fall in the road . . . so where lay the far side of the valley I'd seen from higher up? Ahead, surely – but if the road ran that way, so could the car.

'Heaton Woods,' the signboard read. 'Vehicles prohibited.' Whether that would halt the Ford I didn't know, but it was a chance and the gateway was stone and sturdy and not wide.

I dashed through – straight into magnificent woodland: big old trees with thick trunks and high foliage. To my left was a steep, rough slope down through the trees, crisscrossed with little tracks. Children's feet, I thought. Far down, I thought I heard a stream.

The other path was the one I took – along the valley wall. I was on a slight down slope, but nothing like the one out of the village. And to my surprise, I wasn't much out of breath – scared, yes, but physically pretty good. Maybe running downhill doesn't use up oxygen.

Running on the near-flat did, though. I'd done maybe three hundred yards *before* I got into the woods, and wasn't even panting. Now, and quickly, my body felt the drag. John Close was never anybody's quarter-miler, and the seconds now tolled up oncoming troubles, an aching calf, a thigh that wandered sideways.

There! That was the squeal as the Ford braked and slid a little on the chippings. Questions: had they seen me come in here? – would they come in after me, or drive on?

They didn't drive on. I heard a door slam. Therefore they were on foot now, like me, and if they were the Americans from the church, they were a bit older than me.

I slowed from gallop to good canter, still running on the slight downhill slope through the trees. It might have been

79

quite pleasant if there hadn't been a man with a pistol back there.

Why? I know I gasped that word aloud. Sergei had told me why two lots of Russians had an interest in me. But why Americans? And were they Americans?

I couldn't think, dared not pause. The pathway roughened and all my concentration was needed to stay on my feet. Then I saw steps, off to my right, and it was plain they climbed another flank of the hill I'd raced down minutes earlier.

I must choose: either race onward, deeper into this very sizeable wood, without the smallest idea where I was going, and how to get out again, or take the steps, which, almost certainly, led up to the village.

Some way back were voices, little cries and yells. I thought: those steps will be bloody hard to climb, but I'm younger and fitter. Veering right on to a well-worn path I started the upward run.

At once it was plain that 'hard' was an underestimate. On those rough steps, cut into the hillside, there were a couple of yards or more between each riser, and though at first the risers themselves were quite shallow, they became higher as the hill grew steeper, and my strength began to flag. Soon they'd reached a height of more than a foot! Tears your guts out, and it ripped brutally at mine.

Halfway up I glanced behind and saw my pursuers emerge into the open, running still, the woman surprisingly just ahead of the man, and both loping along effectively. I heard the yell. Both of them stopped and she pointed at me and yelled again. I set off, and soon I was reduced to that kind of upward running that needs hands to push on knees and much grunting and gasping, and really isn't running at all. And she was on the steps, I saw, in another glance behind me.

While the man . . . There was a chestnut fence, and he was leaning on it with his hands lifted to shoulder level. There was a distant little cracking sound. Then another. My brain must have been starved of oxygen, because I completely failed to realize then that he was firing at me.

The third shot convinced me, though; it hit me.

*　*　*

At fifty yards or so, uphill, that shot *must* have been a fluke, but it certainly hurt! It hit me in the rear ribs, four or five inches above my right kidney, and it brought me instantly to a standstill, of course, and as my hand flew round reflexively to the wounded spot, I could actually *feel* the bullet, feel it embedded in my flesh! As I touched it, it came away in my hand. My blood was on it, and my back hurt. I flung the bullet away and pounded on up the steps, wondering if I was already dying, if I could even make it to the top.

Then, suddenly and wearily, I was raising my foot over the last long upward step, and in moments my feet were on the old stone cobbles of a back street: gratings, gardens of old cottages, everything leading *down*, almost funnelling me *down*. Thank God!

I went with it, letting gravity take me. One last glance back told me the woman was now floundering on those murderous steps, and the man had taken a mere few paces and then stopped. They were both in those stoop-shouldered, long-arm stances that tell at once of physical defeat.

So was I. But I was at the top. Yes, and with a bullet wound. Putting my hand round my back beneath my jacket, I felt for the hole. There was sticky blood, and it was very tender. But I didn't feel too bad. We've all seen too many movies and I remember I felt at the corners of my mouth to see if blood was emerging there. And when I then looked at my hand it was bloody. That's the point when I came nearest to dying – of a seizure.

I managed to propel myself forward, gasping a lot and aching even more and it was only a matter of a few moments before that little sloping, sandstone back street took my feet back to the main road, where a bus was passing, probably the next along the route after the one that had put me down.

Damn it, I was only a matter of yards from the bus stop – and from that short road opposite – Parson Drive, where Pavel Blanck lived. Dare I go there now, with those two behind me? I could be dripping blood, and they'd follow the trail of red spots to his door. Too many movies, again! I listened and heard the bus going off down the hill – yet *another* hill; this place was all hills and all of them steep –

81

but I heard nothing of my pursuers. I walked quickly across the main road, turned left into the one where Blanck lived, and knocked on the door of number 11.

The door was painted green, I noticed, and the curtains were green. But the leaves on pot plants on the stone steps were yellow. Apart from the white . . .

9

There was a fair-sized lump on my head, and it throbbed like a big amplifier in a small, cellar disco. My knuckles also felt sore, and when I lifted my right hand, it was scraped. So was the left. I was naked from the waist up, and flat on my belly on what looked, and felt, like a scratchy nylon carpet.

Footsteps. I succeeded in looking up. A small elderly man loomed over me, plastic bowl in his hand, box tucked under one arm. I smelled antiseptic. He had a kind of triangular face, with high cheekbones and Slavic eyes. 'Tear the shirt,' he said. 'Am sorry.' Then he was on his knees on the floor beside me, muttering, 'Zis will hurt a little.' As it did.

I told him I'd actually got the bullet out, but he said, 'Maybe not all,' and probed about, and that hurt some more. Meanwhile he murmured conversationally that I not badly hurt, that I lucky man, that he do such thing many times. The English he spoke was highly efficient, but there was an error or omission every other word. No one would ever doubt what he meant; equally, no one would ever think him anything but foreign. 'I open door, you collapse,' he said. 'Not bullet, this bullet nothing. But you have no breath.'

'Been running,' I said.

He nodded. 'Sweat hard. You get cramps soon, maybe.'

He was taking it all remarkably calmly, I thought. 'I'd better tell you who I am. I'm John Close and I'm a lawyer from –'

'Australia,' Pavel Blanck said. 'City of Perth.'

'How d'you know?'

'Passport in pocket.' He laughed. He was a little Slav pixie, gap-toothed and, I guessed, permanently cheerful whatever horrors the world might have brought to his threshold.

I said, 'Do people collapse on your doorstep very often?'

A pause. 'Here, no, in Heaton. Other places, well, some-times it is known.' Then, still on his knees beside me, he took my hand and shook it. 'You are welcome in my house, though it is very sad, for he must have gone to God.'

'Peterkin, yes, he –'

'The man Pyotr, of him I speak.'

'Same man, different name.'

'He die how?'

'Fell down stairs. He was in prison.'

'Was murder?'

'I don't think so, but it's a possibility.'

Pavel pursed his lips, then rose from his knees to his feet in one youthful movement. He'd be seventy, at least, I thought.

I said, 'Some people were chasing me. I ran through the woods down there – and then up.'

'Up steps,' he laughed delightedly. 'I not surprised you faint.'

'Those people could be outside somewhere.'

'Yes.' Complete lack of concern.

'And they have a gun.'

'I also.' He pointed. In the corner by an oak sideboard stood an old army rifle. 'Three-oh-three Lee Enfield,' Pavel said. 'I marksman, also.' He went to the window, edged aside the velvet curtain and peered out through a net one. 'Coast quite clear,' he said cheerfully. 'What you bring to Pavel?'

Well, I'd brought nothing except myself.

'What should I have brought, Mr Blanck?'

'Pavel, *Pavel*! Not Mr Blanck. Never. He tell me you bring something.'

'Who told you?'

He was silent, pixie-smiling, shrewd eyes on my face.

Who could have told him anything about me – the priest? 'Has Father Franklin phoned you?'

He shook his head.

I thought about this. Who else could 'he' have been?

'Sergei?' I said.

'Who this Sergei?' Pavel snapped quickly.

'A Russian.'

His expression said very clearly that he disapproved of Russians. 'Why you talk to Russian?'

I said mildly, 'He talked to me. He wants to know about Peterkin – about Pyotr.'

'He know Pyotr, this Sergei?'

'Not as well as he'd like to.'

'But he know him?'

'I don't think so, not until Peterkin was already dead.'

'Where is Sergei?'

'Now? In England.'

He hissed between his teeth. 'Sergei chase you up steps?'

I said, 'I think those two were Americans.'

He was now a frowning pixie. 'First it is Soviet, then Americans.' Pavel paced the small sitting room on his bandy little footballer's legs. 'Secret Pyotr have, keep many years.' He turned and stared at me. 'Is secret no more.'

'Oh, it's a secret, all right,' I said.

'*You* know it!' He spoke accusingly.

I shook my head. 'No. Only a bit. His daughter knows the same bit. Probably *you* know.'

He laughed shortly. 'For what Pavel need secret! My friend Bodinski, he know. He last five minutes, then pfft.' Snapping pixie fingers indicated Father Bodinski passing. 'Pyotr, he know, he die. Maybe is murder, you not know even this.'

I said, 'He's guiding me towards it.'

'Who is?'

'Peterkin – Pyotr.'

Pavel said harshly, 'Is spirit guide, eh – hah!'

'He's left papers. Other things. Hidden in different places.' I began to get to my feet and my head throbbed where I must have banged it on his door as I passed out. I remembered that I'd seen something as I went down. What was it? I said, 'Leaf.'

He chose to misunderstand. 'Leaf if you want to. Do as you want.'

I said, 'Pavel, I have another of them – just the same.'

'What you have?'

'A leaf,' I said. 'Pyotr gave me directions and I found it where he'd hidden it.'

'You bring it here? Go now – fetch it.'

'It's in Australia, Pavel; his daughter has it.'

'Daughter's name?'

'Alex.'

'Sergei – he know you. He know Alex also?'

'Yes.'

'Then he know already – everything she have.'

'She's hiding,' I said, 'and she's good at it. Learned it from her father, and he was *very* good at it.'

He cocked his head to one side, thinking. I didn't interrupt. Finally, he said, 'Why you not bring leaf?'

'It didn't seem necessary. I do have it.'

'But this leaf – I do not see.'

'It's like the one at your door. Made of pottery. Rough glaze.'

Pavel said, 'You *say* this. How I *know*?'

'Perhaps we have to trust each other.'

'Trust! You crazy?'

I had to smile, aching head and the flesh wound notwithstanding. 'Some people do it.'

'Much good they do themselves! I am Pole, do not seek trust inside Pole, it taken away by many thieves!'

'When you asked me if I had brought something with me, did you mean the leaf?'

He shrugged.

I said, 'So we can go no further?'

He shrugged again. Then he said, 'This Pyotr, I meet him once in my life – when he arrive first in England. He receive instruction in the faith from my friend Father Bodinski.' He crossed himself. 'After he go, the Father tell me this is most dangerous man alive.' Pavel repeated the words, slowly. 'Most dangerous man *alive* – you understand?'

'Yes.'

'Why you think this is?'

'I can only guess. Why do *you* think?'

Pavel closed his eyes tightly for a moment. 'I do not know. I do not *want* to know. I hope I *never* know!'

'I'll try,' I said, 'to make sure you never do.'

He said, with great insistence, 'Also Sergei, all Soviets, all Americans.'

'Yes. But, meanwhile, Peterkin – Pyotr, if you'd rather – is trying to direct *me* towards something. It's probably this great secret of his: the one that made him the most dangerous man in the world. I don't know – But he's pushing me straight *at* something – I can feel the pressure in my back!'

He looked at me aslant, the pixie face drooping. I said, 'Pavel, why would I lie?'

'Why does everybody lie, John Close, lawyer from Perth? Lawyers worst liars in world. Lie, always lie.'

'How did the leaf come to you, Pavel?'

He blinked, once, slowly.

'Speaking of lies,' I said.

Suddenly the pixie was scowling.

I pursued it. 'You're lying, too.'

'Me – why I lie?'

'I don't know *why*,' I said. 'But you *are*. You must be. About three years back Peterkin paid a visit to friends and family. In Montenegro, so he said. Everybody thought he was a Jugoslav at that time. I know I did. But he wasn't Jugoslav, nor Montenegran, was he? He was as Russian as Lenin's whiskers, and when he flew off to Europe it was here he came – probably to this house – to *you*.'

Pavel blinked again, the little sloping eyes very bright.

'He brought you the leaf, didn't he, and told you to keep it until somebody came who had another one just like it? And that's why the leaf's by *your* door. It's innocent. It means nothing to anybody else, including Sergei. But it means something to me because *I* found one just like it a yard under water in the Abrolhos Islands, twelve thousand miles away. Did he mention the Abrolhos?'

There was a little shake of the pixie head, but otherwise a silence, which went on for a while, until I said, 'It's a matter of trust, Pavel. If both of us stick to the truth –'

'Wait,' he said, rising. 'Here you wait!' And vanished from the room, closing the door behind him. I heard other doors open and close in the next minute or two, and then he came back and said, 'Tomorrow we talk again.'

'All right.'

'Is good,' Pavel said. 'For you rest, for me thinking. Go away sleep.'

Truth to tell I didn't mind a bit. Between jet-lag, long-distance sprints and minor bullet-wound, the plug had been pulled on my supply of vitality, and I felt decidedly droopy.

'Where you stay?' Pavel was asking.

'Victoria Hotel.'

He was standing by the sideboard, holding a little pile of books and he said, 'I take you. Then, I library.'

'There's no need. You could phone me up a taxi.'

But he was insistent. With the books under his arm, he led me out of the back of the house. There was a short garden and, at the bottom of it, a wooden shed. I could hear, some-where nearby, the plunk-plunk of tennis balls. Pavel cocked his ear, listening. 'Always is tennis. Is happy place.'

'You like tennis?'

He shook his head. 'For Pavel – always football. But Pavel like people happy. See too much other.'

I wondered idly where his car was because there seemed not to be much room here. But then Pavel opened the door of the little cedar shed, unveiling a huge old motor-cycle made for anything but a pixie. He beamed proudly at me. 'Is Ariel Square Four. Pavel's first bike he own. Is only bike he own.'

It was a monster. Four cylinders and a 1000cc engine. He pointed out its important features one by one like a guide in an art gallery. It was thirty-odd years old and gleamed as if they'd only made it this week. He was tucking his library books into one of the bike's vast black panniers, when he said, 'Is fast.'

'I bet it is! What's CH.AD.11 mean, Pavel?'

'Get you there damn quick. You read this?' He held up one of the books.

I looked at the title. 'No.'

'Archaeology' – he had no difficulty with that word, or any word, just an idiosyncratic way of stringing them together – 'is interesting, very. Tomorrow we talk of all things maybe.' He put it in the pannier with the others, then tossed a crash helmet to me, and stepped lightly aboard. The monstrous thing had no modern nonsense like electric starters; it had to be kicked and there was an old-fashioned valve-lifter to help. He gave one thrust on the kick-start. Nothing. Then he winked and said, 'Now,' and kicked again and the thing came to roaring life as though telling us it was A-okay for lunar lift-off.

I will not deny a certain nervousness as we trundled forward, with Pavel's little legs barely touching the ground and an engine that would drive a small car along stroking away under my knees. Bloody dangerous, I thought, with memories of my earlier down-hill plunge very fresh at the front of my mind: surfaces with loose stones, sharp bends. Really, I should have insisted on a cab.

We roared out into the road, turned right and then flashed down one of the steepest hills I've ever seen. Pavel could ride, I'll say that. 'Nobody follow,' he yelled over his shoulder as we slid smoothly to a halt at traffic lights half a mile on. I yelled back, 'Who could keep up?'

He laughed delightedly and accelerated into space as the light showed amber/green. We did a couple of miles in a few minutes, smooth as silk through thick traffic, and I climbed off, shaky but exhilarated, outside my hotel.

'In morning,' said Pavel, revving his thousand cubic centimetres. 'Ten o'clock.'

'Yes,' I said.

'My place. And no drink this night. You are shock.' He raised a gauntlet and went rasping away like a flea on the back of a tiger.

I went up the steps and through the revolving door with his final words turning temptingly through my mind. In the lobby, my eye lit on a sign that said, 'American Bar'; as I collected my room-key I thought how soothing a drink would be. I went in, bought myself a dry Martini, drank it in three, and took the lift up to my room. It was one of those old hotels, to which bathrooms have been added by cutting off part of the room with a new wall; so from the door the bedhead was invisible. I closed the door behind me, put on the light and walked into the room, and they were sitting there, out of sight, by the bedhead. She was holding the pistol.

The man said, 'Tell me this, Mac. You a man or a mountain goat?'

10

I told them to get out and stay out. He laughed shortly and she smirked. He was below middle height, broad-bodied, with glasses and a lined forehead; Kissinger, more or less, but without the same evident glittering intelligence or the gravel voice.

'Okay, I'll go.' I turned for the door.

'At this range we don't miss,' the woman said. 'And this tube thing here is a silencer.'

For some reason I wasn't especially frightened. Perhaps there wasn't any fear left in me after Pavel's bike. I said, 'What is the American bid?'

'Bid?'

'We seem to be heading towards an auction,' I said. 'Don't we?'

She said, 'Don't get clever, sonny.'

They sat and stared at me. I stood and stared at them. I said, 'You'd better tell me, don't you think?'

'Tell you what?'

'What you want.'

'Don't get cute with me!'

I said, 'For God's sake – what's happening here – are we all rehearsing the words for a gangster film? You come into my room – break in, I expect – you threaten me, you talk like something with Cagney and George Raft in it. This afternoon you didn't just shoot at me, you did shoot me. First chance I get I'll call the police.'

'Oh dear,' the woman said, 'how you *do* frighten us.'

'All right, then, if the police don't worry you, I'll call Sergei.'

They looked at each other and stood up and told me to sit down. This whole scene, I thought, was on the verge of

91

comedy. Still, I sat. The man said, 'You don't understand, feller, do you?' And at that point I did begin to laugh. Hysteria, beyond a doubt.

He hit me then: back-handed, just as they do in the movies. He did so confidently. It hurt like hell and suddenly I was looking at him very soberly indeed.

He nodded. Then he said, 'Yes, we're American. I'm going to ask you a question that'll give you a clear perspective on all our positions here, ours and yours. You ever hear of American agents being flung out of Britain – or Australia for that matter – for exceeding their authority?'

I shook my head. And ran my tongue round my mouth. There was blood, but not much.

'We do as we like, right? This country here, Britain, United Kingdom, whatever, it's a client kingdom, old Roman style. What America wants is what you want. We need it, you give it, we take it, right? America comes *first* – okay?'

I nodded.

'So you're going to tell us what you know. Everything you know.'

'About?'

'Don't get –'

'Cute – no,' I said. 'I don't know anything.'

'Sure you do.'

'Not that's worth the knowing.'

The woman cut in. 'You know Sergei, you said so!'

'I sat next to a man on an aircraft. He said his name was Sergei. No surname, no patronymic. Not even the middle initials America always demands. If *you* know Sergei – who is he and what is he?'

She said, 'KGB. Must be.'

'It's plain you know as much as me,' I said, 'and *that's* bugger all.'

We sparred for some time. Then she picked up the phone and asked for a number, and after a moment, muttered a few words into it. 'Now we wait,' she said. I suspected by now that she was the senior of the two.

We waited. I asked if we could ring room service for some

coffee, and was surprised when it was done. By the man. When the knock came on the door I thought, here's the coffee, but it wasn't. A man came into the room: one of your English black beetles, nose in the air because of the frightful reek of inferiors in the vicinity, dark suit, tribal tie – and a gold watch-chain, for God's sake. About forty and trying hard to be sixty-odd.

The woman said, 'Rupert – you know anybody name of Sergei?'

'Not presently operating,' Rupert said. 'Is this the –?'

'Creep,' the American said sourly. 'The Australian creep. This is him. Tell him the state of play.'

Rupert looked at me, down his nose, naturally. 'What precisely is your difficulty?'

I said, 'There are several. The first is that I was shot in the back this afternoon by this homicidal bloody lunatic here. The second is that I'm being held prisoner here and now, at gunpoint. The third is that they keep demanding information from me without saying what for, or what it's about. The fourth difficulty, I suspect, will be with you.'

'You've been informed of America's primary status in this matter, I imagine?'

'You Poms can kiss America's nasty spotty bum if you like,' I said. 'I'm Australian, thank God.'

'Oh dear. You do have the traditional chip on your shoulder.'

'Both shoulders.'

'Yes, well, look. How to put it? Let's say it seems there is a matter of enormous delicacy up there in the air at the moment. Unspecified, but of importance to the other side.'

'How do you know?'

He tried hard to look mysterious and said, 'Sources.'

'And the other side is still Russia, is it?'

Rupert looked at me. He disliked what he saw. 'You are obliged to answer me,' he said. 'I am under no similar obligation to you.'

We wrangled some more. His view was that Bob Hawke and our sainted government would side with the Poms, and compel me. Mine, as an Australian lawyer, I said, was that

Bob had more sense, and they could try phoning Canberra if they liked. And then I got a bit shirty and asked why it was that government employee selection techniques produced nasty bastards whose first thought was always to twist a man's arm up behind his back, and whose mothers never taught them to say please. Doesn't matter what country, I said. Brits, Americans, Australians – all tarred with the same authoritarian brush. 'Although, come to think,' I ended up, 'Sergei's pretty civil.'

'You're a goddamn communist!' the American accused.

'What are you doing here anyway, Mr er –?' Rupert asked.

'In England? I'm dealing with a client's affairs.'

He fished in his pocket and produced a piece of plastic. It said 'Ministry of Defence' and 'authorized' and so on. I said, 'Try it this way round. If you think I know more than you know, just tell me what you know. If I *do* know more, and if telling you doesn't clash with my confidential relationship with a client, and if you say please very nicely, I may consider your request.'

That was when I began to understand. I was told they'd had leaks from Russia. Names weren't mentioned, but one leak had to be from the immediate area around Yuri Anastasovich Gusenko. Gusenko was after a great security secret that had somehow got loose. And if Gusenko was after it, then the matter *must* be important, because, although nobody knew what it was, Gusenko *was* head of the First Chief Directorate KGB, and was well known for not wasting time on trifles.

So that was it, and my turn now. I gave them a description of Sergei, stressing his education at The Queen's College, Oxford, and his accent to match. The news did not please Rupert, who muttered 'Queen's' contemptuously. I said I had a number of clients, and one had been a New Australian gentleman whom I believed to be Russian by birth, and who was now dead.

'Tell us all about this guy,' the American woman said.

'Certainly. He was a manual labourer for nearly forty years,' I told her, thus disappointing her greatly.

'I'm not sure I believe you.'

'Please yourself. Finally, the client on whose behalf I'm in the UK is a Japanese lady.'

'Japanese?' Rupert repeated. '*Japanese*? Where do *they* come in?'

'Through Immigration, in general; however this one was born in WA.'

'In where?'

'Work it out for yourself.'

And there we ended. My release consisted of the three of them walking out of my room, leaving behind a miasma of dire warnings, veiled and unveiled threats, and bafflement. I was baffled, too, but to a more limited degree. I lay on my bed, on my left side, and worked out for myself that the clever Mr Gusenko had now contrived to have armies of people hunting down his badly needed information; not only me, but two secret services – three if you counted Gusenko's own.

My own bafflement was limited because, unlike my (assumed) CIA and SIS acquaintances, I actually *knew* a few things. Gusenko also knew quite a bit, and so did Alex, but I was out in front – and wondering how Pavel had conned me out of his back door without my getting a good look at the leaf. Never mind, I thought. I'll see it in the morning. I dined, then slept, not very well in either case.

Being watched is a strange sensation. You read a lot about it – skilled shadowers lurking in busy streets, as people even more skilled shake them off. (They don't teach any of that stuff in the law department of University of WA.) What I now had to do was to reach Pavel without leading the intelligence army to him. And how, I wondered, do you do a thing like that?

Not easily, I soon realized. Yesterday I'd lost the Americans by being younger and running uphill; effective, but couldn't be repeated. Or could it? I flexed my stiff legs and felt the calf muscles complain, so I filled the bath with hot water and sat in it, kneading. When I got out, they felt better. After breakfast I asked for a taxi, then told the driver I wanted the gate at Heaton Woods.

'Goin' 'oggin'?' he asked with a laugh.

'Sorry?'

' 'Oggin',' he said. 'Watchin' courtin' couples. You need big boots and a long stick wi' a feather on t'end. Find a lot of 'oggers in 'Eaton Woods.'

'Bit early in the day, isn't it?'

'Ah, but 'oggers are optimists.'

'Do you always ask people that?'

'Only alternate Thursdays.'

I've had sillier conversations, but not much. When I asked him if there was a more roundabout route, he said, 'Is an' all, we'll go Six Days Only,' and took me along roads I hadn't seen before, until suddenly we began dropping down a road that was very steep indeed, plunging in among high old trees, then rearing up the other side, and stopping at the stone gatepost I'd run through the day before. I had money ready, and handed it over as the car halted. As I got out he called, 'Watch out for 'oggers. You can allus tell 'em by their boots!' I heard his laugh disappear up the hill, as I began to canter along the track for the second time.

It was very quiet. A breeze rustled the boughs high above me, but otherwise there was only the sound of my feet on the path, and the stream below. I felt surprisingly fit. My bruised and holed back ached, but was nothing like as sore as I'd expected. Pavel had dressed it with genuine skill, probably born of practice. In the cool morning air I even felt a sense of well-being.

It evaporated pretty quickly on the steps, but I was buoyed up when I glanced back, by the absence of other runners behind me. I had had one fear beforehand: that they'd guess what I was up to, and await me in comfort at the head of the stairs. But when, gasping, I reached the top and began to walk down the back street to the village, there was nobody about except a couple of women with shopping baskets walking together, gossiping.

I stopped on the corner and looked round it at the main road where the buses ran, quite excited at being *still* ahead and at the thought that the leaf Pavel had had from Peterkin would put me further ahead. Knowing the way now I slipped round the back of Pavel's house, to go to the rear door. This meant passing the shed. Its cedar door swung open. The shed was empty. I looked at the space, and thought of the gleaming machine and its doting pixie of an owner, and swallowed as I wondered where they could have gone.

Heart hammering, I went up the path to the back door. It, too, lay open. I called 'hello' and when nobody responded, stepped inside.

11

Gradually, nervously, I moved from room to room through that small house, aware from the beginning that it was empty because an empty house and one with people in it respond differently to sounds, and you can tell the difference at once. Pavel simply was not the kind of careless man who left his doors unlocked and swinging. Something, therefore, was wrong. I was afraid all the time that I would find him dead in one of those quiet rooms. I didn't. Dead or alive, Pavel wasn't there. As I worked my way up to the attics though, one thing was blindingly clear: every room had been thoroughly searched. In two of the bedrooms, carpets had been rolled back and floorboards prised up; in a first-floor bedroom a small scatter of soot in an old cast-iron fireplace indicated a search of the chimney. It would be wrong to say the search had created chaos, because the pixie's home, though neat as a pin, was frugally furnished. What the house was . . . was newly disordered.

Except, that is, in the room I'd been in with Pavel the day before: the sitting room that held his desk and books. That *was* in real chaos: papers all over the floor, drawers pulled out of the desk and sideboard and upended, contents strewn about.

All this is my fault, I thought, in a sudden and painful spasm of guilt that had my throat momentarily full of vomit. Whoever had done it had been led to Pavel, and only I could have led them. The contents of my stomach rose a second time at the thought of Pavel himself – and what might have happened to him, because *that*, too, was my fault. My own clumsy blundering had led somebody here, to Parson Drive, to this house, to little Pavel.

Who was it? Who'd done this? Who had him now? I knew with awful certainty that the door was not going to open suddenly; that I was not going to hear Pavel say, 'Is morning, hello, hello!' No, somebody'd managed to track me yesterday. But who? The Americans and the SIS man, Rupert, had professed their ignorance forcefully when I'd talked to them the night before. Sergei was, as far as I knew, nowhere in the area, and did not know I was here.

Sergei, of course, might have supporters in sufficient number to watch me day and night, people who'd stepped in as soon as I left with Pavel, the people who did *this*. I was still staring with deep sadness at the scatter of Pavel's possessions when I saw his books. There were plenty of books on the floor, many of them in Polish. What made me notice these was the heavy plastic film in which they were covered – lending-library bindings.

I bent and picked them up. When he and I had left this house, Pavel had taken three books and recommended one of them to me – what *had* the title been? Something about archaeology, something about gods, was it? The three books in my hands were all detective stories. I looked carefully at each; none was based on archaeology, nor were gods in any of the titles. But did it all mean what it seemed to mean – that Pavel had been to the library and then returned here with these new books? That he'd then gone out again on his motor bike?

If so – what was it all about?

I pulled back the edge of the curtain and looked out. Parson Drive is a quiet place and I could see nobody at all. Front door next: I opened it just enough to look at the short path and the steps. Where Peterkin's pottery leaf had been there was now a large, pale pebble; one which neatly fitted the space.

Which seemed to show that he'd been and he'd gone again. On his Ariel Square Four, which could probably reach the stars in half an hour, and which he rode beautifully. The books had been left here, the leaf taken. What did all *that* mean?

Well, just possibly, I thought, it *could* mean that Pavel

might be safe. I puzzled over it. Pavel had been mates with Father Bodinski, who'd vanished all those years back, and Pavel didn't want to travel the same involuntary route. Pavel, therefore, had perhaps disappeared voluntarily. But why? Probably because he thought he was in danger. He may have been followed, though given his chosen mode of transport that was a bit unlikely; or he may have found he was being watched, and decided to get out.

Yes, but he'd arranged to meet *me* here this morning. And what would I do in his place? Run like a rabbit, that's what I'd do. And maybe, just maybe, try to leave some kind of sign behind. If there was time.

Well, the library books could be one kind of sign, the missing leaf another. Also there was Peterkin's own contribution: CH.AD.11. Whatever that meant! Who might know – the Bishop? Or Father Franklin, whom I hadn't asked? Pavel might know, but he hadn't answered when I had asked, and was in no position to answer now.

Or – there was the book about gods and archaeology. Which came first, the chicken or the egg? The most direct thing, in that it had come direct to me, to John Close, solicitor, was Peterkin's own part of it, and Peterkin had planned his obstacle race damned carefully. Therefore, I shortly took the trail after CH.AD.11 via Father Franklin. On the other side of the city.

Telephone: I could call him; no need actually to go there. And there was a phone box close to the end of the cobbled street.

I said, 'Father Franklin, my name's John Close, we met yesterday, you may remember . . .'

He said, of course, and hello, and had I managed to talk to Pavel?

'Yesterday,' I said disingenuously. 'And he's set me a bit of a puzzle which I'm hoping you may be able to help me solve.'

'Puzzle!' said the Father, and his sudden frown came down the phone at me. 'I'm not much for puzzles, Mr Close.'

'I realize that, and I'm sorry, but it really may be very

important. It's the meaning of some letters and numbers.'

'I hope,' he said, 'that you aren't wasting my time.'

'The sequence is a capital C and an H together. Then a full stop. Then an A and a D together. Then numeral one twice. Could it be a chapter in the Bible, perhaps? And a verse?'

'That,' said Father Franklin, 'is something one might expect an educated man to know, Mr Close. Have you not *got* a Bible?'

'At home,' I said. 'In Australia.'

'Go and buy a pocket edition.'

'I will, I will,' I gabbled, sensing that this growing disapproval would lead in a moment to a hung-up phone. 'And I've a contribution for your church as well. I'll bring it to you some time soon. Please trust me.'

He sighed audibly. 'C and H *could* mean Chapter, of course, and the full stop indicates abbreviation. But I know of no book in the Bible which begins with the letters A and D. So I'd guess it wasn't that.'

'Anything else strike you about it?'

'C-H-A-D,' Father Franklin muttered irritably. A pause, then he said: 'Chad was the little man looking over the wall and saying "Wot no anything." Remember him – a cartoon figure?'

'No, I don't, but I'll look him up. Well, thanks for your time. I promise you will get the money for the church.'

'And, of course, Mr Close, Chad, or rather Saint Chad, is the name of one of the churches here in the city.'

'With the full stop?'

'Without.'

'Father Franklin,' I jabbered. 'You're a –'

'Priest,' he said, 'not a quizmaster. I'd be humbly grateful if, in the future, you'd try to remember the distinction.'

'One more thing.'

'Just how great is your contribution to *be*, Mr Close?'

I thought of Peterkin and the money he'd left behind to fund my search. Peterkin had attended that church, taken instruction there from Father Bodinski. 'A hundred,' I said. 'No – make that a thousand.'

I sensed his frown recede into the handset, like water going down a plug. 'For that amount of money,' he replied, 'you may ask me two questions.'

'Where is it – St Chad's?'

'In Toller Lane,' he said. 'That's T-O-L-L-E-R.'

'Would a 74 bus go near it?' From the phone box I could see one grinding towards me up the hill.

'Within about a quarter-mile, I'd think.'

Sprinting for the bus stop, I neither saw nor sensed any surveillance.

The Pakistani conductor didn't know where I should get off for St Chad's Church, but one of his passengers did.

'It's Duckworth Lane you want, love,' said a large lady, turning with difficulty to look back over her shoulder.

'Thank you.'

'I'll tell you, don't worry, when we get there.'

'Thanks.'

She gave me a running commentary on the way. 'See that house there, the detached one up there. That's Garden Lane and it's Sutcliffe's house is that – the Yorkshire Ripper.' And a few hundred yards further on, 'See there, Saltburn Place. J.B. Priestley was born just there.' Then, 'Off you get, love. And walk down yonder. It's on the right.'

The absence of a full stop worried me a bit as I looked at the board outside St Chad's. Name of church and parish, times at which Mass was said, name of priest. Chad here was one word, unsplit by punctuation. Perhaps Peterkin, writing it, had simply made a slip, or, more likely, had known that Chad would be recognized for what it was by local cognoscenti, by people like Pavel or Father Franklin.

Inside, all was quiet, the morning Mass long over. Inspection of the pews at the back showed no numbers. I moved forward, a bit hesitantly, because something about an empty church does that to you, and then began counting. One . . . two . . . three . . . four. Here was pew eleven, its wood worn smooth from wear and polish.

But no message that I could see. I dropped a coin deliberately to make a reason for a hands-and-knees search, and thought: how silly to have to create an excuse for being on my knees in church. I turned to look beneath pew eleven, and saw a smooth stone floor, dark wood . . . and something pale lying deep in a dark shadow; pale and almost out of reach. To touch it with my fingers I almost had to lie down, but touch it I did, and *when* I did, knew this was something I had touched before. In a moment I had pulled out one of Peterkin's pottery leaves.

'Found it, have you?' said a voice. Another priest in rubber-soled shoes.

'Er – yes.'

'Heard the coin fall. Sound carries here. And you know what we priests are like about money!'

I ached to examine the leaf, but had to talk, however briefly. He was a pleasant man, and grateful when I handed over a note for church funds. In return I got a short tour. But at last, after what seemed aeons of time, I was out in the street again, turning the leaf over in my hands. I'd felt with my fingers the little roughness on the base. There *was* lettering there. I looked, and sighed.

'Pol cc.' These conundrums of Peterkin's seemed never to stop coming. Where in the world did that big, essentially simple man suddenly develop this taste for tortuous cunning?

'Pol cc.' Pol must, I thought, mean Polish. In most places I knew – in Australia, for instance, or New Zealand, or here in England – the letters cc would stand for cubic centimetres or for cricket club. Somehow I doubted the existence of a Polish cricket club, however complete the integration of one people into another. What was it then?

Father Franklin told me, on the phone and not without audible sighs of irritation, that there existed in the city a Cavalry Club, whose membership consisted of those gallant Poles who in 1939 had fought Panzer tanks from horseback. 'Those who survived *then*,' he added. 'A lot fewer survive now. But they go there still, to their club, and take their sons and grandsons.'

I went, once again, on the apparently miraculous number

74 to a house behind Grange Road, where they met. The door was open and an elderly man mopped away at the bar floor.

'What you want?' he demanded. 'Bar open twelve o'clock sharp.'

I said, 'I'm not sure. Somebody sent me here.'

The normal response might have been to ask who had done the sending. It's what I expected, anyway. Instead, this man walked across the room, opened a door, and yelled upward something in, presumably, Polish. A reply came. He bade me come over, and pointed. 'Man awaits for you,' he said.

The man waiting for me was Pavel, perched on top of a bar seat like a pixie on top of a toadstool and grinning happily. 'You find?'

'I find. Pavel, your house is –'

'Of course, of course. It searched, yes?'

'Yes.'

'Expect this, Pavel expect this very much. See men, know Pavel must go. You clever find me.'

'Not so clever. I thought at first you must be dead!'

'Soon you know not, I am right. You see books?'

'On the floor, yes.'

'Not matter where. You find leaf in church of Chad?'

'Yes.'

'Pavel put him there.'

'I know you did. It couldn't have been anybody else.'

'And so you are here!'

'And so I am here. And now that I *am* here, what do I get? Is there, at long bloody last, something from Peterkin?'

'From Peterkin?'

I don't often lose my temper. *But* this time even when I'd counted to ten it was still fizzing, and I grabbed Pavel by the lapels and roared at him to play straight, to stop lying.

'What lie this?' he asked innocently.

'The lie,' I bellowed, 'that you only met Peterkin once.'

He looked at me quizzically. 'Maybe is two times with Pyotr.'

'The second time,' I grated through clenched teeth, 'being just over three years ago.'

104

'Was some time.'

'When he came here,' I said, 'with this bloody leaf, and left it with you with certain instructions, yes?'

He nodded.

'He told you to expect me one day, because I'm thirty years younger than he is and could be expected to live longer. Right?'

He nodded again.

'He told you to make bloody sure I was who I said I was, and that I was persistent, and then to be sure I got my hands on the leaf.'

'True. Is all true.'

'So while everybody'd thought, including Alex and her mother, Peterkin's unofficial wife, that the old fellow was tramping Montenegran mountains, he'd been in Yorkshire, fifteen hundred miles from there, setting up this devious trail for *me* to follow. Why, Pavel?'

'Why you ask why?'

'Because there was already a scheme to protect Peterkin's secret. It was concocted by Father Bodinski originally, wasn't it? Papers put in a convent. All very secure.'

Pavel said promptly, 'Convent close. To find Pyotr is big problem, long search, but he found. We wait. He need money to come. He save money. Then Pyotr come. Take paper from hiding place, make new place.'

'Where?' I asked.

'Here,' Pavel said. 'In Pavel's hand,' the hand producing it like a magician from behind his back.

The hand held another of Peterkin's brown manila envelopes, much tied up in sticky tape. My fingers told me there might be a substantial wodge of paper inside. And a leaf.

'Read and learn,' Pavel said.

'Do you know what's in here?'

'Never. Pavel not want know *nothing*.'

'Can I read it here?'

'Of course.'

'Pavel,' I said, 'was there any significance in that book you mentioned pointedly yesterday? The one about gods and things.'

He said, 'You must for this decide. I not here after now.'

'You're here, all right.'

He shook his pixie head. 'All for me is done. Holiday for Pavel. Go see friend far places. On Ariel Square Four cannot be follow. Pavel return when all finish. Only then.'

At that point he ups and outs, and soon I could hear him, out the back somewhere, kicking the mighty bike into life. After a moment he throbbed off on it and I looked round for a knife with which to open the envelope . . .

12

Peterkin wrote:

So I come to UK one more time. You know I have to do this. How I hear convent has close? This I not tell. But paper must go to new place. Secret – I must move it.

But first I start to think. It is now all these many years. Private secret very old now. Like me it is old. Maybe it have lost much important weight. Maybe now I hide always for no reason? This must I learn. But I have not money, anyway little money, so how to get cash I need? I remember man in Fremantle Gaol, he tell me how make money from Americans. He say American is clever man at his home, but fool on vacation. I think much about this. All his life had Peterkin been honest man. Peterkin find coin on ground, he always look for man who drop it. Pay tax on wage, pay landlord, borrow but pay back. Keep out of trouble always. When fools try rob Peterkin, I fight them and who go to gaol? Peterkin go and when Peterkin in gaol he learn tricks. Not use, but learn. Also remember.

Much is there to think of. Yet of these things nothing that is new. All thoughts are thoughts what I think many times. I think them when Nikita Sergeyevich make himself General Secretary. When Kennedy come almost to war over Cuba, I think I give to USA my secret. Many times after, I struggle to decide. But after – always I am certain it was right to keep. It is right. Still it is right. Except secret may not exist any more. I hope it not exist, hope it destroyed and I am free, not

107

carrying secret for life. Then I can go live in open with wife and daughter and fear nothing ever.

You know what happen. Peterkin buy gold. He use savings, make nugget, find Americans. Plenty Americans in Perth, in Fremantle, some are rich men in big yachts. Is good time for me, very happy, very easy. I sell many nugget before am given away by American woman. Before trial, not tell you how I play nugget trick. But I tell now.

First you find American. If rich, always he tell you quick; if he no rich Peterkin go find another. Talk. American always tell you how he get all his money. He say real estate, he say stock market, he say make shoes. I tell him I find money. All I want.

He say what kind money? I say, this kind. I wear small nugget on leather string round neck. Take out, show him. One ounce, maybe. Let him hold in hand, feel weight. He like, maybe for wife.

This nothing. This I tell him. Bigger nugget I have. Big, big nugget too heavy for Peterkin wear round neck. Also too big for American to buy. There is much talk, much drink, beer for Peterkin, Swan Light, no alcohol, Peterkin keep head clear. In Fremantle Gaol my friend tell me all this happen. It happen like he say, so easy. Two things, always. American say where this place you find gold? Tell me, he say, we become partners, use machinery, find much gold. Peterkin say no. Say he find some place, this place his. Show nugget many times. Ask American ever go Las Vegas? All Americans go Las Vegas. See Golden Nugget? Certainly he see. This big nugget, I say, is from Western Australia, is found in WA. One day I find like that, another big piece gold. I tell him nugget have extra price over pure gold.

Soon he say he wish see big nugget I have. Peterkin say in two days, three days perhaps. Not want to sell, but show him.

And so it is done. American in his head see himself with nugget in America, show to friends. Friends not have big nugget. Friends envy him. He say, oh boy, oh boy.

Peterkin reluctant, American determined. Big price he pay. Peterkin go away.

To Europe I go away. Always in Australia I am man from Montenegro, but passport come from New Zealand when migrant. Out of date but easy I get new passport. Fly on Greek charter, and from Athens on to London to move papers.

In London I walk up Piccadilly one day. Stop in big surprise. Here shop belong Aeroflot, Soviet airline. In window posters say Visit USSR. Say Moscow beautiful, visit Leningrad, sunshine in Sochi. Not say visit Vorkuta, not say Lubyanka lovely or barbed wire sharp, also electric, say come see USSR!

Peterkin stare, go on with walking. He think, is this thing possible? Can Peterkin go? If Peterkin go, he can find out about his secret. But is big risk. Always USSR will be big risk for Peterkin. Walk and walk. In Regent Street is British Airways shop. There also is poster, Visit USSR. Here I can ask.

Big surprise. Visit is easy. Pay three hundred sterling pounds, go with many people in big party. Visa not hard to get. Take few days. Girl smile to me, say is fun trip.

I think is not fun for Peterkin. Go into park, sit, look at passport. Peter Kinsky, it say, New Zealand citizen, born Skopje, Montenegro.

But I know Soviets have biggest file in world, this called Great Index. My name in it as Kremlin Guard, also as escaped criminal. Fingerprints in file, also height, weight, eye colour, wound scars, size feet, colour hair. Soviet border guard at airport check with Great Index, there is Pyotr Kinsky. It is all computer, easy for this guard.

Passport say born Skopje, Montenegro. I look long time at this. Pyotr Kinsky born Ukraine. Is more Kinsky in Great Index? Many, of course. How many same height, weight, age, scars? If they make serious check, they check fingerprints, then Peterkin go Lubyanka immediate. In my head is picture of Gusenko, Yuri Anastasovich. Old now. Cruel. He be glad to torture me, in person, himself, Yuri, my old comrade.

I find New Zealand House in London, go to consular office, talk to young lady. She very pretty, smiles always, is optimist, say many NZ passports go into Moscow, out again, no trouble. Never trouble. Never? She say never. Soviets not enemies of New Zealand. I think, Soviets enemies of Pyotr Kinsky!

Three days I think and worry myself. Can criminal false passport be got for me? I try find answer but cannot.

Peterkin must choose.

Cannot decide. Coin must decide, like two-up game. Toss coin. Heads I go, tails not go. Not dare look, leave coin lying two hours on grass in park. When I look, see head of Queen!

So I go. I am in terror, but is easy. Try remember through many years every lesson in security. In travel party are many women. I inspect with care. Two are old, from Scotland, I hear strong accents. One strong accent like another to stranger. I talk to ladies, at airport, on plane, in line to show papers. We all nervous because this is USSR. Therefore nervous laughs. I laugh myself past the border guard. Am in – have now three days.

This Moscow I visit is not Moscow Peterkin left. Then are German tanks near city, no German people in city. Now are many Germans in city, no German tanks outside. I go to theatre, to circus, to parks, to ballet at Bolshoi, is Swan Lake of course. Go also many times to Red Square, walk in Kremlin where tourists go, walk round outside, visit graves in Kremlin wall.

All this time, eyes in back of head. Peterkin watch, watch, then watch more, watch everybody. Nobody watch Peterkin. Nobody follow him. Other people not spied on, also. Maybe am blind, but not think so. Here

110

is new regime, no following, no spying. This mean is no secret police. Is ridiculous! Russia has spies, always.

Then is second night in Moscow for me. Moon is thin, sky cloudy. I been to theatre. I take Scottish ladies to hotel, say in loud voice I take quiet walk before sleep. Go to Red Square.

Plenty light here. Plenty people also. Lenin mausoleum now closed, but still plenty people, walk slow, look at everything. I am slow also, walk until I am among tourists at Kremlin wall graves. Here is Voroshilov. I saw him many times, also Budenny, his friend with the big moustache. I look at names I have forgotten, most I not want to remember. I look also at my position.

Soon I am there. I see mark. It is as I remember. I stop, I bend, I touch . . .

And there, damn it, he stopped, like a serial writer trying to tease people along. He'd more *cause*, I'll admit, but it was maddening!

He left a blank space on the sheet, enough for three lines or so, then started again. By this time it was next morning in Moscow.

It was not hard. There was bureau Intourist at hotel. I say to girl I have interest in art. She say go this museum, this gallery. Peterkin shake head, say he wish see sculptors work. She tell me where school. I go. Find young man, buy him drink and food, show him my leaves, say what I want.

He say tomorrow too quick for kiln, for glaze, for everything. I say tomorrow. I say if he betray me he be killed. He say work will be done tomorrow, but not be perfect. We agree.

So now is here. I have my leaves. Take to airport, say proudly, 'Have sculpted leaves of weeping birch'; show leaves to customs officer. He smile, say how beautiful, Soviet sculptors full of sensitiveness and Peterkin lucky man, how much he pay?

111

*We talk. Scottish ladies arrive. They very happy, have
dolls and toy balalaika. We all laugh. I am on aircraft.
Goodbye Moscow. G'day London.*

I thought how strange it was to be sitting in this rather
dingy upstairs bar, reading about Peterkin's misbehaviour in
Moscow. But then strangeness is always comparative, isn't
it? To be in a club for Polish lancers in a terrace of sandstone
houses in Bradford is pretty strange to begin with.

But nothing like as strange as what Peterkin had been up
to!

I began to think about it, and realized that, like Peterkin
flying with relief out of Moscow, I, too, needed a bit of G'day
London.

'Have you a phone?' I asked. I called a taxi, then put my
papers and my new leaf in my pockets and went to the hotel
to pack. I felt really quite light-hearted, and there were three
reasons. First that I didn't have Peterkin's secret – not yet.
Secondly, and very important indeed, I could actually *prove*
I didn't. To whom? Well, to Sergei, or the charming CIA
couple, or the posh Englishman, Rupert, whose profession
was contempt. One of that happy band, confronted by the
gap in Peterkin's Moscow tale – assuming they got it from
me, and then read it – would be compelled to admit that,
while I knew a good bit, I didn't have what the Americans
sometimes call the total enchilada. For a start – what about
the leaves that kept falling my way? Why leaves anyway? I
hadn't the faintest notion. There *must* be a reason though.
Peterkin had always reasoned pretty hard.

So I felt much reassured a while later, as I sat in another
hotel bedroom, this time at Heathrow, and telephoned
Jane.

She's Jane Strutt. In my optimistic moments, it pleases
me to think we're almost engaged. I'm her solicitor, and I'm a
trustee of Stringer Station in the north of Western Australia,
which Jane inherited from her great-aunt and gave to a group
of Aboriginals as a place to carry on the Dreamtime. Jane is
an engineer by training, an officer in the WRAC by pro-

112

fession, and formidable by nature. I always have the feeling
that if I lived nearer, we'd be that much closer to the altar;
but trying to carry on a courtship at long range has its diffi-
culties.

She has one of those swift ways of answering the phone.
'Major Strutt,' she said briskly.

'Since when?'

'Since August, John.'

'Congratulations. Bet you're a colonel in a fortnight. Move
over Montgomery, watch out Wellington –'

'Thanks, and where are you?'

I told her, and she said, 'Taken root at the Penta, have
you?'

'How d'you know I'm at the P–?'

Jane said, 'Shhh!'

'I want to see you.'

'I'm glad to hear it. But why when you've been here so
long, are you only now ringing me?'

I said, 'Well, there are questions.'

'Not on the telephone, John. Over dinner, if you can spare
the time.'

So there's me, panting to see her and already wrong-footed,
waiting for her that evening in a niceish, Greekish sort of a
place in St Martin's Lane, Beotys by name. Eight o'clock
she'd specified, and at eight o'clock something unrecogniz-
able as an army officer came down the stair, wearing dark-
blue and shimmering – did I say that Jane was prosperous? –
hemline somewhere twixt knee and ankle, a broad smile,
and a question on her lips:

'Did you come all this way to see me?'

'Well, er, no,' I said.

She sat carefully. 'Good. Mind – you've taken your
time . . .'

'Been pretty busy,' I muttered.

'Doing what?'

'No,' I said. 'My turn with the questions. How did you
know I was at the Penta?'

She winked. 'You fly around with a little flag on you.'

'Do I – what kind of flag?'

113

'It's an electronic one. When your name comes up there's a flashing light and quite a rude little noise.'

'Which computer?'

'Immigration,' Jane said.

'How come you get to see it? The likes of that aren't for oil-caked engineers.'

She glanced round. The restaurant wasn't full yet. 'They seem to be trying me out. For the last couple of months it's been port and airport security. Before that it was Codes and Cyphers.

'MI what?'

'Dunno. It's MI something though. Five, six, eleven. It's all in the air.'

'You want to do it?'

'Dunno, again.'

I said, 'Who does the bomb disposal job in Belfast?'

'Ordnance Corps. No women – just big, strong men.'

'You think that's wrong?'

Jane breathed out through her nose, the way she does. It's not a snort, but it would be from most people. She said, 'Women are deft –'

'You did say *deft*?'

She grinned. 'Neat fingers and a light touch we've got on our side. In my case a degree in mechanical engineering. I volunteered once. They wouldn't entertain even the thought. There, there, dear – go on with your knitting!'

'Still, they've made you a major. What do you wear?'

'Crown on each shoulder.'

'You could swap them for dungarees and go into coal-mining – I see they're going to have to let women down the pits, so great is the demand.'

'Thanks.'

'Or come on out to WA.'

'Yes, I know.' She looked at me straight. 'Thanks. But . . . John, what *are* you up to?'

So I looked around me for cocked ears, and then the waiter came and we ordered drinks, and while we waited I said, 'How'd *you* know I'm up to anything? And *wasn't* that a smart change of subject!'

'Alien under observation. That's how I know.'
'*Alien!*'

Jane grinned at my bared fangs. 'Austr-alien,' she said. And then, 'There was a report about you.'

'I bet there was,' I said angrily. 'Nasty nerd of a Pommy bastard, Rupert by name. Works with some equally abhorrent Americans. Tried to push me around in –' I paused. 'You actually come from Bradford.'

'Thornton,' Jane said, 'but near enough.'

'I've just been there.'

'I know.'

We drank and ate and were interrupted and tried to start again, but restaurants are no good for quiet conversations about things that need to be kept secret. So at last we left and started walking towards Holborn, murmuring quietly, and I began to tell Jane about Peterkin. Matter of fact, I'd introduced him before, months before, in earlier conversations, but in those days he'd been alive and merely a comic New Australian with a nice line in swindles.

The new (dead) Peterkin wasn't funny at all, and at some point as we walked along Theobalds Road, Jane said, 'You'd better not say more.'

'Oh, come on!' I said. 'I need to talk to someone I can trust. This whole business is getting too big for just me!'

She squeezed my arm. 'You can't trust me, sport.'

'Why not?'

'Because I'm a perfidious Pom –'

'Oh, Christ!'

'– What's more I'm sworn. To defend the Queen, her Crown and Majesty. And her Dignity. Official Secrets. The whole shooting match.'

'Look, Jane!'

'What's more, I'm curious. Intrigued. Nosy. And probably duty-bound to worm it all out of you.'

'Sounds like it would be fun,' I said. 'That bit, anyway.'

'I'd better say good night.'

I said, 'No – please don't.'

We'd stopped walking by this time. She said, 'He knew, didn't he? Peterkin knew.'

'I assume so.'

'And you know, too, don't you?'

'Not me, no.'

'But you must!'

'He didn't tell me. Left that bit blank.'

She blinked at me.

I said, 'Since everybody else is already following me about hopefully, you could join in – perhaps as Rupert the Despiser's right-hand, er, girl, er, woman, er, person. Couldn't you?'

'And betray you?'

'Nothing to betray, not at the moment.'

She said, 'There will be. You're near, and getting nearer. What you know is valuable.'

'Not very – not at the moment, it isn't.'

'And probably only you,' Jane said very seriously, 'can make all their dreams come true. Just you. Nobody else. That's true, isn't it?'

'Reckon it probably is.'

'Do you know what happens next?'

'What I have to *do* – I know that.'

'Then don't tell *me*, John.'

I said, 'For God's sake, Jane, I've been banking on your help!'

'This time you can't, I'm sorry.'

I said furiously, 'Who was it said, "If I had to choose between betraying my country and betraying my friend, I hope I'd have the courage to betray my country"?'

'Forster said it.'

'I agree with him.'

She said, 'How soon can you go back home, John?'

'Soon as I like.' I was glaring at her. 'There's not much to stay for, is there?'

She had her eyes lowered, lids down: first time I'd seen her like that. Then her hand came up and it was a tear her hand brushed at. She muttered, 'I'm sorry.'

'I'll bet!'

At that Jane's eyes came up. Even moist with tears those eyes were like a pair of gun barrels, and she spoke now with flat determination. 'I have a duty,' she said. 'I've accepted it, I hold a commission, I've sworn an oath. What's the point of all that if I cop out at the first test?'

'So that's it, then?' I was turning away with lumps of lead where my heart should be, when she said, suddenly, 'We're still on the same side!'

I looked at her.

'Well, aren't we – Britain and Australia? When were we anything else?'

'What you imply,' I told her, 'is that what is Britain's is Britain's and what is Australia's is Britain's, too!'

'Not what I mean at all. I mean we're in the same alliances, we sail ships together, we fly together, all those things.'

'You're not taking *me* over – understand that!'

No trace of the tear now. Jane was smiling the same steady Jane smile. 'I'm coming to the aid of an old ally – that's what I'm doing. You need help; maybe I can provide some of it. And, at the same time, stay closer to you than the others.'

'You can stay as close as you like.' A powerful sense of relief was growing in me.

'It's purely a matter of one's own viewpoint,' Jane said. 'And in my view we should be working together.'

I said, 'Agreed. We work together to the end.'

'Yes.'

'At which point,' I went on, 'the decision is mine.'

'What decision?'

'The one where everything's in the open. At that point, if and when it arrives, *I* decide.'

She gave me a beady look and changed the subject, leaving me to wonder whether she'd agreed or not. 'These leaves,' she said musingly, and I forgot the rest. 'What's in them, do you suppose?'

'In them? I don't suppose there's anything *in* them. They carry messages – that's their function.'

'You think that's all?' We were strolling now past Holborn Police Station. I'd have headed for Lincoln's Inn Fields – old, stylish and romantic once – except it's all dossers nowadays

117

and hardly romantic at all. So we turned right and walked towards the railings and austerity of Gray's Inn. We lawyers are homing pigeons.

'All,' I said. 'Yes, it's all. What makes you think –'

'Are they heavy?'

'Heavy-ish,' I said. 'Solid lumps of pottery – they're bound to be heavy.'

'Normal, you'd say? Not exceptionally heavy, not exceptionally light – that's your estimate?'

'Yes – why?'

She stopped and turned to face me. 'While the lights were out in Moscow,' Jane said, 'your pal Peterkin was up to no good, at least according to what you told *me* – and you have read what he wrote. Then, when the lights came on again, Peterkin is already off, hurriedly finding himself a young sculptor who'll apparently do more or less anything for a square meal. Next thing after *that*, he's smuggling his weeping-birch leaves past a most unusually sentimental customs man at Sheremetyevo, and successfully, too. From what I hear they don't select frontier guards for their sentimentality, but old Peterkin still slides by. Probably had his two tame Scots ladies doing his carrying for him.' She paused. 'No, my lad – if those two leaves didn't *contain* something or other, or conceal something or other, then I'm Margretta van der Alster, the celebrated Dutchwoman. Where's the nearest?'

'Dutchwoman?'

'Leaf, before I throttle you with these here hands.'

'At the Penta Hotel.'

'Then take me to the Penta Hotel,' Jane said, 'at once, if you please.'

I was just opening my mouth to say, 'With pleasure,' when Jane said, 'As you were,' and I saw she was blushing. 'I believe,' she said quickly, 'that I could have phrased that rather better.'

'You certainly could. You could have said, let's *both* go to the Penta Hotel.'

She said, 'Want me to find out about that leaf you've got?'

'All right.'

Jane thought for a moment, the blush subsiding. 'From what you say, we'll already have been seen together. If we separate now, maybe they'll think it's just been a dinner date. Look – leave the leaf at the hotel desk tomorrow, and I'll call round and pick it up. I'll get on with it lickety-spit, and let you have the news by tomorrow night.'

'And you won't tell Her Majesty before you tell me?'

'Nope. G'night.' She kissed me on the cheek and skipped off into the brightness of High Holborn.

I went back to the Penta by tube, and the journey was like a bloody obstacle course. Drunken larrikins menacing everybody on platforms and trains, a couple of escalators not working, little old ladies struggling with their bags past the averted eyes of the paid help. Heathrow's an unlovely place, and the English, a lot of the time, are unlovely people. One of the unloveliest of them was waiting for me in the foyer of the hotel – the one I knew only as Rupert. He knew me, it seemed, as Close.

He was sitting on a low couch. He rose out of it, looked down his nose at me, and said, 'Close, you've twelve hours to get out of the country.'

'Expect that's the notice you're going to serve me,' I said, pointing to a paper in his hand.

'Correct.' He handed it over. Home Office stationery. 'You are hereby warned . . .' I read, and stuffed it into my pocket.

'Twelve hours,' he repeated. 'That means –'

'Noon. Tell me, who's going to make sure I go?'

'Me,' he said. 'You've a seat on the 12.15 Qantas. Tourist class.'

'I hope you'll have a comfortable night,' I said. I went to the lift and to my room, made a little parcel of the leaf, addressed it to Jane, and got the porter to come up and collect it.

Then I lay in bed with my head wondering what the hell I was playing at; and my heart knowing very well. I could have taken the leaf to pieces myself, quite easily. Drop it on a hard floor, in the bathroom, for example, and its secrets would doubtless be revealed. But only to me, and that wasn't

119

quite enough, was it? No – because I wanted Jane involved. When you live in Perth and your girl's on the other side of the world most of the time, and you're not too sure whether she's yours anyway, you tend to look for any link you can find, especially on the day you're going back. Furthermore, if there *was* anything inside the leaf, which I strongly doubted, then Jane, in London, and with assorted military and/or intelligence assistance behind her, would be better placed than I to deal with it. Perth isn't strong on things like that: sunshine and sea-food, yes; intelligence operations – well, hardly.

The telephone woke me at seven. Rupert was on the other end of it, all charm. 'Up you get, Close, and quick about it! Take-off's 12.15 and you check in two hours before; that's at 10.15, and you've got to get over there. So if you want any breakfast . . .'

I listened in sullen silence, dropped the phone back on its base at that point, and went to shower. Room service sent up the great Aussie breakfast which Jane and most of Australia pronounce as Stike-niggs, and I ate with pleasure, hoping the waiting Rupert was starving. Packing took all of a couple of minutes, and *The Times* not much longer. I then spent half an hour thinking about the message on the leaf Jane was due to collect from reception.

There were three words in small letters. On one side the word was PUSH and on the other it was PULL. I had already pushed the one and tried to pull the other entirely without effect. The third word was ALBANY, which was no problem at all, thanks. I knew where Albany was.

But PULL? And PUSH? Like notices on doors, I thought. Still, I'd find out in Albany day after tomorrow.

That's how I thought. But events have a way of making changes.

13

There's a story they tell about the Duke of Edinburgh. Old Philip has just flown in to some far-off fly-blown dump in the middle of nowhere, and isn't in the sunniest of humours as he comes down the aircraft stairs and begins shaking hands, and some grovelling fool says, 'How was your flight, sir?' So Philip pauses a moment, then he says to the bloke, 'Have you ever flown ten thousand miles?' The bloke says yes. 'Well, it was exactly like that,' says Philip. True or not, it's in character, and generally it's correct.

My flight home wasn't 'like that', though it had its moments. For some reason the plane was half-empty and I had a bank of seats to myself all the way to Hong Kong. Peace, quiet, Australian champagne and a good movie, for once. As I waited on the ground for my connecting flight, I was remembering, naturally enough, my meeting with Sergei, and wondering why I hadn't seen him since. Sergei had seemed like the kind who elbows his way into your life intending to remain. Maybe, I thought, he had been a mere inch or two behind me in England, watching as I pounded up those damned steps and following (as best he could!) as I rode upon Pavel's power-packed pillion. Or maybe Sergei had become bored with what to me had seemed like great adventures, but must, to someone like Sergei, have seemed to be adventures at the level of Percy Pig Goes Fishing.

I had kept my eyes skinned for him both on the flight out and now on the ground at Kai Tak Airport. Not a whisker. As I looked around me, it was perfectly clear that there could be, and probably were, spies of every possible persuasion and pigment milling around, grabbing cups of coffee and purchasing duty-frees and paperbacks between flights. No Sergei

121

though, and I'd be sitting in the Weary-Mums-and-Screaming-Offspring Enclosure again, if I knew my Qantas. Sergei wouldn't, that's for sure.

But no, not this time.

There was I with a heavy heart from kissing my girl good-bye and a spinning brain from all the obsessive calculations about how far away from me Jane was at this particular moment. For two pins I'd have got off the plane, gone back to London in disguise and got a job sweeping the London streets to be near her. Not selfishness: the streets need the sweeping. Yes, and I need Jane. I had my aisle seat; my goods were in the locker, when . . .

Well, I tell you! This slender number could have come direct from the front cover of *Vogue*, or perhaps all that blonde hair got swung around in shampoo ads; she could even have stood with a pair of wolfhounds in front of a super-gracious stately home. What's more she was speaking – and to me.

'I don't want to squash your hat,' she was saying, and smiling at the same time. She held a coat up halfway to the locker.

I said, 'Go ahead – it's made to be squashed. It's shapeless to start with. Can I help you with your coat?'

No, she could manage, thanks. But I got up all the same to let her in to the seat by the window. She travelled in suede and silk and designer jeans. *Très élégante.*

To say she knocked me sideways would be overdoing things, but I'll admit that for a while all the attention cells in my brain formed squares and turned right and marched towards her.

Once we were in the air, she dropped a glove – oh, yes, *gloves*! – and allowed me the privilege of retrieving it. She also thanked me, prettily, and after a while she began to chat. She was on her way to Mandurah to see an elderly relative, now ill. The elderly relative used to live in Perth, but had moved south a few years back and Elin – her name was Elin Gundarsson, she said, and she was half-Scot, half-Icelander – had once visited Perth, but never Mandurah. Did I know it?

Oh, yes, I said, thinking at once of Mandurah's man-eating mammoth mosquitoes which come out at dusk and turn strong men into moaning, twitching heaps. You also sometimes get a shark or two – biggies – in the opening of the Peel Inlet, but I'd swear that of the two the mozzies attack faster and more violently. I said, 'Nice place for seafood, Mandurah.'

She also liked seafood, it seemed, and we spent a chatty couple of hours: she told me how to pickle herring in Madeira sauce, and I told her about the Blue Manna crabs she could catch in Peel Inlet and how to cook them on the barbie. I mentioned the mosquitoes as an afterthought. 'Get some repellant,' I advised.

Elin shrugged. 'Insects don't bother me,' she said, and I thought, good luck, lady.

Then we ate and drank, and after that she slept most of the way south, awakening an hour from Perth, just in time for the pre-landing wash and brush-up, and the people-processing.

Queue for Immigration, queue for Customs; no seats and hard standing. I'm well separated from Elin by now, because man after man has said, 'Oh, *please* – after you!' Said it to her, that is, not to me. I wave before she vanishes out of my life. Little wave back.

A while later I emerge into the meeting and greeting area, which is packed and suffocating as usual.

I took a deep breath and a firm grip on my flight bag and plunged in and I had excuse-me'd myself about ten yards into the crush when I glimpsed an Akubra hat and blue glasses and Sergei murmured, 'So nice to see you again,' and bound himself to me like a second-row forward at scrum-down time. Together we rucked and mauled our way towards the exit.

'Have a good trip, old feller?' Sergei inquired as we stood outdoors in the heat getting our breath back. 'Discover a great deal, did you?'

'Not a thing,' I said. 'I'm just as baffled as when I started.'

He sighed. 'So all that frantic galloping around Yorkshire was wasted. That's very sad. Can I give you a lift?'

123

'Thanks, but I'll take a taxi.'

'Taxi drivers,' Sergei said, with a rather languid, Oxonian gesture, 'are all far too greedy. They should be avoided whenever possible. Anyway, I've a car just over there, and we need to talk, don't we?'

'Do we?'

He took my elbow in a firm grip, murmuring, 'Step this way, sir.'

I went, partly because I was too jet-lagged to argue, partly because he'd make me go even if I summoned the energy to refuse. So we wove our way into the ranks of parked cars until he pointed to a metallic-blue Commodore and went to the driver's door while I wheeled off to the passenger side, where I was standing when somebody behind me said, '*This is your car, Mr Close.*'

I turned my head. 'No,' I said, 'this, er –' and stopped in mid-denial because the bloke behind me was holding one of those hunting knives with black Teflon coating on the blade. The Teflon means the metal doesn't shine, but its real purpose is to prevent the steel catching on your ribs as it's withdrawn.

'In the back,' he said.

In apprehension, I glanced over at Sergei, who was looking startled, and I must have looked pretty startled myself, because Sergei now stood face-to-face with Elin Gundarsson, and, since she was all smiles and he was not, it was plain enough that she had the advantage.

Obediently, I climbed into the back seat. A big man got in the other side, produced handcuffs, and fastened me to the grab handle, then got out again.

The car moved off. I didn't see any more of Sergei and Elin. She must be part of the Other Side, whatever that was. I remember wondering where she could be from: Paramount Pictures itself might be ranged against me in pursuit of Peterkin's secret. Or perhaps the Bolshoi?

But there was nothing amusing about this; I stopped having amusing thoughts. If you wonder what it feels like to be kidnapped, I can tell you: it feels horrible. You wonder frantically *who* and *why*. Above all you think – but it takes a minute or two to get round to this – you think, where are these bastards taking me, and *what will they do to me when we get there?*

There were two men in the front seats and I asked them all those questions, together and then individually.

They didn't answer, either singly or in unison. But the geography gave me a clue. We'd turned south on to the Kwinana Freeway and were about to cross the Canning River into Brentwood. We could still, of course, be running anywhere, but this route seemed to offer the alternatives of Murdoch University (unlikely) and Jandakot, the number three airfield for Perth.

Twenty minutes later, Jandakot it was. The car rolled into a car park beside a hangar, and was then carefully positioned well away from the other cars. After that we sat and waited, and kept the air-conditioning on and the engine running.

In a while the other car rolled in beside us and Elin got out. Sergei didn't. I could see him in the back, looking a bit woozy. As I turned my head I could also see a helicopter warming up.

Ten minutes later we were all aboard it, and the chopper was on a curving northward flight with the city on the left and a lot of space ahead. Elin Gundarsson sat up front with the fliers. Opposite me sat a man who had a gun, but kept it in his belt, and opposite Sergei was another, similar bloke who wore his pistol in his hand. Both looked wary and alert, though it was hardly necessary, since both Sergei and I were once more handcuffed safely to the metalwork.

The noise was considerable, easily drowning my voice when I yelled to Sergei in the hope of information and enlightenment. He must have heard something, because he looked my way and raised an eyebrow, but I doubt if he understood anything more than that I *was* shouting.

The chopper soon swung to the west, once the city centre lay behind us, and headed over the northern suburbs till we came to the ocean around Trigg Island beach. After that, we flew in a settled kind of way, a little west of north. We were following the coastline, so far as I could tell. Not that I could tell very much – looking out of the window required painful contortions – but after an hour or so, as the pilot made some sort of correction, I got a glimpse on the right side of what looked like the little town of Eneabba with the Yarra Yarra lakes behind it.

In which case, I thought, we could be Geraldton-bound and I wondered why, and what secrets Geraldton might still hold. Peterkin *had* lived there, of course, but only for a while, and in much the way he'd lived in other places, infrequently and leaving few marks. And I reckoned I knew those marks already.

So why was I being returned up here?

The helicopter descended, not long after, in an area of open land that stretched flat to the horizon in every direction. I could see through the window what looked like part of a run of power cable. It was still there when the engine was cut and the blades slap-slapped down, and then I saw a yellow/green truck – the top of it, anyway, – slide past the window.

No mistaking that – refuelling by BP bowser, the old Yowser Bowser of song and story.

I shouted loudly for help.

'Save my breath, if I were you,' Sergei said.

'Christ – we've got to *try*!'

'Out there,' he said, 'there's a diesel engine and a pump. This dragonfly of ours is sound-insulated. Locked too. Save your voice.'

'Where d'you reckon we're going?'

'I'm sure your knowledge of these parts is greater than mine,' Sergei said, 'but we're an hour north – wouldn't you say? – of the great throbbing metropolis. Geraldton's a possibility, I suppose, or maybe further north still. You never know with these people!'

'Who are they? Who's the girl?'

'Ah, yes. Charming little creature, she is, wouldn't you agree? Shade older than she looks, I suspect. Must be. Senior captain or major, at any rate.'

'In what?'

He was saying, 'Well, there's quite a wide choice, really –'

126

when the door slammed open and they came clambering back in, and in a few moments we were in the air, swinging now to the west, and with the nose-down attitude of the aircraft, I was able to look for a second or two over the pilot's shoulder. We were now over the ocean, and heading west, which I thought meant either South Africa, which lay rather beyond the chopper's range, or – back to the Abrolhos!

And I was right. Could hardly be wrong, in fact. It had to be the Abrolhos, somewhere, or a watery grave for all. As it was, when the handcuffs were unlocked and Sergei and I were herded outside, it was on to a flat acre or two of damp rock – Mother Nature's perfect helicopter pad, in the middle of nowhere. Nothing to be seen as I looked around me. Just the ocean swell, and the rock, and the helicopter.

Plus a low, black and deadly submarine! (Not the rounded nuke, this time.) I felt my jaw drop open in surprise, felt an electric tingle as my senses suddenly struggled to come to terms with this extraordinary sight a few feet away.

It sat still and flat – and intensely practical – in the water alongside; the little rocky island had turned into a jetty for it. A small boarding ramp ran from dock to deck, and a few seconds later I found myself crossing it, under the control of a couple of pistols; Sergei, behind me, was being shoved along.

'Up the ladder,' Elin's voice was snapping crisply from the rear.

I climbed up what in the days of U-boats used to be called a conning tower, and is now known, I believe, as the sail. At the top a sailor waited, pointing downward into the interior. I looked down: at blazing lights and men, at faces turned up towards me.

'Down. Go down into the vessel.' Elin's voice again, melodious in the way cracking icicles are melodious.

She said, 'It's simple, Mr Close.' There was a small space beside and behind the periscope – I haven't the slightest idea of submarine nomenclature, so I won't attempt to name

127

anything – and we sat facing each other, knee to knee almost, and with one of the guards from the aircraft to see fair play. He stood a few feet away, out of earshot, his back to the ladder we'd just descended.

'Simple,' she repeated, her clear grey eyes looking into mine. They were intense, those eyes, and oddly powerful, almost as though lit from behind.

I told her that it certainly *ought* to be simple. 'But it isn't,' I said. 'What I'm doing, *all* I'm doing, is looking after the estate of a client. Other people seem to imagine I'm doing other things.'

'As you are,' she said. 'You are handling the affairs of the traitor and runaway, Kinsky, Pyotr.'

'A working man, named Peterkin,' I said. 'And I find myself kidnapped at gunpoint, transported two hundred miles in a helicopter, and now on board a fully operational ocean-going submarine.'

'On patrol,' she said. 'This vessel is on patrol. And she is scheduled to return to her home port of Vladivostok in five weeks from now.' Elin paused, then added, 'If necessary with you on board.'

I said, 'What would make it necessary?'

Her pale nostrils flared as she took a deep, disapproving breath. 'Mr Close, you possess actual and intellectual property which belonged formerly to Kinsky but belongs now to the state.'

I shook my head. 'To his family.'

She shook hers. 'There *is* no family, therefore –'

'You have proof?'

'My friend, there has been an elaborate search. There is no family.'

'Be that as it may,' I said, preparing to slip into lawyerese, 'and even were his property to revert to the state –'

'As it must.'

'Even then, it would not be to *your* state, but to the Crown.'

'The British Crown! Nonsense. Kinsky was Russian.'

'Ukrainian, I rather believe. No proof, of course.'

'The Ukraine is part of USSR. He was a Soviet citizen!'

'After that he became a citizen of New Zealand. He owed allegiance to the Crown.'

She looked at me fiercely down her perfectly straight, chis-elled-ivory nose. It was like being glared at by a magazine cover, but chilling all the same. 'No Soviet citizen,' Elin said, 'can cease to have responsibilities to the Soviet state.' All this was happening, mind, as the Soviet empire was well embarked upon the process of disintegration. News bulletins were about fighting in Armenia.

'Is that so, *still?*'

'Unless,' she went on, 'a specific decision has been taken, by appropriate officials, to exempt him.'

'In his case it wasn't?'

'In his case,' she said, 'there was a sentence of death *in absentia.*'

'*That* will take some carrying out!'

'It has *been* carried out, Mr Close.'

I stared at her; she stared back. Peterkin was undoubtedly dead. I'd been inclined to the coroner's recorded view that he'd fallen by accident down those stairs at Albany Gaol. But maybe not. I said, 'If you got that close to Peterkin, why kill him? If there actually *is* any information, Peterkin was the one who had it. He was the organ-grinder, after all. I'm just the bloody monkey.'

'You will be a very cold monkey, if we take you to Siberia, and I believe there is a saying about —'

'That's brass monkeys,' I said. 'How did he die?'

'I understand his fall was deliberate, Mr Close.'

'Understand?'

'I wasn't there. Women are not usually permitted in men's prisons.'

'But he saw your bloke and just jumped.'

'Something like that, one imagines.'

She smiled a shiny smile. 'So much for the history. May we return to the present? The man left behind him a piece of information of great importance. It's clear he left it to you.' Now the smile slid away and the eyes seemed to glow even brighter. 'You,' she said, 'will give that information to me.' They were curious, compelling eyes, and I wondered for a moment, as her gaze seemed to pin me into my seat, whether Elin Gundarsson might be a hypnotist, natural, or trained.

'He left me the wherewithal to pay for his burial, that's all.'

'You're lying.' No tinkling ice in the voice now: she spoke softly, in not much more than a loud whisper.

'Nope,' I said. 'And I don't know what's got into you all. I'm just an ordinary solicitor. A bloke hears about me and I defend him. And lose! Happened twice. Now look, Elin, I didn't even save him from chokey. He went inside for three long years. D'you reckon that's a basis for a deep relationship, for a matter of great trust? Because I don't. I wouldn't have trusted Peterkin with a three-dollar note! But I was his lawyer and I deal with his legal affairs. That's all of it.'

She said, 'Oh, no.' Her eyes still glowed, but I now felt in no imminent danger of coming under their control. If I had been, I really wouldn't have cared.

Not then.

What I cared about *then* was that somebody might yell those commands you see in the movies, like 'Dive, dive, dive!' and 'Make me a course for home!'

She knew it, as who wouldn't! She sat staring at me for a while, and then said, 'You should tell me voluntarily, Mr Close. That would be the easy way – for me, and certainly for you.' She paused. 'If you don't, think what happens.'

'I get tortured.'

'Not yet. What happens *next* is an injection. A drip that makes you talk, to tell everything.'

'So why waste any time?'

'It can have unpleasant side effects, this drug. And anyway, we have nothing against you personally. You aren't a traitor – you are merely what you say you are, an obscure lawyer with duties to his client. It is simply unfortunate that your duties have put you in possession of information which is important to us.'

'Unfortunate?'

'For you, yes. For you the information can have no purpose whatever. You can't use it.'

I said riskily, 'I could sell it. Any number of people seem to want it. Maybe I could hold an auction.'

The superb nostrils pinched. 'And maybe we could hold an execution. What would you sell, Mr Close?'

'What I know.'

'Yet you tell me you know nothing.' Elin gave a little smile. 'I shall allow you a brief break so that you can think. You like tea with lemon?'

'Yes.'

Moodily I prodded lemon slices with a teaspoon, and sipped the tea, trying to work out what it was that I knew. Because, although I'd been in the odd tight corner before, I'd never been in one quite so tight as this, or one from which no possibility of escape existed. I was, after all, in a submarine: pressure hull several inches thick, crew of a hundred plus, only one way out – and that up a ladder guarded top and bottom by armed men.

But what *could* I tell?

What facts did I know?

All I'd succeeded in doing was finding out that Peterkin was Ukrainian, that he'd been to Moscow three years before, and that he'd brought out some pottery leaves with cryptic messages on them.

Of which the latest was meaningless; even to me with my supposed specialized knowledge of a) Peterkin, and b) Western Australia, the words PUSH and PULL and ALBANY didn't mean anything very much.

So would it really matter if I told her?

I sipped some more tea, uncomfortably aware of my own problem, which was that if I went off to meet my Maker, the Great Secret, whatever *that* was, went with me. *And everybody knew that.* Sergei knew it, and so must the unsuave Americans, and the awful Rupert. I knew it, and so must Elin. The only thing on my side was that not one of them, so far, was prepared to write off the Great Secret.

But sooner or later . . . well, one fine day, somebody on that list would say, 'Ah, the *hell* with it, what's the use?'

131

and would bring about my death, ensuring that nobody else could ever learn the secret.

'Go on!' I said to myself: go on and make the decision; *tell* them! Them, I thought, *them*? The only person available to tell was Elin Gundarsson, whoever *she* was. So the first thing, I told myself, was to find out everything I could about her.

'I hope,' Elin said to me when we were knee-to-knee again behind the periscope a few minutes later, 'that you have decided to cooperate.'

'I've thought about it. I see the sense,' I said. 'But there's a but.'

'Which is?'

'Put it this way. Imagine that what I've got is, for instance, a diamond. You come to me and you say, give me the diamond because I am your friend, and I don't want to hurt you and, anyway, I have this damn great submarine. Well, the first two are meaningless. You're not my friend unless you've given me proof of friendship; and your protestation that you don't want to hurt me is quite worthless. That leaves the submarine. Why don't you give me some motivation?'

'Of what kind?'

'Tell me about yourself.'

She gave a little nod, the kind beautiful women give to hotel doormen when they want a taxi: a mixture of the aloof and the impatient. 'I am a Soviet officer. That is all you need to know.'

'No,' I said. 'Whose side are you on?'

'I don't understand your question.'

'How do you feel about *perestroika*?'

'It is the official policy of my country.'

'And Comrades Gorbachev and Yeltsin – what about them?'

'Civilized debate?'

'And you are what – a loyal comrade, a committed citizen?'

'Both.'

'And in command of this vessel?'

'The vessel has a captain.'

'Whom you can command?'

132

She shrugged.

'Which makes you what – a political officer, an intelligence officer?'

Another shrug.

Now, I've read the papers like everyone else. 'I'll bet,' I said, 'that you're a GRU officer.'

'And if I were, what does it matter?' Elin said. 'All armed forces have their intelligence organizations.'

'Sergei,' I said, 'is KGB. I think, anyway. And yet you're holding him prisoner. Isn't that a funny thing!'

'A defector,' Elin said.

'He didn't seem that way to me.'

'You would hardly know about such things.'

'I had a strong impression that he considered himself to be both patriotic and pragmatic. He wants whatever he thinks I know. So, tell me this,' I went on, 'if anything I've got is of value, and if I were to give it – or wish to give it – to a representative of your country, should it go to you, or to Sergei?'

'To me.'

'Sergei's here, on board. And I'm a very reasonable man. Couldn't he join these discussions?'

'I've told you, he's a defector.'

As she spoke, a buzzer sounded nearby. There followed the sounds of a phone being lifted and a voice speaking rapidly. Elin cocked her head, listening, and after a moment, frowning.

'What's going on?'

She said, 'Believe it or not, we have a caller!'

'Hostile?' I asked. 'Australian frigate, American aircraft carrier . . . ?'

'A man selling fish.'

'There's nothing like salesmanship,' I said. 'It's what makes the world go round. Are you buying?'

She was only half listening to me, the beautiful head still held cocked. 'The impudent fool has come alongside without permission!'

'Just foot-in-the-door tactics,' I said. 'Buy his fish and he'll go away.'

She looked at me. 'This fish – what will it be?'

'Schnapper. Shark, maybe. Barramundi if you're lucky. Herring – for pickling, eh?'

Elin allowed herself a smile. 'Pickled herring? Then we must have some. Captain –!'

Then something began to happen . . . first the phone buzzed again and was answered . . . rapid speech in Russian followed, angry now . . . The phone slamming down . . . Elin rising angrily, shouting an order . . . a sudden heavy splash, clearly audible through the hull . . . Then a deep Australian voice with a laugh entombed somewhere in it, echoing down from above . . .

'Look out below,' it boomed, 'and get yer bloody great feet off the floor!'

Which I did. Jokers are jokers. I jumped up on my seat like the lady getting away from the mouse, and from where I stood had a perfect view, around the periscope housing, of something pouring down from above – lengths of something, colours bright green and yellow, plus jelly-like stuff, a shower of it, all pouring down from the hatch up there.

For a moment or two, I was simply astonished. Elin stood four feet away, gun in hand now, also temporarily transfixed. But that second or two was enough. *She* didn't know yet; I did. I now knew the green-and-yellow for what it was. God alone knew who was up there! I flicked out an arm for Elin's pistol and plucked it from her hand as she stood, still gaping . . .

Then the voice boomed again from above, so deep and authoritative it could have been the Deity himself! 'Up the bloody ladder, John!' came the words.

Elin tried to grab me as I leapt across to the periscope housing and, I'm half-ashamed to confess, I kicked her. But I did – I was in a panic, reaching hurriedly upward now for a pipe on the roof and swinging myself across to the ladder, lifting my feet high as I hurled my body across the narrow space . . .

Because – well, the deck beneath me was alive now with writhing sea-snakes – and jellyfish too, those almost transparent little things we call stingers and with damn good reason.

The few men I could see had backed away fast – and rightly so, because those snakes, handsome as they are in Australia's gold-and-green national colours, carried a venom several times more deadly than any of the land-snakes. Seven tiger snake bites equal one from a sea-snake.

Breathlessly I grabbed for the steel rung in front of me . . . felt my right hand slip on oil as it took my weight . . . felt the great pound of my heart at the thought of tumbling down to the wriggling mass of sea-serpents a couple of feet below me. I grabbed with my left, and held tightly –

'Climb, you bastard!' The deep voice roared at me, and I began instantly to obey. Oh, but was I nimble on that ladder! Below me all was confusion – but it wouldn't be for long. Orders were now being shouted and I heard the clang of metal on metal – and then a shot! That sound put great flapping wings on my heels and I tore upward, expecting another shot, directed upward and into me, every instant, and I raced for the circle of pink light above me. Hurtling out on to the little deck on top of the sail, I glanced back to see that Sergei was inches behind, his face contorted with pain and exertion. As he emerged into the eerie glow of dusk, and turned to slam down the hatch, I saw he was wounded somewhere round the shoulder, his shirt stained with blood.

'Don't hang about!' snarled the deep voice; and a big hand slapped my back, and Joe Hag was almost throwing me over the rail, on to the stepway down. He, meanwhile, had put his two-hundred-and-fifty-pound frame on the hatch cover, which hadn't prevented his grabbing Sergei and flinging him after me.

In seconds my scrambling feet were on the rock and I stood for a moment waiting for Sergei to join me. Above us the great metal superstructure seemed to tower darkly into the sky, silhouetted as it was against that pink and grey and blue sunset. Then a stream of light came, as the hatch cover was lifted, and I thought that any second the tower's rail would be lined by submariners with assault rifles.

'Quick!' I said to Sergei, 'Run!' Not much more than a

hundred yards off I could see *Abrolhos Lady* alongside at the other edge of the little outcrop island, and as we set off, Joe Hag's voice boomed again. 'Now try some of this,' he yelled, and you didn't have to be Einstein to work out that another load of the ocean's rich store of poisons was being tipped down into the sub, directly on top of my pursuers.

Seconds later Joe Hag came swarming down the side of the sail with a seaman's swift surefootedness and was pounding after us.

Abrolhos Lady was already turning as we reached her. I could see Alex's small figure busy in the deckhouse, swinging the *Lady*'s bow out, manoeuvring the sturdy vessel so that the stern was turned to face us as we ran. I remember hesitating briefly as I came near, and trying, in the disappearing light, to make a clear judgement of the jump – one foot up on to the wide, wooden stern planking, then a deep step down into the well. Difficult, but it had to be done and I hurtled up, out over the water churning beneath the stern, got my foot down on to the boards, then went down the drop like a sack of sand somebody'd thrown off the truck!

It hurt, but nothing broke and I scrambled up and grabbed at Sergei as he came flying over behind me – in far better control of his movements than I'd been – and then the great bulk of Joe Hag blotting out the sky a second or two later, landing, graceful but heavy, in the stern well, with a crash that made me suspect momentarily that he'd gone straight through.

Now Alex threw in the big diesels and *Abrolhos Lady* surged away from the rocks, picking up speed as she made for a mass of volcanic outcrops less than a quarter of a mile away. She must by now have been making ten or twelve knots, speed still increasing, and heading into all that miscellaneous rock looked pretty perilous to me. I said, 'Alex, they can't chase us!'

'They can shoot us though!'

'No. No-no-no!' This was Sergei, wounded, but laid-back as ever. '*You* are aboard, old chap. They can't shoot. Not and be sure. They'll think you might have put a message in a

bottle, or something.' He smiled. 'Anyway, you're with me!'
Then the smile collapsed at the edges and he slid to the deck
in a heap. Delayed shock.

'I don't care what he says!' Alex's hand moved on the
throttle, urgently ordering more revolutions; and the *Lady*
roared ahead, straight at a black lump that reared six feet or
so out of the dark ocean and which, as I cringed and turned
my eyes away, proved to conceal the entrance to a channel.
Joe Hag leapt up to the bow, the revs dropped right back, and
suddenly instead of hurtling, we were nosing slowly forward.
I was on my knees beside Sergei, who was now coming
round, blinking a lot, and swearing. It was in Russian, all
that foul language, and I don't understand Russian. But
curses sound like curses.

'Wound hurts?' I asked.

'That's a bloody silly question,' Sergei said, wrathfully.
'Bullet in my damned shoulder, damn you, and you gave it
an extra damned wrench dragging me aboard. Of course it
damn well hurts!'

'Then let's have a look. And watch your language – ladies
present.'

'I'll do it, thanks.' Sergei was ripping at the left sleeve of
his shirt when there was a bellow of amplified sound, and
Elin's voice on a loudspeaker was carrying to us, 'Be aware
of this, Mr John Close – there is no escape . . . no escape for
you.'

Cheerful words.

But Sergei evidently saw no harm in them. He was busy
inspecting the punctured flesh of his upper arm, and he said
in a pleased voice, 'Entry hole here, you see, and exit hole,
yes, *here*. Point three-two. Bandages, if you will, some hot
sweet tea for the shock. Oh, yes, and don't give me any
whisky, even if I ask for it, all right? Not for twenty-four
hours.'

'If we live that long,' I said.

'Live?' He looked up at me. 'She's given up. Till the next
time, that is.'

'How do you know?'

'Get the tea, old chap, it's urgent. I'm in shock.'

137

So I went and got the first-aid kit and gave it to him, then boiled water and made tea, and ladled in sugar and brought a steaming mug to him where he sat on the deck with his back against the woodwork holding a big pad of wadded bandage against the wound.

'Thanks,' Sergei said, 'and now if you'd bring the rest of that water you boiled, plus a little antiseptic, we can get all this cleaned up.'

Which we did. After that he called for one of Joe Hag's spare sweaters against the evening chill. It fitted him like a marquee, big though Sergei was, and though he looked a bit funny, you couldn't say he was a complaining patient.

Meanwhile I'd asked, 'How d'you know she's given up?'

Sergei said, 'That's a new sub she's got over there. Wouldn't be very clever to lodge it up on all these rocks, would it? Her masters wouldn't be precisely thrilled.'

'Who d'you reckon she is?'

'GRU,' he said.

'That's what I guessed. Told her as much.'

'Did you?' He grinned. 'That would take her somewhat aback, I expect.'

'Also told her you were KGB.' It was dark now, and I couldn't see his face.

He said, 'What did she say to that?'

'Said you were a defector.'

Sergei gave a merry laugh. 'Priceless, isn't it! All these old dinosaurs –'

'She didn't look like a dinosaur to me.'

'No, she's a pretty little bit of nonsense, I agree. Trouble is, you know, that some of them get bitten by the military bug and turn all intense. Met her on the plane, did you?'

'Yes.'

'You,' he said, 'will certainly have to give up flying, the way you keep picking up undesirables!'

I left him and climbed up to the wheelhouse.

'Can the sub follow us?'

Alex turned a taut face towards me. 'Not directly, I shouldn't think. Sub's too long to try threading her way through at night. But she'll have a good speed – maybe enough – to run south and then back and head us off before we make Geraldton.'

'She wouldn't want to enter territorial waters on the surface, though,' Joe Hag put in. For a big man he moved very softly: I hadn't sensed his approach. I said, 'Thanks.'

'No worries. Matter of fact I almost enjoyed it.' He gave a big, square-toothed grin. 'How in hell did we know, right?'

'Absolutely right.'

'I saw a chopper heading out here. They don't do that much, not civvy choppers. I told Alex; she phoned her mate at Qantas; they confirmed arrival of J. Close in Perth. Guesswork. But not exactly complicated.'

'And the snakes?'

'Hobby of mine, marine life. I have a pool where they breed. And I was thinking – how *do* you attack a sub? Then I remembered the pool. Fine mesh net to scoop them up. No worries at all, mate.'

I looked around me. Sergei sat leaning against the cabin housing, tea in one hand and cigarette in the other; Alex, the wheel in her brown, strong little hands, her stance alert and confident, guided us through the rock-strewn dark. Joe Hag, having single-handedly defeated a Russian warship and its entire crew, was picking his big, square teeth with a gutting knife.

Calm everywhere, except inside me. *My* heart still thudded, *my* hands had a tremor, *my* mouth was still dry.

'Anybody any suggestions?' I asked.

Silence. Then Sergei turned his head. 'I'd avoid Geraldton if I were you.'

'Right,' I said. 'We head south.'

14

Albany lay south – a long way – and rough it would be, too, because you're in waters where two great oceans meet; and though the meeting may be a mere matter of marks on a map rather than the clashing of great currents, even knowing *that*, when you reach the point off the Pig's Nose where the Indian Ocean joins the Southern Ocean, you're in the Thirty-Fives, which aren't *quite* the Roaring Forties – not *yet* – but are close enough to raise in your head all those stories you've read of storm-wracked clippers battling for Albany and the wonderful, calm Princess Royal Harbour where they could lie and convalesce in safety.

Albany's where I'm from. It's where I grew up. I know the place well. But rake over my brains, and their miscellaneous contents, as I could and did, those final words of Peterkin, the last clue he'd left me, stirred no recollections. As *Abrolhos Lady* corkscrewed south on a good swell – stiff, but nothing like the seas you get approaching Albany – I tried to be logical, to think of places where the words PUSH and PULL might appear. It did me no good. I thought of doors: in pubs, in entrances to lavatories, in department stores. Could be any of them, I thought, could be none!

We didn't make it to Albany. After twenty hours under way, *Abrolhos Lady* was coming abeam of Rottnest Island when several nasty noises occurred in swift succession. First, a loud bang, then a kind of metallic, screaming sound, followed by something reminiscent of an uneven burst of machine-gun fire.

A noise one knows.

We'd hit something.

Not only that: whatever it was we'd hit had fouled the starboard diesel.

And the propeller blades were stripped.

Nice, that was. Bloody nice.

We swore quite a lot in our different ways. I noticed young Alex did her cursing in Japanese. And fluently.

Well, there was Rottnest just over *there*, full of expert yachtsmen who'd be delighted to help, but the island hadn't much in the way of repair yards. Over *there*, fifteen miles or so, lay Fremantle, with miles of first-class yards. Not much of a choice, really: except that Fremantle would probably have some of Elin Gundarsson's GRU underlings standing about with high-grade binoculars and other equipment looking for us. It was also reasonably likely that somewhere out at sea the sub sat watching us, through all the fancy prismatics in its periscope.

But it had to be Fremantle. We dragged ourselves over to Rous Head with a staysail up, and worked our way to the Boniface yard and tied up like an advertising hoarding with *Abrolhos Lady* in lettering a foot high across the stern, where anybody entering harbour was bound to see it.

'We'll leave her,' I said, pointing to the *Lady*'s name, 'and go on down to Albany by any available means – and that's preferably one at a time and separately.'

'I'm going with you,' said Alex at once.

I shook my head. 'You're with Joe.'

'But *I'm* with you,' said Sergei.

'No.'

He gave me a confident nod. 'Just try and shake me.'

'I will.'

And I did, and I went via Perth city centre to do it. There, safely in the shopping streets I dodged from Aherns' sports department to Myers' food hall and back again, slid round the corners of an arcade or two, traversed a crowded cellar full of assorted Oriental restaurants, and left him somewhere in my slipstream.

Next, a telephone. From a pub in Wellington Street I rang my own home number, got my answering machine, and had

141

it play back my calls. Assorted voices jabbered at me. None was important. Little bits of the practice of law, parts of my social life, news of a barbecue at Pete's, a Law Society dinner dance. Really, I remember thinking, I'm quite a busy little fellow. And it was hard on the heels of *that* thought that I realized it was Jane who was speaking now, with a low throb of urgency in those unmistakable Pommy tones, and she was using carefully meaningless phrases. 'Seem to confirm my original hypothesis,' said she, and, 'May perhaps be something of a surprise.' And then she said, 'Arriving,' without specifying when.

I hung up, with some small feeling of relief. We needed an answer or two to some of the bloody questions, and Jane had some answers and, bless her, was bringing them direct to me. Fine. But Jane would be walking straight into Elin's grip; if, that is, she wasn't walking into Sergei's; because both would have known, almost before I did, what was on the tape of my answering machine. They only had to call my number to find out. There was a pathetic little built-in protective code, but both of them would go straight past that. They were, after all, elite Moscow-trained hoods.

So I began to worry and wonder. Jane was sharp, all right, but was she sharp enough? She knew I was a target and so, therefore, by extension, was she. Yes? Yes, of course.

What would she do? Come in by another flight, or another airline – would she do that?

Possibly. Jane had flown around the north of WA before. The idea wasn't strange to her. So if she came in from Britain on a flight to Darwin, and then chartered a light plane, as she could – and could well afford . . .

I rang Bob Collis, and asked if he'd had any calls lately.

'Yair. Had a major one.'

'When?'

'Last night. Could have been a problem but it isn't. Hey, listen, I opened a bottle of one of my Rieslings.'

'Good, is it?'

'You wouldn't get better from Lampe's.'

'Oh?' I said, and then, 'Ah,' as my understanding came. 'Help you drink some soon.'

He said, 'Tonight's a good time.'

I hung up, found a newsagent, bought a paper, and riffled through it. If anybody had listened in to my conversation with Bob – unlikely, but one never knows – then the word Lampe would have them foxed. It would have had me foxed if Bob hadn't taken me off one Sunday the previous fall to introduce me.

Jane was, I guessed, tucked away, probably at Bob's cottage at Dawesville on the Inlet, where she'd been tucked away before; so she was safe, and would meet me that night at Lampe's place.

I used the phone to rent a car from an outfit on Adelaide Terrace. They came to pick me up, took me to their HQ, watched as I signed the forms, and probably wondered what the hell *this* was all about. But they were courteous, and I avoided running by chance into Sergei or Elin or other perils.

I drove west and then took a route out of the city through the suburbs. Some nice names: Applecross and Como, and some intriguing Abo names, like Myaree and – my favourite – Coolbellup. I don't know what it means except that anything ending in 'up' was so named for the presence of water, named by the Aboriginals, and they were people who knew the value of water.

Hours to go, still, and hot hours at that. The temperature was about thirty degrees. It wouldn't be hard now for me to stay out of sight, provided I was indoors in some café or walking in an area off the main roads. But I'm West Australian and, like the rest of us, there's a fancy for beach and surf bred in my bones. Suddenly sunlight and seashore were calling hard.

I made for Busselton, where West Australia's old-time Grace Bussel, on horseback, rescued the crew of a wrecked ship in the big seas. I stopped and bought board shorts and a towel, then drove on to Cowaramup and paused at the top of the hill to look down at the best surf in the world. And I'm not kidding. The best known? – well, it may not be famous. But the *best* – oh, wow!

Below me the breakers were marching in: straight as

rulers, one two hundred yards behind the other. They were forming maybe a mile off, then rearing up and racing towards the beach. Out where they formed, all the surfers trod water and waited to pick up their piece of perfection and ride it in: the long sweet thrill of the surf-board.

In any case it was a good place to stay out of the way, I thought. Who'd come looking a mile out to sea? I let in the clutch and drove down there with my heart almost aching at the beauty of it all. Months, even a year since I'd done this – so maybe I'd be rusty.

But I wasn't rusty; the skills you learn as a kid last you a lifetime. What I was, after a couple of hours of surf, was tired in bones and muscles. I hurled myself down in some shade and slept an hour. When I woke, I grabbed the board again, tied myself to it, and went back in to begin the long paddle to the point where the breakers formed. To do it, to get out there, you have to butt your way through the breakers, and I was doing that competently enough until I misjudged one and found myself scrambling up its face and, when I was momentarily poised on top, looking straight at something that could have been the tip of a periscope, perhaps a quarter of a mile away!

Instantly the sun grew cold and reality returned. Had I been seen? Probably. Recognized? Almost certainly not – a man with wet hair plastered round his face and only his head visible is pretty effectively disguised. But the possibility that I'd been spotted *did* exist. I looked for the next respectable roller, climbed aboard, and rode straight and fast to the beach, and, no, I didn't fall off. What I did now was dress quickly and take my rental car on to the back roads, in among the pink dust. It leaves a trail behind that you can see a mile, but mine wouldn't be the only such dust trail. Within the next hour or so, dust would erupt over the entire area.

Because down there, on the Pig's Nose, culture was coming in with a capital C, and it was heading there by every means you can think of: in planes and choppers, in every kind of car from ancient bangers to new Rolls-Royces to drovers' wives in four-wheel-drives: eight or nine thousand, so the newspaper said, plus the London Philharmonic. There's a winery in a natural amphitheatre out near the Cape, run by men with money, and tonight the air was to vibrate for once with something other than mosquito music. The orchestra, having played in Sydney, was to continue its tour in Singapore, but had been persuaded to break the journey in WA for a concert with two purposes: the first inevitably commercial (i.e. to launch a new branded Chardonnay made on the premises) and the second to let Perth's prides of social lions put on their dinner jackets and gowns and travel 'out of town'. Lets the pretty ladies show off themselves and their jewels, and there's no shortage of either in Perth.

It was a nice idea altogether, provided you believed that Australia's nervous-but-lethal snakes would *all* get out of the way, and leave the vineyard to music-lovers and picnickers. Yes, a nice idea, and the first ('I know exactly what you mean, darling – I was at the *first* one!').

There'd be chaos, and I'd meet Bob in the serried ranks of Zinfandel vines, and he'd have Jane with him. Furthermore, in the inevitable confusion, Jane and I could slope away together in ways and directions which would make following difficult.

With that in mind I positioned my hire-car very carefully for the getaway; far enough, I hoped, from the concert site to avoid being parked in. Then I waited.

It had been a damned hot day, and it was going to be a damned hot evening. The car had no air-conditioning, so the alternatives were to keep the windows up and swelter, or to roll 'em down and be eaten alive. I kept 'em up.

Around six the sky began to fill with flashing lights as Perth's glitterati flew in to land on local airstrips. Dust from big knobbly tyres would certainly be climbing the sky, though I couldn't see it yet. The snakes might or might not be heading for the hills, but the mosquitoes would certainly be licking their lips, for dusk was descending. I climbed out of my car – and headed in among the vines, stamping my feet a bit to warn the dugites and tigers to wriggle away. By

145

the time I reached the lines of Zinfandel vines, the crowds had begun to assemble below me in the base of the amphitheatre where batteries of lights shone brightly. Here I could stay comfortably out of anybody's sight, and watch as the crowds flocked in.

I suppose I was fifty or sixty feet higher than the long lines of chairs set facing the acoustic shell inside which the orchestra would play. To my left was the old house which had been modernized and extended into a winery-cum-restaurant. People entered through a gap in the trees opposite me. To my right was the acoustic shell, and behind it an area of handsome old gum trees, into which numbers of imported and decorative trees had been planted. I remember thinking that what with the coloured lights strung between branches, and the spotlights highlighting specimen trees and old stone, it made a very handsome setting for ... and the train of thought ploughed to a dead halt right there, as I saw Sergei, accompanied by his blue lenses and his Akubra hat, sidle to the rim of the amphitheatre, pause very briefly, and then start to descend the path. By that time I had binoculars on him. There was coloured paper in his hand, ticket no doubt, and a cigarette in a holder between his teeth. He was dinner-jacketed. And confident, too, judging by the way he looked around him.

He set questions jumping in my head. How, for a start, did he know I'd be here? Were others with him? That kind of question. Plus – what did he know of Jane? Knew she existed, of course. But what she looked like – did he know that? She'd be with Bob Collis, of course, and that would be camouflage of sorts, and, as I've said before, Jane's sharp.

So I kept my head down and waited, squinting all the time through a gap in the vines, and thinking. What I was thinking was principally this: I just *might* fail to spot Jane. Oh, yes, I know – girl I love and all that, so how in God's name could I fail to spot her? In my mind I tried to count the time we'd spent together and it wasn't a lot of days. Nothing like a month in total, and certainly not *enough*; part of the time she'd been in slacks and an old shirt, part in army uniform, and women can change themselves like chameleons with a hairdo and a new dress. I had to spot her before others did. *Had* to!

And I didn't. Thanks to Bob Collis and his Pommy manners. If he'd been your average Ocker moneybags he'd have come in first, with a bottle in one hand and a glass in the other, and his mates on either side and the sheilas trailing behind, aware of their station in life. But Bob Collis, in spite of forty-plus years among the colonials, preserves some of the punctilio of his cavalry mess on social occasions, and led Jane forward gently and discreetly. But that's not what I actually saw.

Truth is, I was a lot less alert than I should have been; after all, watching a crowd of several thousand file into an arena is a bit like watching sheep go over stiles and has much the same soporific effect. I thought I was looking carefully. And wasn't.

Sergei certainly was, though.

I'd been idly watching one particular WA Lady Out For the Evening, with her cocktail frock in peacock-blue taffeta, earrings, and necklace in diamanté, bag and shoes in white and her bloke done up in a pastel tuxedo with tie and cummerbund to match the dress, when suddenly I saw Sergei materialize beside them. The bastard was quick as a snake! One second he'd been leaning nonchalantly on a chair, and the next he'd popped magically out of some bloody trapdoor right beside the woman and was chatting away. But why — why *her*?

It was only then, and far too late, that I realized, a) that the girl in blue was Jane in disguise and a black wig, and b) that the symphony in glitz beside her was poor, formal old Bob, also in disguise.

Plainly neither disguise had worked and Sergei, having been ditched, had unditched himself with aplomb and efficiency. He hadn't spotted me, but then he hadn't had to. John Close would go straight to Jane, and Sergei knew it.

So I did, quick. I shoved my way hard through the accumulating throng, intending in my petty way to tap Sergei on the shoulder without his seeing me coming; but I wasn't good enough. Well before the shoulder got tapped, he was saying politely over it, 'Good evening, Mr Close, and isn't this all frightfully exciting!'

A magician, no doubt of it. He now asked sweetly, 'Where are your seats?' and when Bob Collis told him, murmured, 'What a delightful coincidence. I'm in the row behind.'

'How'd you swing that?' I demanded.

He shrugged a little. 'A nothing,' he said, and handed me a hundred-dollar note. 'Nice if you could find some fizz, old chap. French, ideally.'

I'd have stayed dismissed, too, if a cool voice behind me hadn't said, 'So nice to see you all again,' and as I turned there was Elin Gundarsson in some elegant little Paris number and what looked suspiciously like diamonds, smiling the delicate smile of the queen of the catwalk. With her, but without cummerbunds or matching bow ties, were a couple of unmistakably seafaring types. Dark suits, with low foreheads above, big hands at the ends of the sleeves, and no pretence at social graces. Armed, I imagined, as was Elin Gundarsson, more likely than not. She carried a little evening bag, small, but squarish: about .32 automatic size.

And there we stood, a little knot of us, while the concert-goers swirled by us, like a river past a rock, and we looked with polite dislike at each other, listening intently as Sergei said, 'Most amusing, really,' in his most insinuating Oxonian tones, and waited for someone to ask him what was amusing. Nobody did. He wasn't fazed. Nothing would, or indeed *could* faze Sergei, I think. He went on, 'Oh, yes, *very* amusing, and almost tragic, you know. I mean the orchestra flew into Perth, didn't they, with all their instruments, and then went absolutely *straight* from one air-conditioned aircraft to another to fly down here, and then they got out and the coach was late, and it really was most frightfully hot . . .' Sergei paused. 'You'll never guess, my dear,' he said roguishly to Elin Gundarsson, 'what began to happen!' She regarded him coldly down her ruler straight nose in disbelief. I knew what she was thinking: could this monkey really be a Soviet spy!

I said, 'What began to happen, Sergei?'

'Thank you, dear boy. Well, the glue began to melt. In the heat, you know.'

Ever the straight man, I said, 'What glue was this?'

'Oh, it was *the* glue,' Sergei gushed. 'The stuff that holds Stradivari together. Oh, and the Guarneri, too. A little bird told me there was at least one of each, plus an Amati. Terrible if they'd all collapsed into a little pile of bits of varnished wood down here on the Pig's Nose!'

Sergei did it all so well that a passing couple actually stopped and the man said, 'Couldn't help hearing, mate. What happened?'

'They put them all in the refrigerated wine stores,' Sergei said sweetly, 'but it *will* be interesting, won't it, to listen to the tones and resonances.'

So saying, he executed a very fast and curious contortion – Kung Fu, or something similar – in which he placed one foot on Bob Collis's chest, and pushed, sending Bob flying backwards down the slope. Simultaneously a hand was shoving indelicately at the chest of Elin Gundarsson, driving *her* back against her minders and the three of them were also stumbling backwards down the slope. Finally, a nanosecond later, his elbow drove into my midriff, and as I fell, gasping, he'd slung Jane over his shoulder and was running off with her, yelling, 'Make way, make way! Oxygen, oxygen!'

I could still hear his shouts as I stumbled to my feet and turned and began to stagger unsteadily after them, gasping and grunting and struggling for air.

For a moment or two I could still glimpse them through the tears Sergei's gut-punch had brought to my eyes, then they were gone, among the old gum trees behind the acoustic shell from which the orchestra was due to play. Multicoloured lights glowed among the trees, and I had the sense to note that they'd vanished right beneath a blue one. Knees buckling, thigh muscles wobbling outward, I went after them, in a kind of despair, mentally reduced in the same way as I was physically reduced – from the sudden and painful cut-off of oxygen – gasping like a fat man who's just had to chase a bus; but, though it was all I could do to muster sufficient concentration, I did keep my eye on that one blue light beneath which Jane had vanished.

149

I was a stumbling collection of grunts and gasps as I tried to drive my wandering limbs towards that one light, on past the acoustic shell, into the trees, and then I put my foot down awkwardly and fell against a tree, bashing my left shoulder. Bruising pain there, now, but a little less in my gut, and breath was shuddering into me as I stood, peering into darkness and listening. And taking breaths so noisily I could hear nothing else; certainly no yells of oxygen-for-the-lady.

But they must be *there*, somewhere. That was thought one as my starved brain now began sluggishly to perform. Thought two was that a man carrying a woman slung over his shoulder could run neither very far nor very fast! I stood rubbing my shoulder for the time it took to take in two breaths, then reeled on into the trees. Ahead of me was blackness; the lights of the amphitheatre were behind me now, and though there was a young moon up there, its dim light helped barely at all.

'Stop!' my brain ordered, and acted upon its own instruction. I stopped obediently and heard ahead of me a crashing sound, direction uncertain, but I blundered off, in the hope I'd sensed it correctly, cannoning off big gums and forcing myself forward. Then, quite suddenly and unexpectedly, there was light, just as the good book says: some vehicle on a road ahead, coming from the right, headlights full on, beams pinkened by the hanging clouds of red dust from earlier traffic, and in a moment the gums ahead were no longer lurking obstacles; now they were black shapes silhouetted against the pink light!

But the light wouldn't last: given a little oxygen the brain works on automatic, and mine informed itself that the vehicle was moving fairly fast, and I'd have only a second or two for looking around before darkness dropped back in place. I looked, pretty damned desperately, for anything moving. Trouble was, everything was moving, as the source of light itself moved. Trees moved, and bushes, and branches and the ground itself, but nothing human – nothing! I'd lost Jane – Sergei had got away!

A thud, over to my left, had my head snapping round, and as my eyes searched feverishly in the now-declining light, I saw something shift. Not a tree – I knew that – nor branch, nor bush. That movement was human. I turned, and hurried, and heard a grunt, and a second later a curse, and it occurred to me, as I moved, that movement was easier for me now: that I could actually breathe, that the pain was lessening – and that the opposite must be true of a man running and carrying a heavy burden!

That thought helped. I had no illusion that I could take on Sergei in single combat and win. But, maybe, if I *could* catch him, he'd have to set Jane down to defend himself, and she could dodge off into the dark. Just maybe . . .

Another grunt. Human, male, and ahead of me. I forced myself on, not running exactly, but trotting, and my eyes were working better now the pupils had adjusted themselves. And now I glimpsed movement again. Close.

Another thirty seconds and I was *very* close, could actually see Sergei dimly. He wasn't running, now, but this was a tough man, and he was striding out purposefully, with what had to be Jane still across his shoulder, in the fireman's hold, wriggling and swearing. One way and another, I thought, he mustn't have heard me. Too much noise around him, per-haps – his own breathing, the noise of his progress, Jane. From six feet behind him I shouted, 'Stop, Sergei!' and stop he did, and turned, saw me and turned back to hurry on, and I was preparing myself to do a rugby tackle when he seemed to spin suddenly out of balance, and start to go down and I plunged in and pulled him the rest of the way to the ground, and realized at once that this was an immense bundle of hard muscular strength I'd grabbed, and that I'd never be able to hold him. Then suddenly he was still!

It was so sudden and complete that for a moment I thought him dead: that he'd fallen on his own knife, or shot himself with his own silenced hand gun. I was still confused when a familiar, confident female voice said with satisfaction, 'That's fixed his damned wagon. It *is* you, John?'

'In person,' I gasped. 'Have you killed him?'

'Much as I'd like to – no. Who on earth is he, and what did he want? He's not the local rapist, I take it? He's the spy – the Russian?'

'One of them,' I said, grabbing her hand. 'What did you do to him?'

She was putting on a white shoe, standing on one leg. 'These heels are really quite sharp,' Jane said.

'You stabbed him with it?'

She shook her head. 'Hit him in the kidney. That's why he dropped me. Then I kicked him.'

'Where?'

'Where I was taught,' Jane said primly. 'Are we safe here? Shouldn't we move on?'

'We should.'

'Who are the others, the other Russians?' She was looking down at the sprawled Sergei as she spoke.

'The girl you saw. And the two men with her.'

'Looked like a model to me,' Jane said. 'And they were just thugs. Should we tie him, d'you think?'

'We leave him, we vanish. Simple. Come on.'

So hand in hand we picked our way through the woods. I was hearing sinister little rustles among the fallen leaves and gum nuts every few paces. Jane seemed not to notice anything, but I was wondering which of our many species was wriggling out of the way. I made a point of stamping my feet to encourage them.

'Aren't you making rather a lot of noise,' I was asked, with a certain crispness.

'Yes, and with a sensible purpose. You're not wearing boots, are you?'

'Don't be –'

'High-heeled pumps and tights,' I said. 'So put your feet down carefully, and stay behind me.' Not, I remember thinking, that my own light shoes would offer much protection. Depends what bites you, of course, and how successfully, but in most cases you're a goner without antivenin injections. It was a pretty spooky walk we set out on, towards where I'd left the hire-car. No antivenin in the hire-car, either.

15

Finding my car wasn't difficult: what was impossible was getting it out, because I'd been brutally parked in by the usual me-first bastard in the usual Ford. One of these days, when I've stopped running, I'm going to do leisurely research – just out of interest, you know – into why Ford drivers behave worse than drivers of, for instance, Holdens, or Mitsubishis. You get parked in, it's a Ford. You're overtaken in a lunatic, life-threatening way, likewise. There's a motorist gives you the raised finger (singular or plural) and what's he driving? Guess.

It was a big, *heavy* Ford, too, beyond our power to manhandle, and my little blue Toyota couldn't be shifted either. Meanwhile, assorted people would already be hunting us – Elin Gundarsson and her GRU drongos for three, and a now-upright aching Sergei for another. I stood cursing, looking at that bloody Ford, and muttering in a panicky way that we had to get away from here! Then I realized I was talking only to myself. Jane was no longer beside me. More panic. I called her name.

'Over here, John,' she called back softly.

I went to where her voice came from, and she was standing beside a big, dark, rectangular shape, and grinning at me. 'See what this is?'

'Land-Cruiser,' I said, now grinning back. We'd once had an unpleasant adventure in the northern desert with one of those things, the pair of us. 'Whose is it?'

'Some culture vulture,' Jane said airily, 'who won't need it for an hour or two. They've only played about six bars of the Mozart. Do we care? Anyway, he's left the door open – he *wants* it to be stolen!'

We left in it about a minute later. I'm honest, myself, but

Jane's a quality engineer and she steals a car like a pro: six seconds to find the wires, ten more to make the appropriate connections (this was a diesel) and about four to manoeuvre on to the road. There was a damn great roo-bar on the front. 'What say,' I said, 'we go and mangle that Ford a bit? Just for our private satisfaction.'

'We're going the other way.'

'Yes, Major Strutt.'

'But I don't know where. Will you tell me, please.'

'Albany,' I said. 'Way down south.'

'How far?'

'Long way. Two hundred miles, near enough.'

'Does anybody else know where we're going?'

'Not that I know of. But they seem to possess uncanny ways of finding out.'

Now the bold thief of moments before switched moral positions. 'It's not fair to take this 'Cruiser that far. Is there another way?'

'Nope,' I said. I was looking out of the rear window, making sure we weren't being followed. It wasn't likely, given the back country roads we were now travelling, but not impossible either. When I turned back we were on a bend, passing a paddock illuminated by our headlights. There must have been forty horses, all asleep standing up.

'Can you ride?' I asked.

'Two hundred miles – is one of those horses Black Bess?'

'We take it steady,' I said. 'Makes a nice little holiday.'

Jane took her eyes off the road for a second and gave me a brief, hard, accusing glance. 'You're serious.'

I said, 'Forest and pasture all the way. We just vanish. Pretty handy.'

'And we just pinch the horses out of a field –?'

'Paddock,' I said.

'Out of a paddock, then. And we *just* ride two hundred miles bare-back!'

'Make a left,' I said, 'about two miles further along, and drive until you come to white-painted rails on your right. We will then be at a farm belonging to a rich dentist client of mine, who keeps a lot of horses at my expense and that of other poor tax-payers, because this is a tax-loss arrangement. He'll be in Claremont, where he drills out his gold weekdays, and the horses will be grazing, and he prides himself on the fine leather saddlery he imports from Italy. Okay?'

'And this?'

'We leave it somewhere. Phone the police, if you like, and tell 'em where.'

'Right,' Jane said, making the left.

We took ourselves a good horse apiece and saddled them up. We borrowed such of old Bluie Martin's goods as we thought we'd need – they were his kids' really because I don't see Bluie actually camping, not with the Cabernet in peril of getting over-warm inside the tent – and off we went with clothes, food, a stove, sleeping bags etc. Gentle pace, cross-country, not a chance of running into hostiles, or much chance of encountering anybody at all unless we chose to, which we didn't.

Personally I'd have been content just to stay forever down there in the huge, beautiful, green, empty south of WA, in the region known as the Great Southern. People don't believe you in Europe when you tell them about the giant karri and tingle forests, hardwoods a hundred and fifty feet high, nor the great pastures and beautiful rivers. Down there you're a hell of a long way in every sense from the red centre. Pretty well a people-free zone it is, and Jane liked it as much as I did. But Jane's get-up-and-go; Jane believes in keeping moving. Accordingly, that's what we did. Each of us happy in the other's company, but both aware, early on, that we couldn't just stick around there in peace and safety. Why not? Because when we'd found ourselves a spot for the night and were lying in sleeping bags, looking up at the Southern Cross, I asked at last what had brought her all of a sudden to Australia. Was it the leaf?

She didn't answer immediately. I sensed she was collecting her thoughts. Then, after a moment, she said, 'Does Schliemann mean anything to you?'

'A name?' She nodded. 'I've heard it. Not sure of the context, though. A man, a place?'

155

'Man. German. Remarkable story.'

'Tell,' I said contentedly.

'Okay. It may take a while, but it's relevant, that much I promise.'

'Tell me.' I settled myself comfortably. Listening while Jane told me a story was, I thought, a good way for time to be spent.

'He was a businessman,' Jane said. 'Born 1822. Successful, made a lot of money, but wasn't really interested in business.'

'What *was* he interested in?'

She said, 'Homer.'

I *knew* I'd heard of Homer. 'Epic poetry.'

'That one, yes. He read Homer like I once read *Little Women* and Nancy Drew. Obsessively. Now, it seems there's a lot of debate about Homer and always has been – what's authentic and what isn't. But the point with Schliemann is that Homer was the chappie who wrote about the siege of Troy. Just legend, most academics thought at that time, all just legend. But Schliemann believed it, like fundamentalists believe the Bible: true, word for word.

'Now, the business part – where he got his money in the first place. Schliemann started life as a grocer's apprentice, then went to sea, but not far. He was shipwrecked on the Dutch coast and took a job in Amsterdam. So far, so ordinary for those times. But now we come to the extraordinary bit, because he started to teach himself languages. Guess how many.'

'Hundred and nine?'

'Oh, *you*!' Jane said. 'Seven. He taught himself seven languages, including Russian. Taught *himself*, mark you, *seven* languages, and he was still only twenty-four when his firm sent him to St Petersburg as its agent. That was 1846 and soon afterwards he founded a business of his own. By the time he was forty or so, he'd made so much money he could afford to retire. But he didn't. Instead he began studying.'

'More languages?'

'Archaeology. Then he went out there.'

'Where?'

'Turkey, as it is now. He began excavating a place called Hissarlik and established it was the actual site of a city.'

'Long lost?'

'Long lost,' she agreed. 'Three thousand years lost – and be quiet while I tell you about it.

'There were a lot of delays,' Jane went on. 'All the usual officials employing all the usual slow-it-down methods, lots of trouble, but finally he started digging. At that time, apparently, it was thought that Troy, if it had existed anywhere outside Homer's head, had been miles away. But Schliemann believed Homer, and eventually, digging into the flat-topped hill at Hissarlik, he found not just Troy, but nine other cities – or the ruins of them, some older ones, some less old – all stacked on top of each other. You still listening?'

'Enthralled,' I said. 'But where's the leaf come in?'

'Be patient. I'll get to it in the finish. Where was I?'

'Nine cities.'

'Yes. Well, each one had been built on the ruins of the one before, over thousands of years, and, out of the nine, Schliemann, in fact, picked the wrong one, not that it mattered very much. He investigated on the second level and the third. In fact, it was found later, that Troy was on level six.'

'Where's the leaf in all this?'

'Hush. Be as fascinated as I am.'

'No leaf?'

'Not at the moment. So here he was, the self-taught enthusiast, the mere amateur, and now he'd made the greatest discovery in the history of archaeology. The world was agog, okay?'

'What did he do then?'

'He decided enough was enough, at least for the time being. The digging could stop on June 15th, 1873. He wanted to move on because Schliemann had other projects. Then, the day before –'

'That's the fourteenth?'

'How do I keep you quiet?'

My suggestion was rejected. It wasn't the first such suggestion, or the first rejection. But I thought – and hoped – that

157

after I'd made it she seemed to have trouble refocusing her mind on Heinrich Schliemann. 'Where was I?'

'The day before, the fourteenth.'

'*Very* dramatic,' Jane said. 'He was just watching the labourers dig that day, when he suddenly glimpsed something. Told his wife, "Send the men away, all of them, at once." She asked why and he said, don't argue, just do it. The way men do. No explanation. Typical, if I may say so.'

'Did she?'

'She protested.'

'Also typical, if I may say –'

'Schliemann said, tell them I've just remembered it's my birthday and they can have the day off.'

'Couldn't he have told them himself?'

'He's a *man*, damn it,' Jane said. 'Why do it yourself when you've got a slave beside you?'

Jane has a taste for riding the feminist hobby-horse. When I'm not with her, it's something I tend to forget; when I'm with her, it's often hard to avoid.

'So the *woman* gave orders and the *men* obeyed, right? How many of 'em?'

'Hundred or so, I think.'

'Must have been a commanding lady.'

She gave me a moonlit glare that told me I was insufficiently serious. 'Sorry,' I said.

'The moment they'd gone he told her to fetch her red shawl, then he scrambled down into the hole and began frantic digging with his knife. There were big blocks of stone teetering above them. They could have been crushed at any minute. But he'd spotted the glint of gold – a vast quantity of gold – and ivory, and silver, too – and what it was, was the treasure of one of the great kings of ancient times. All buried for three *thousand* years, until Schliemann piled it in his wife's pinny that day. I'll bet,' Jane added, 'that *she* had to carry it out of the hole.'

'Isn't that recorded?'

'It's inevitable!'

'Is the leaf a part of that treasure, then?'

'No.'

158

'Then why are you *telling* me all this?'

'Do as you're told, John. Listen.'

And listen I did. Tried to, anyway. But it had been a long, trying day, and my mind was trying to cope with assorted matters, and somehow my eyelids must have tumbled down like iron shutters . . .

Next morning, though, I was up bright and early, which Jane wasn't. Body still catching up on jet-lag, I imagine. I lit the little gas stove and got a brew going and then put on a frying pan for bacon and eggs, all of which I'd swiped from Bluie's place, and the smell of cooking bacon wakened Jane. I always reckon myself, that if you fried bacon in the morning in a graveyard, two-thirds of those under ground would rear up and smack their lips. Jane certainly did. And she said, 'What's that Australian word?'

'Billabong?'

'No –'

'Swagman?'

'No. It's –'

'Bonzer?'

'It's drongo,' she said. 'And it's what you are, you louse. Falling asleep like that!'

'I was tired and it was peaceful.'

'And dull, too, was it?'

'The eggs,' I offered meekly, 'are just about ready.'

Jane glowered briefly, glanced round, then smiled. 'It's hard to be cross on a morning like this. Especially when you saved' – the smile became a grin – 'my bacon.'

'Or whatever.'

'Why did he grab me, anyway – how could I help him?'

I said, 'Sergei's after what he's always after – information. You had news!'

'How did *he* know?'

I shovelled bacon and eggs on to one of Bluie's tin plates. 'Well, for a start, he's probably tapped every phone for miles – mine for sure, and probably Bob Collis's too. Then, well, he knew about you, from England. And it was a fair bet – see things from his point of view – that you had worthwhile news. He wouldn't imagine you'd fly all the way over just to see me.'

'What about the others, then?' she asked, past a forkful of bacon.

'The other Russians?'

She nodded.

'Rivals,' I said.

'His rivals?'

'Nobody tells me anything, Jane. But so far as I can *tell*, Sergei is KGB and pro-reform. The girl, I think, is GRU – military intelligence, Red Army, etc – and so, therefore, are her cohorts. Who include, by the way, and in addition to the two thugs you saw with her yesterday, an entire ocean-going submarine and its crew, plus, probably, a lot of other assorted resources.'

'And Sergei and the girl –'

I interrupted. 'Her name is Elin. Elin Gundarsson. Or so she says.'

'Doubt that,' Jane said. 'Icelandic name. It'll be a false one. But she and Sergei are enemies?'

'My oath, they are!'

'So she'd kidnap me, too?'

'I reckon,' I said, 'that Sergei only grabbed you because if he didn't, she would.'

'Better be careful, had I?'

'You need somebody to look after you,' I offered hopefully.

Jane speared a precisely cut piece of fried egg. 'You did a great job last night, and I'm grateful. Any coffee?'

There was coffee. While we drank it, I learned yet more about Herr Schliemann. The treasure he'd unearthed in what he *thought* was Troy, he smuggled out of the country. Illegally, it seems. My old tutor, an academic lawyer if ever there was one, was fond of observing that the pursuit of knowledge must always take precedence and Schliemann must have agreed. In spades. No doubt he wanted to study all that gold very closely.

Over the second aromatic cup, I brought up the matter of the leaf again, and was again ordered to listen and wait and see.

After Troy, Schliemann, it seems, conducted another great expedition, at Mycenae, on the Greek mainland, digging into what again turned out to be royal remains. And once again we were back into Ancient Greek history/myth, and this time it's a famous tale. We all know about Agamemnon, don't we: away ten years at the Trojan Wars, while at home the dirty rat Aegisthus made a play (successful) for his wife Clytemnestra. Nor did Aegisthus stop there. When Agamemnon came home, Aegisthus invited him to a celebratory banquet, and there "struck him down as one slaughters the ox at the crib". Years later, the son, Orestes, came back to murder both his father's assassin and his adulterous mother. You may have seen the movie (Aeschylus) or read the book (Homer). Either way, there was nothing new about all this, even then, when Uncle Heinrich sank his spade into the earth.

But Heinrich Schliemann *introduced* something new. Homer had described Mycenae as *golden*, and, as we know, Schliemann believed – and by now had plenty of reason to believe – every word Homer wrote.

'So,' Jane said, wiping her lips with a tissue from her bag, 'to cut a longish story short, he made another great discovery – the graves, and in them, the bodies of the men (Agamemnon and his men) murdered by Aegisthus and Clytemnestra. He sent a famous telegram to the King of Greece: "I have today looked upon the face of Agamemnon."'

'What about *Mrs* Schliemann?'

'You're right to ask,' Jane said. 'Her name was Sophia, and for three weeks and four days, she had explored the earth with only bare hands and a penknife. Women's work, you see. I imagine Schliemann himself was smoking his pipe and thinking lofty thoughts.'

It seems that five graves were found. 'I'll just bet,' Jane said, 'that Mrs S. found them and dear old Heinrich hogged all the credit. At any rate, he announced to the King "my discovery of the graves".'

'Any other names I'd know?'

'Cassandra,' Jane said. 'Daughter of the King of Troy.'

'She was the one with all the bad news?'

'The gift of prophecy,' Jane said. 'She foresaw the fall of

Troy, but nobody believed her. When it fell, Agamemnon captured her.'

'And what – tucked her under his arm and brought her home?'

'Something like that. You have noticed already, I imagine, that sauce for the goose Clytemnestra was *not* sauce for the gander Agamemnon?'

'I'd have thought guilt in this one was a bit tricky to apportion. Did Cassandra wear a leaf, then?'

'No.'

'Because I'm getting impatient. Please can we get to the part with the leaf?'

'We'll get there soon.' It's one of those things. If Jane would say yes – and I keep hoping she will – I'm not entirely sure whether I'd have a wife or a commanding officer. The correct descriptive word for me, I suspect, is wally. Or wimp, if there's a difference. The thing is, it doesn't deter me. 'Bear with me, John,' she went on. 'Now, where was I?'

'Cassandra's grave.'

'Yes, okay. Except it wasn't Cassandra, and it wasn't Agamemnon. The graves date from four hundred years earlier.'

I said, 'Schliemann boobs again!'

'Depends what you mean by boobs,' Jane said too quickly, and gave me a hard look when I sniggered. 'They may have been the wrong bodies, but they were covered in gold, silver, precious stones. By way of compensation.'

'Leaves? Covered in leaves like the Babes in the Wood?'

She went on remorselessly. '"All the museums of the world taken together," Schliemann wrote, "do not have one fifth as much."'

'Was he right about *that*?'

'I expect so. Let me tell you what he found.' She opened her little evening bag and pulled out a sheet of paper. 'The inventory. Ready? Well, in the first grave he found three skeletons and on each were diadems of pure gold, laurel leaves and crosses of pure gold –'

Greatly daring, I interrupted. 'Are those leaves . . . ?'

'Nope,' said Jane. 'Another grave had the remains of three

162

women in it, and buried with them were all *sorts* of orna-
ments – animals, flowers, butterflies, golden decorative
pieces, figured lions, beasts of various kinds, warriors in
battle. Oh, John, the list just goes on and on! One of the
skeletons wore a crown. It was gold, of course, decorated
with golden leaves.'

'Are *those* –?'

'Nope. The head with the crown on it had almost turned
to dust.'

'As I shall, soon.'

'And in this grave –' She grinned at me. 'Shall we forget
the others?'

'Please!' I said. 'Oh, *please!*'

'In this grave were thick golden leaves.'

'Oh, goody!' I clapped my hands. 'Peterkin's among them?'

'Very likely. It's hard to be positive. There were a lot of
them.'

'Well, Peterkin had a few, didn't he? How many
altogether?'

Jane laughed gaily. 'Seven hundred and one. Imagine the
value!'

I thought about the value for a moment, at four hundred
dollars an ounce. 'Beats me,' I said. 'We've got the seven
hundred and first, right?'

She shook her chestnut head. 'Dunno what we have, but
it's one of them. I checked. Went to a woman at the British
Museum who's tame.'

'Tame?'

'SIS can consult her when need arises.' Jane plainly was
quoting. 'She took one quick look and began jumping up and
down. While she was doing that, she produced a few words,
hissing with excitement.'

'Said, "Stone me!", did she?'

'Said, "My God, it's Mycenae!" Then did six more little
jumps, then said, "Schliemann!" and jumped about a bit
more. And *then* she said –'

'Where the bloody hell did you get *this*?'

'No, she didn't. Not her job to ask questions. She's retained
to supply answers.'

'So what *did* she say?'

'Next word was "Berlin". I asked her, "Is that where Schliemann took his finds?"'

'You're going to tell me another little story, aren't you?'

She held up finger and thumb, a millimetre apart. 'Very short one. Let me pour you another cup of coffee.'

'Go on about Berlin.'

'What we do now,' Jane said, 'is we move forward in time.'

'To the present?'

'Not quite, but we're getting nearer. Schliemann's collection went to museums in Berlin, principally to one for ancient history. Now – what happened to Berlin?'

'The wall came down.'

'Before that.'

'Hitler,' I said.

'Okay. And after that?'

'The war. Bombing raids. The –'

'Hold on. With the bombers coming, lots of important material, lots of valuables, treasures, were moved for safety, out of galleries, and museums, and *into*, of all things, the Tiergarten.'

'That's the *zoo*, isn't it? They didn't put all this material in with the lions?'

'Still less the hippos, no,' Jane said. 'But there was a huge flak tower there, bristling with guns, supposedly indestructible, and impregnable. Make a guess?'

'It wasn't.'

'Right again. It was knocked flat, destroyed. Most of the contents were crushed in the rubble.'

'Except,' I said.

Jane nodded. 'Some was recovered. But not for a while. All of Berlin was rubble, because of the long pounding by –?'

'Bombers.'

'And?'

'The Red Army, if memory serves.'

'It serves, John. You see what it all means?'

'Yes,' I said. 'I see very clearly. The Red Army got there first, didn't it? Before the Brits and the Yanks?'

164

She nodded.

'And *we* have a leaf or three which we got from Peterkin, who got them from . . . are you thinking what I'm thinking?'

16

There was to be no more talking, until we had washed the dishes and ourselves in the stream close to our campsite. I didn't even shave; the thought of who was looking for us made me wonder if a few days' growth of whisker might not be useful. Jane looked at the stubble like a sergeant major – one eyebrow raised and lips tight. We saddled the horses, packed the saddle bags, and rode away at a walk.

A beautiful morning was all around us: sky blue, air cool, grass green, trees numberless and handsome in that uniquely Australian way native trees have. There were grazing animals in every paddock, cattle, sheep, horses, and 'roos, and only the 'roos took any notice of us, hopping cautiously away at our approach. One was a very big red bull and Jane said, 'He reminds me.'

'Of what?'

She dropped the word into the sunlit freshness of morning, and it landed with a thud. 'Stalin,' Jane said. 'The big red in person.'

'I'm not sure it doesn't fit too well,' I said. At that moment we were about as far from Stalin as it was possible to get: forty years, ten thousand miles, an ocean or two, and two or three generations.

'You're just nervous of it.'

'Well, I am, but it's not just that. We're in among myth and legend now. I mean, for God's sake – it's possible to draw a line, ruler straight, if we're to believe all this, direct from King Priam and the siege of Troy, via Hitler's Berlin to Stalin's Moscow, and from Moscow to Peterkin in Albany Gaol and then to me!'

'To us,' Jane said firmly. 'I have the leaf.'

'Where?'

'Security at Perth Airport.'

'Good. So it goes like this, and correct me if I'm wrong. Herr Schliemann digs it all up. He's German, so after he's done his bit of piracy and got everything out of Turkey –'

'Greece.'

'Mycenae's Greece? I see. Okay. It goes to a museum or museums, where it stays till Hitler. It then goes into secure surroundings, but destruction arrives. Agreed?'

'Go on.'

'Enter a million Russians – guns, tanks, planes. Then there's a gap of forty years or so. Until us. We *know* about Schliemann and the discoveries, yes?'

'Yes.'

'We *know* about the Berlin museums, yes?'

'Yes.'

'All that is *fact*, then. Is the Tiergarten flak tower fact? I mean, it seems crazy to me to take all your most precious possessions and stick 'em in a tower, no matter how impregnable, in a city that's being bombed day and night and is number one target for the guns of a fair few armies. I mean, it's just not a sensible precaution. Imagine how they'd look at you at the Legal and General or the Norwich Union. They'd chase you off the premises with dogs.'

'Hitler,' Jane said, 'didn't have to deal with insurance companies.'

'I've dealt with 'em, Jane. I know.'

She sighed. 'I expect the state bore the risk. Like it does with ships and banks.'

'Mmm. Who told you about this tower?'

'The lady at the British Museum.'

'As fact?'

'I asked that. Well-established truth, that's what she said.'

'Said so to you?'

'To me. The tower had deep foundations, but the upper works collapsed and everything was crushed.'

I said, 'But not *everything*. Our friends the Russians came in, and among the raping and looting and burning, which would be impulse activity, there were obviously real souvenir hunters. Systematic blokes with lists, looking for rocket scientists and gas manufacturers and war criminals, and among them must have been a guy who was after Schlie-mann's treasure.'

'And found it, and delivered it to his boss!' Jane's eyes sparkled. 'Who could only be, surely, the man Peterkin stole it *from*.'

I raised my hand. 'Hold it, Jane. The Red Army's in Berlin. This drongo knows where to look and he finds the ancient treasure. Or a bit of it. What's he do – first plane to Stalin? Not him. It's *your* world, this one. Please, sir, may I have an interview with the colonel, or whoever?'

Jane said, 'Maybe he was a colonel.'

'There was a general, though, I happen to know. Iron Man. Marshal Koniev. He took Berlin. He'd know – he'd have to know one way or the other – about this.'

'Why?'

'Because it was important enough to wind up in the hands of the bloodthirsty tyrant himself.'

Jane shook her head. 'Doesn't hold water, John. There were political commissars everywhere. One of those fellows, carrying a laissez-passer from Stalin *himself* could do as he liked, Koniev or no Koniev.'

I said, 'I'm talking about *how* the leaves got to the Kremlin, because it seems obvious they must have done. So if Stalin had sent the kind of special commissar you're talk-ing about, then it pre-supposes that he had a detailed knowl-edge of archaeology. If he'd just wanted gold, he could have helped himself, couldn't he? Because Russia's a big gold producer.'

'So what are you saying, John?'

'That they were found in the ruins, got to Koniev or some-body on that level, and must have been *presented* to Stalin. Who kept them not because they were gold, or ancient, but because they were a convenient, portable, personal, private reminder of what he'd done to Berlin, to Germany, above all to Hitler.'

'Okay. You listened to me, so I'm listening to you. But why does it *matter*?'

'I've read about the Kremlin. I've seen film. It's stuffed

with treasure – the Tsar's jewels, God knows what. But it wasn't the Kremlin in general that these came from, was it? And Peterkin didn't carry a pocketful of solid gold leaves with him when he ran out into the night – knowing Stalin would have him killed just for knowing his greatcoat was wet.'

'You're saying . . . ?'

'That when Peterkin went back to Russia, he *knew* how to get in to Stalin's old quarters.'

'Would they still be kept as he had them?'

'Dunno. They preserved Lenin's. Why not Stalin's? No, damn it, they *must* be preserved! It would be stupid to think anything else. Peterkin went back to Russia, a few years back, looked for the entrance he'd left by, found it, and went in. When he came out, he'd a few knick-knacks in his pockets, certainly *one* leaf – only one has been broken open – but probably others.'

We rode on in silence, or as near silence as you'll find on horseback. Then after a bit Jane said, 'But it isn't the gold leaf from Mycenae that Sergei wants, is it? Or that Gundarsson woman – '

'Or those bloody Americans in England. No, it isn't. And there's *your* comrade in arms, too, Rupert whatever, the one with the PhD in unpleasantness. Though I'm not sure the Americans or the Brits even know what it is they're hunting.'

'What do you mean?'

'Well, they know the Russians are hunting for something, so they hunt for it, too, whatever it is, as a matter of principle.'

'The cold war's over, John!'

'So the story goes,' I said. 'Don't forget history's long-term. How old's the Kremlin? Maybe seven, eight hundred years. What is it? It's a fortress. How many tyrants has it housed? Dozens. Now you *can* say all that is over. But would you make bets? What are the chances of a new tyrant a decade from now, or five decades, or a hundred years ahead?'

'But, John, the Soviet *Union* is breaking up! Give it a bit of time and you'll have a dozen independent countries – '

'Fighting each other,' I said. 'It could be like the Balkans

169

all over again. Or like it was centuries ago – Mother Russia surrounded by the hostile tribes, Ukraine here, Tajiks there, Georgians and Letts. Everybody armed with nukes. Oh boy! Not to mention the Golden Horde, but they'll be riding tanks, this time, instead of ponies. You know what Stalin did?'

She turned her head and smiled at me. 'Yes, I know what he did. Stalin breached the Kremlin walls.'

'And?'

'Something else?'

'And *left* them breached! Peterkin got in. So anybody else can – spy, assassin, you name it, and it could be this year, next year, some time or never. But Peterkin was always right. The secret he held *was* the most deadly thing there was. Imagine if the CIA in, say, 1951 when the Russians were building their first nuclear bombs – imagine if they'd been able to send in an assassin straight to Stalin's quarters!'

Jane was still smiling. I said, 'It's nothing to grin about, you know. Peterkin kept his secret till he died, and he was determined not to hand it on to his daughter. But he handed it over to me, blast him!'

'Us.' Jane said.

I really don't know why we were smiling, now, the two of us. No, correction – I know why *I* was smiling. I liked the idea of a secret shared with Jane because it brought us closer. Not close enough, but closer. That was the cause of my smile. What caused Jane's, I have no idea. Perhaps we felt secure, for the moment, wandering gently on horseback through a beautiful, timeless stretch of land which man has barely touched.

Several hours later, over lunch – corned beef and bread – Jane said, 'We could escape, you know.'

'Mmm.'

'All we have to do,' she said musingly, 'is tell them every-thing we know.'

'They won't believe it's everything. People like that always think there's more.'

170

'Ah, but . . . we *don't* know, do we? Either of us. But you know where to find out.'

'I have a clue Peterkin left. A riddle. If I can solve it –'

'If *we* can solve it.'

'Fine by me – if we *can*, we find what Peterkin has hidden –'

'And only *then* do we have the big secret,' Jane said. 'Ergo, we can duck out if we choose to. All we'd have to do is give *them* the clue, the signpost, whatever. Let *them* find it. It'll be clear enough that we don't know anything. So we're safe, no longer sole custodians of all that's deadly. Freedom!'

'Yair.'

We rode on after we'd eaten, thinking, quiet. Personally, I was also beginning to be a little bit saddle-sore; don't know about Jane, and was too delicate to ask. What she'd said was basically true, I thought, except that you don't *need* to know it all to get the bullet in the back of the neck. Often, just a little knowledge is more than enough, and we knew *more* than a little. *We* knew there was a secret door into the Kremlin. We might not, and indeed did not know exactly where it was, but we knew where to find out. Quite enough death warrant evidence for your average tyrant.

I said all this as the afternoon wore on.

Jane listened, then thought a while, then said, 'And there's the oath.'

'Her Majesty?'

'That's the one. John, what *should* we do?'

I said, 'There's only one way to unload it.'

'Give it to someone else. Our side, not theirs?'

'Something like that.'

'Then we go ahead. Get the information if we can. And before you say "who's we?" I mean Britain *and* Australia.'

'You know what I am, Jane?'

She grinned. 'More or less. You want all the descriptive words?'

'I'm Peterkin's cat's-paw. I *was* once his lawyer. Maybe in a sense I still am. But principally I'm his agent – I've taken his money to do what he wanted me to do. I have to think what he'd have wanted.'

'Well, what *do* you think? We're near enough two parts of the same country – certainly the same civilization. If our two governments get the information jointly, I don't see how Peterkin could have objected. After all, Britain took him in when he was a refugee.'

We looked at one another. No smiling this time. This rural idyll was very pleasant and all that, and personally I'd have liked it to go on. And on. But it couldn't . . . and when we emerged, the people who wanted to lay their hands on us would want us *still*; and furthermore would still be searching.

But Jane *was* right, and now she said, 'What is it we are looking for anyway? What's the next pointer Peterkin put down, and where do we find it?'

'Albany,' I said. 'And all we've got is two words: one is push and the other is pull.'

17

Six days we spent getting down to Albany, and we emerged from the back country in the hills behind the town, from the Porongorup Range national park, having seen literally no one since we were chased out of that concert on the Cape. For the record, we were still unwed in both the common law and more formal senses. Not to say what'll happen one day, but . . .

So now we sat up there looking down on my home town for nearly an hour. I ran my eye over the broad spread of the place, trying to think of what or where push and pull could be, and meanwhile giving Major Strutt a quick visual tour and reciting vital statistics. The town's, that is.

The place you look down on is built around a harbour – Princess Royal Harbour, it's called – one of the greatest landlocked harbours on earth. I'm not kidding. Albany's a match for Hong Kong, or San Francisco, for Savannah or Sydney; it's a huge anchorage, safe in the worst storms. In the days of sail, Albany was the haven after the lashing that ships took in the Southern Ocean; later it was a coaling station for steamships. But after coal-firing was superseded, Albany's harbour became less important. In my young days, grain was shipped out, and some wool, and wood and phosphate, but none of it was big commerce. Also there was whaling then. The continental shelf's only thirty miles or so offshore. Whales used to be plentiful there; the whalers went after them. But along came Save the Whales. The outcry grew ever louder, and the whaling company ceased operations at Cheynes Beach in 1978. Now it's a museum, and they'll tell you there that out on the continental shelf, the whales are getting thin and may even be starving, because there are more whales now, and less food, because the krill, off which they feed, is now being commercially harvested, and there's no Save the Krill campaign.

So I pointed it all out to Jane, from Frenchman Bay on the west to the Nanarup surfing beach, where once I idled time away, in the east.

'Very handsome,' I muttered, 'but there isn't a push or a pull anywhere.'

'Department store doors?'

'There's only one of any size. We'll just have to make a search.'

'Pubs?'

'Likewise.'

'There must *be* doors,' she said. 'I never look at the signs, I must admit. Always push when I should be pulling. Then feel like an idiot.'

'Everybody does that. Bob Collis says he once saw a sign that said LIFT and there was a bloke trying to lift the door.'

Jane smiled for my sake, but she's not a great one for feeble quips. 'What does a person push, apart from doors? There's nothing, really, is there?'

'Broken-down cars,' I said. 'Lawnmowers, prams, bikes on steep hills.'

'Okay, what does one pull?'

'In the vernacular, birds. Otherwise, ropes, chains, carts if you're a horse, ships if you're a tug, teeth if you're a dentist.'

'*Must* be doors,' Jane said. 'What we'll have to do –'

'Salesmen push products,' I said.

She shook her head. 'Describe Peterkin.'

'Big, strong, very quiet.'

'No, not that. Was he – well, bright?'

'Einstein he wasn't.'

'How good was his English?'

'Peterkin's? It was serviceable. Heavily accented. You could tell he was foreign. But he did physical work all his life; he wasn't drafting statutes or writing theatre notices. Why do you ask?'

'Well, he left his clue, didn't he? Only two words, so he *had* to be precise. Had to know the meaning. Had to know they'd tell the right thing to the right person, which means *you* – John Close, solicitor.'

I pondered this. 'You mean, was his knowledge of words exact? Let me think about it. Tell you this, though: the description he wrote of his escape – that was pretty well done.'

'Explain that. What does it mean?'

I sighed. 'He was clear. He wrote down what happened, and there was nothing confusing about it.' I thought some more, remembering. 'Wrote as he spoke. Even the prose had a strong foreign accent.'

'You understood every word? You don't remember startling misuse of language? He didn't get things badly wrong?'

'No. But it's weeks since I read –'

'Doesn't matter. Concluding question: he'd know exactly what the two words mean – push and pull?'

'He'd know, yes.'

She looked down over Albany, spread below us. The sun gleamed on flat calm water in the wide harbour and on the great sweep of King George Sound, with the Southern Ocean beyond and apparently calm. 'Strange,' Jane said. 'So peaceful and remote, and to think it's where such a sophisticated secret is.'

'Where it may be,' I corrected her. 'We don't know if this is the end of Peterkin's trail or not.'

She said, 'He wouldn't send us off again. Not from here.'

'Maybe,' I recall saying warningly. 'Don't rely on the peace and calm though. Never. Not here.'

'But look at it!' she protested. 'Flat as –'

I said, 'She's a treacherous old cow, the Southern Ocean. I'll tell you how treacherous. At school I had a mate called Bruce Ross. Twelve, at the time. Day like this, it was, and he was standing on top of a granite cliff beyond that golf course way over there. Place called the Gap. Well, he was eighty feet up, just standing there. You'd think he'd be safe. But there are unpredictable surges. They start hundreds of miles south and the continental shelf is just too close to shore to break them up. Bruce was bloody unlucky. But he

175

was bloody careless, too, because we'd all been warned a million times. Big wave reached up and plucked him off the rock, neat as you like. Never seen again, Bruce wasn't.'

'Eighty feet!'

'It happens,' I said.

There's a trotting track with a bit of stabling just north of the South Coast Highway. For a few bucks I was able to leave our horses there. Now we needed things. I'd no illusions that disguise would help if we were actually spotted, but they might help us blend with the local scene, and Albany's a tourist town. In summer the population goes up from twenty thousand to forty, and they're all kinds: bathers, fishermen, bowls players, all the usual. There's tennis, golf, squash, sightseeing, you name it, hillwalkers, rockhounds, climbers in the Porongorup, sailing, waterskiing.

We strolled over to the caravan park on the Mount Barker road, and begged the use of a phone, and I called up Dr McQueen – Dr Jim McQueen, that is, whose phone message about Peterkin's death had started it all. When I got his answering machine saying, 'We're sorry, but the doctor is busy just now and please leave your number . . . etc', I grinned at Jane through the glass, and said to the recorder, 'It's John, Jim, and I want to borrow your Land Rover. Coming over right now.' Then I called a taxi.

'What's so amusing?' Jane demanded.

'Local joke, don't worry about it.' I'd been thinking. There was no knowing who else would be in this town. In theory nobody knew *we'd* be in Albany. I hadn't told Elin Gundarsson, though I'd contemplated it; Sergei didn't know; even Bob Collis didn't. The only ones who knew about the Abrolhos leaf were Alex, and Joe Hag, both in faraway Fremantle getting a bent propeller straightened and balanced. Could be that we'd be safe here right out in the open. Or maybe not.

Jim McQueen's Land Rover, parked in his wide driveway, had dark-tinted glass. On a separate hard standing were a Mazda sports car, a Toyota sedan and a nice Bayswater-built twenty-eight-foot Leeder with twin Volvo diesels. By the standards of Australian doctors, the poor bastard must, I reflected, be close to starvation.

And they like to keep what they've got to themselves. When I told him that he'd got me into a mess which was now a matter of life and death, and probably worse, he wasn't much impressed.

'Have to do better than that, John,' he said. 'You forget in my job life and death's everyday stuff.'

'Even mine?'

He considered that. 'Anything happens to my vehicle,' said Dr McQueen, 'you restore it. Showroom condition. All over. How long d'you want it anyway? Come to that, *why*?'

'Dire need, Jim.'

'How long?'

'Two or three days.' I'd just spotted the Scottish lion rampant flying over his garden, and said, 'Meet my fiancée, she's a Scot, too, Lady Jane Fraser.'

That got to him: Scot plus title!

'Fraser,' he murmured respectfully. 'Of Lovat, perhaps?'

'Cadet branch,' I said, 'cousins of the Saltouns.' All this nonsense I knew from my mother who'd come to Australia from Skye, mainly to get out of the rain. But McQueen was entranced. Honoured, he'd be, to let the Lady Jane see the Great Southern from his carriage. There are marked resemblances, says he, to the west coast of Scotland.

So off we went, Jane not knowing whether to giggle or rage, me with McQueen's final hiss: 'Not one tiny scratch, mind,' still sibilant in my ear. At assorted stores we spent Peterkin's money, kitting ourselves out as tourists, me in those plaid board shorts and a dazzling crimson shirt, Jane in a rig she'd worn once before to avoid attention: white shorts, Ken Done T-shirt of Sydney Harbour Bridge, yellow trainers, and white baseball cap. We both wore big sunglasses. Among the holidaymakers in York Street we felt anything but conspicuous, and behind the dark glass of McQueen's Land Rover, we were almost invisible. The sense of security, while it lasted, was pleasing. What we needed now was a hidey-hole and a phone, and we got both at a motel I knew that was convenient for, but nicely away from, the main drag.

There, while Jane had a bath, I sat and thought for a moment, then began telephoning old schoolmates, former neighbours. It was years since I'd spoken to most of them, so an excuse was needed. I said my visit to Albany was for only a day or two and on business, but that there was a bet at stake (nothing like a bet for rousing Australian interest). A mate in Perth, I said, had bet me I wouldn't notice a door that said pull when it had to be pushed, and it was a door I was absolutely bound to use. Had anybody any knowledge of this phenomenon? Interesting little wager, they thought, all of them. But . . . sorry. Ring you if I think where it is . . . nice to talk . . .

So no short cut possible.

When Jane knocked and came in, I said, 'No luck.'

'We have to search – quarter the whole town?'

'The only way.'

She took a deep breath. 'Right then. We need a system.'

'Stroke of luck would be better. There are shops and stores, pubs, hotels, lavatories, golf courses, hospitals. Push and pull could be at any of them.'

'Or all,' Jane said. 'And how will we know? I suppose we'll have to assume Peterkin thought of that and arranged things so that when we see it, we'll know. Or *you* will.' Her face fell. 'Perhaps I won't know. It's meant for you!'

For a minute or two we simply sat, disconsolate. Then Jane sat up sharply. 'Did Peterkin know you came originally from Albany?'

'Don't think so,' I said, slowly, contemplating it. 'I don't tell my clients anything. Not about me. All they know is I'm a shyster in Perth.'

'*Could* he have known?'

'I suppose so, but I doubt it.'

'Did you visit him in prison?'

'Not here, no. Only in Fremantle. What's your point?'

'Well, if *you* were doing this . . . imagine it . . . you're leaving your cryptic message on a piece of pottery. Albany, push and pull, it says, and it's intended for some Perth shyster, right? Now . . . if he knows Albany well, the job of finding it becomes impossible for all the reasons we've been over. But if he *doesn't*, if he's more or less of a tourist, he'll know, or get to know, a lot fewer places.' She was animated now. 'Very few, in fact. John, where do tourists go?'

'Well, golfers go golfing – there are seven courses around here. There's *miles* of fishing –'

Impatient now, she interrupted. 'Where do *all* of them go?'

Now I understood. 'Boat trip on the harbour, the Gap, maybe Jimmy Newell's, the Residency Museum, the Brig Amity. Whaleworld, of course.'

'You told me about the Gap, didn't you – where the boy was washed away?'

'Bruce Ross, yes.'

'What's the Brig Amity?'

'Replica ship. Local timber. Interesting if you like history.'

'In its place, yes. Not now. What's Jimmy Newell's?'

'A little harbour. Old Jimmy was caught in a sudden blow out on the ocean and was driven in there by chance. He was a lucky bloke, believe me – ought to have died.'

'What's left? The museum – any good?'

'Quite good, yes. Small, but –'

'And Whaleworld, you said, what is it?'

I said, 'That's the biggie, Jane. It's unique in the world. The old whaling station at Cheynes Beach. Remember I pointed it out this morning?'

Jane nodded impatiently. 'What's the "world" part?'

'It's a whaling museum; they made it out of a working whaling station. You can see the whole thing. There's a whale chaser – a ship – the flensing decks, the reducing tanks, harpoons – the lot.'

'And everybody goes there.'

'Once,' I said. 'If you like your entertainment bloodthirsty, fine; if you're queasy, once is enough times to look at the head saw!'

Major Strutt is not the fainting, smelling-salts, eyes-averted type. Or so you might think. Major Strutt is a clear-eyed, clean-jawed, look-the-world-in-the-face type, and no bones

179

about it. All the same, I noticed, we didn't begin at Whaleworld.

'Better if we actually behave like tourists, I think,' Major Strutt observed, as she turned the good doctor's gleaming vehicle into Princess Royal Drive, and parked beside the Brig Amity. I paid the price of admission, or rather Peterkin did, and aboard we went. It's a little ship, a replica of the vessel that brought the first settlers. Forty-five people were on her then, in 1826. Today, with just Jane and me and one elderly lady on board, she seemed badly overcrowded; Lord knows where forty-five people stowed themselves. Certainly there was no hidden pottery leaf because there was no room to hide anything.

'Where next?' Jane asked briskly.

We went next to the Old Gaol, now restored. One look reminded me how my father used to threaten to have me locked up inside. Never did it, and didn't mean it either, but those granite blocks kept my little feet on the straight and narrow right enough. After that to the Residency Museum, which is a branch of the excellent WA Museum, and is, as a consequence, good, if small. No leaf in either place, though, not that Jane or I could see. And we looked. It's a strange feeling guiding somebody else around the scenes of your childhood: these were familiar places, but because of Jane's presence I was seeing them in a new way and through eyes which, if hardly new, were focused differently. I could see with clarity that Albany, which for more than half my life had been the entire universe, was just a small town. Plenty of pride and history, lots of natural beauty and amenity, but *small*. The realization somehow sent an offended shudder down my spine. I'd seen London now, and Rome. Beside them, even the throbbing metropolis of Perth was also just a small town. But beautiful, like Albany.

We did not see any leaves, nor anything to push or pull, until we went to the Old Post Office, now a restaurant where there were doors bearing the words, on plates of polished brass. We spotted them, nudged one another, searched minutely, and found only a cup of coffee apiece. After which,

180

on to the Vancouver Arts Centre. Albany was yet another of the discoveries of Captain George Vancouver, Cook's sailing master, who left his name on assorted new shores around the world, all of them a long way from his birthplace, a few miles from Nelson's.

We saw all the tourist sights, and enjoyed both the experiences and, I'm content to think, each other's company. 'Where next?' Jane now asked brightly.

'Better show you the Gap,' I said.

'Okay, which way?'

I pointed.

She said, 'Oh,' in a quiet sort of way. 'Isn't that the way to –'

'Whaleworld. Yes, it is.'

There was reluctance in her every movement, and I thought a breath of sea air might help, so we postponed Cheynes Beach for a bit and went out for a boat trip around the bay . . . round Princess Royal Harbour, that is. Saw nothing in the way of hand-made pottery leaves, naturally, though I had a good look round the boat and Jane kept a beady eye on the shore while I was doing it. I said, as we headed in towards the town jetty, 'There's a sort of inevitability about this.'

'Not finding it, you mean – you don't think we will?'

I shook my head. 'Been thinking about Peterkin.'

'And?'

'Well, there's really only one place here that's his style.'

'He had a style?'

'Wrong word, I suppose, if it suggests fashion pictures and sculptured domestic rubbish. It's more . . . well, he had a way of life.'

Jane nodded. 'You told me, in London. But tell me all over again. Maybe it'll help.'

I said, 'Big man. Strong, physically. Independent to a degree – and we know why. Secretive likewise, and we know about that too. The life he led, here in Australia, more or less from the moment he arrived, consisted of physical work in remote places; unskilled work, mainly; he kept moving on for good reasons, which we also know. But he worked on shell –

mother of pearl – in the boats out of Broome. He worked in the jarrah forests, the karri forests, worked with cattle in the north, and he fished out of Geraldton. What I was thinking was –'

'That perhaps he went whaling!' Jane said quickly.

'Yes. He never said so, not to me. But it would be his *kind* of work.' I pointed. 'See that headland? Frenchman Bay is just beyond, and that's where Cheynes Beach is, the whaling station. Now – Perth is the remotest *big* city on earth. It's twelve hundred miles from the next major city. Okay, Albany is four hundred and twelve kilometres from Perth.'

'What's that in miles?'

'Two hundred and fifty something. And you an engineer! Listen, Frenchman Bay is remote even from Albany – pretty well a self-contained little colony. Was when I knew it, anyway. And most of the time half the whaling men were out in the catcher boats –'

'Remote even from the whaling station!' she said.

'Absolutely in character.'

'Would anybody have records?'

'Probably, but I don't think we need records. "Albany–Push–Pull" was what was lettered into the pottery. We're *in* Albany, and I'll bet you what you like, he's left the leaf at the whaling station. It was territory he knew.'

The boat came alongside and a sailorly hand helped passengers ashore. We walked to the Land Rover and hopped in. 'Direct me,' Jane said. And as I did so, she added, 'Anybody followed us, d'you think?'

I shook my head.

'Me neither.' Jane gave a little shrug. 'But it's hard to believe we got clean away, walking slowly on horseback.'

'Big place to search, Western Australia.'

'But they will be searching,' Jane said. 'It's important. It *matters*.'

18

Whale-hunting stopped in 1978. Now they hunt the tourist dollar, and get it, too; and that's a funny thing: there's a kind of worldwide revulsion against the killing of whales, but there's no shortage of people wanting to see Death's equipment. Just like the Tower of London, I suppose: big queues to see the headsman's axe and block; smaller numbers for the armour.

There's a diagrammatic map of Whaleworld where you buy tickets, and you can run an anticipatory eye over such delights as the Cutting-up Deck, the Carcass Hoist, the Flensing Deck (where the blubber was peeled away) and the Digesters (*everything* was used). Having seen that little lot, and had the process explained, you could go on to take the Wildflower Walk, keeping an alert eye open as you did so for dolphins and whales frolicking in the bay. A guided tour leaves every forty minutes; we joined one, and duly observed, and the system was all very simple. Thirty miles out on the continental shelf, the whales cruised their feeding grounds. An aeroplane flew out to spot the groups of whales ('pods' they were called) and then summoned up by radio a whale-chasing vessel equipped with a gun that fired exploding harpoons. The carcasses were towed into Frenchman Bay, cut up and then boiled down. The oil extracted from the head of the beast was of a fineness and quality unobtainable from any other source, animal, vegetable or mineral, and there's a flask of it for you to admire. The rest, flesh and bones, guts and gristle, were 'reduced' to whale meal.

That was the industry. A decade and a half on, the machinery was beginning to deteriorate through rust and verdigris, the wooden decking was old and exposed to the weather. There were sheds and crew's quarters and a boiler house and a so-called bottom factory which referred more to its location than to output or input. Our eyes searched every nook and cranny, every bone of the huge, displayed whale skeletons, every corner. We kept catching one another's eye, and shaking our heads, or muttering, 'Nothing there.'

And so on. It was hugely disappointing. When the tour was over, we wandered around again, by ourselves, without a guide, trying to work out where in the place Peterkin might have hidden the leaf.

I said angrily, at the tank shed entrance, 'Surely he wouldn't put it inside one of those damned great tanks! They're impossible to enter. But if he didn't, where is it?'

Jane was looking thoughtfully down towards the next group of visitors, starting their tour. 'See the man in blue, John?'

'Donkey jacket?'

She nodded. 'Looks a bit like one of the two with the Russian woman at the concert –'

I looked. He had a nautical air, certainly, because he wore a blue donkey jacket in spite of the temperature; he also had a low forehead, of the kind noted earlier.

'Can't say I recognize his face,' I said.

'Well, I think *I* do!' Jane said.

'How sure are you?'

'Not at all sure. It's a feeling. Shuddery.'

'We'll go.'

'In a place the size of Albany, there really isn't anywhere *to* go,' she pointed out reasonably. 'It's too small to hide in, that's why we've been found. Question is what they'll do.'

'Nothing,' I said, 'because nothing has changed, has it? We haven't found the answer to Peterkin's damned puzzle, and until we do they daren't do anything that might endanger us. Or – well, you know the alternatives!'

Jane wore a thin, thoughtful smile. 'Another matter if we do find out, isn't it?' I said nothing, and she went on, 'Queen's Commission – I *have* to go on. But you're not bound,' and then she grinned. 'I'll bet there's no Shyster's Oath!'

I was pompous. 'It concerns justice, not espionage.'

* * *

184

We drove back towards town. Soon, on the right, a sign pointed up a little side road to the Gap. Jane said, 'I don't think so, not today.' I said nothing, but she was dead right: when you're looking down at the powerful swells that surge into the Gap, the last thing you need is the thought that an enemy's lurking behind you. We weren't followed, not so far as we could tell.

Bath. Early dinner, there being little else to do. We drove over the neck of land beside King Point to a place I've known all my life, at Middleton Beach, for some food from the sea.

'No whale steaks,' Jane said warningly.

'No whale steaks,' I promised.

But we ate steaks (local beef) and drank a Cabernet (also local) from Mount Barker that was red-black in colour and smoothly potent, and we were just finishing, and using napkins on our lips, when the door to the dining room opened, and I glanced over at the bloke who came in. Familiar face in a kind of a way. White hair, glasses . . . he met my eye and came straight over, hand outstretched. 'You little bastard!' he said. Cheerful Aussie greeting, and that voice told me who he was.

I took the hand and shook it. 'Speaking of bastards,' I said, 'where've you spent the last ten years?'

His name was Craig Brindell, and it was astonishing, in a way, that he'd even survived to get white hair. Craig was the local daring aviator when I was a boy: trips round the harbour for a pound. He was also a man who enjoyed the company of boys – and *don't* misunderstand me! If your bike went wrong, Craig didn't just put it right, he showed *you* how. How to make a kite, how to fly it; how to bowl leg breaks and googlies; how to throw a boomerang; how to catch fish and gut them. Great man, Craig.

He'd been living ten years in Eucla, he said, after his wife died. One of his kids was a dentist there, but now he'd moved back because the son needed the space and *he* missed Albany.

I introduced him to Jane and warned him not to call her names, because she was a Pom and anyway had a good left hook; she plainly warmed to him at once. Then, as we were talking she said we'd been at Whaleworld.

'Used to service the engines on their spotter planes,' Craig Brindell said. 'Some winters it was just about the only work there was.' He talked a little about whaling, and a little about fishing, and a little about dentistry. He could talk about most things, and he seemed, just as he always had, to *know* most things. Knew the Royal Engineers, Jane's outfit. 'Served with 'em in forty-four, I think it was, on airstrip construction.' She was delighted and so was he, and as they nattered on, so was I. After a while it occurred to me to ask Craig a question and I waited for a gap in the conversation. There were no gaps. They were talking fast about some RE camp on Salisbury Plain and finally I had to pick up a spoon and tap the table, which brought the waiter tripping over. I waved him away and said, 'You know just about everything. Did you ever know a bloke called Peterkin?'

'Name's familiar,' Craig said. 'Where was this?'

'Possibly at Cheynes Beach.'

He screwed up his eyes. The lines round them were deep seams, and he looked for a moment like a basking gecko. 'What'd he look like? Funny name, that one.'

'Big, powerful, foreign accent . . .'

The eyes snapped open. 'Got him, yair. He worked out there at the factory, didn't he? Big, shy bloke who never talked to anybody. Strong bastard, too.'

'You wouldn't know what he did?' Jane asked.

'His job?'

'Yes.'

'He was a flenser. That'd be . . . let me see . . . about '76, maybe '77. Yair, he was up there on the deck with – did you ever see a flensing pole? Long bastard with a damned sharp blade on the end –'

'Saw one today,' Jane said, smoothly but I suspect queasily. 'You didn't know Peterkin, I suppose?'

'Nah, nah. Nobody did, that's my guess. Wasn't in town long. Wasn't in town much at all. Stayed out there at Cheynes Beach most of the time. God, he was shy! Why the hell d'you want to know about him?'

I said, 'He died. I'm his solicitor. There's a small estate, that's all.'

Craig Brindell nodded. 'He was always ready for work, that much I'll say. I'd do the servicing work in the evenings, and if I needed help, he was available. Never in town in the pubs, he wasn't! But he didn't talk. You could spend an hour with the bloke and never a word from him.'

I was thinking that one thing at least had been confirmed. Peterkin *had* worked at Cheynes Beach, so it was a racing certainty the leaf was there somewhere. But where? We'd been all over the place today, and there was absolutely nothing – he'd left no clue, we had no suddenly surfacing instinct. I felt tensely that we'd have to tear the whole place down and search the rubble to get any idea . . .

My mind had wandered and I was only dimly aware, at that moment, that Jane was chatting up old Craig. She's good at that, Jane is: asks people about their work and their families. Now I heard her ask him quietly what sort of planes they'd had. Pointless, I thought, because we knew already. We've seen it this afternoon!

Old Craig answered her, just as quietly. But his words banged round in my head like a thunderclap!

19

Heaven knows what old Craig thought; we were barely civil, gabbled our goodnights quickly and perfunctorily; we couldn't wait to get through the door and shriek at each other. God, but it was an exciting moment! No sooner had the door clattered shut behind us than we'd thrown our arms round each other and were doing a kind of extemporary polka out there in the street.

'Gotcha!' Jane yelled in my ear.

I said, 'Nothing new about that. What's new is – oh, you bewdy!'

We disengaged, climbed into the doctoral 4WD, and moved off. Jane said, 'Now?'

'Too bloody right, now!'

'It'll be locked, bolted and barred. There's cash money on the premises.'

'Till when – when does it open?'

'Leaflet's in the glove box,' she said.

I found it and looked. 'Till 9 A.M. Can't wait that long! No, look, I'll get in one way or another if I have to swim round to the whales' entrance.'

She shuddered. 'Don't!'

'Because Sergei,' I teased, 'might be there to switch on the machinery?'

But you can't push Jane's emotions around. The efficiency of the slaughterhouse may horrify, but her mind stays clear. She said, with her usual briskness, 'Wouldn't do him much good. Nothing in there works. Is anybody following?'

I turned in my seat. 'Don't think so.'

She said practically, 'These are trained people. They know how to follow. You're sure?'

'Can't see anybody. No following lights.'

She breathed sharply. 'You'd better drive!'

'Why?'

'*Pretend* somebody's behind us, whether there is or not. This is your home town, but it's not theirs. Lose them!'

'But there isn't anyb–'

'Slither into hiding,' she said, 'like a frightened snake.'

So we exchanged seats and I began a complex drive through the streets of my childhood that led us first to Nanarup then back over the Yakama Bridge – I won't recite the details, if only because I can't remember most of what I did. We visited all the suburbs and most of the streets, a lot of the time with the lights off. By great good luck we didn't meet the police. You look at one map and there's only a single route out of Albany to Frenchman Bay; look at a bigger map, and there's another, and that's the one we took, out by the racecourse, meeting nobody, lights off the whole time. But they went on again when we joined the Bald Head Highway. There aren't many people about after dark out there, and any lights glowing behind us would be instantly detectable.

It must have been about 11 P.M. when I turned the Land Rover into the car park at Whaleworld. We had to leave it there; the place was so laid out that a vehicle couldn't be hidden out of sight, but we tucked it into a corner, then got out and looked around us.

Albany was, by now, a thin sweep of lights across the Harbour; it's a place where people sleep early, and long, and as we watched, light after light went out. Behind us, along the road we'd travelled, the dark was complete and unbroken. Nothing was moving out there, nothing except the relentless, violent Southern Ocean.

Earlier that day, when we'd toured Whaleworld, just about the only thing we hadn't been looking for was a way *in*, because we were in already. Accordingly we hadn't noticed how expertly fenced the site was. The only torch we possessed was a little penlight of the doctor's that had been on the dashboard, and such light as it gave revealed no weaknesses in the wire.

But at last we found a place where a little rise in the ground reduced the fence's height. It was the best we could get. I took out our little diagram of the entire site and studied it. The big shed we wanted was only a few yards inside the perimeter. With luck, and if the thing was there . . .

'We ought to be in and out in a few minutes,' I whispered.

'Can you climb it?'

The squares in the mesh were about one and a half inches. 'Should think so.'

And then I tried, with her whispered 'Good luck' in my ears and my heart in my mouth, because breaking and entering would mean being struck off if I were to be caught. Lawyer's thieving has to be more subtle than that.

But I couldn't get my feet into the mesh at all. The trainers I was wearing were too broad. Jane watched me make several futile attempts, then put her hand against my shoulder and pushed gently. 'Let me try,' she said.

Need I say that Jane's feet and the trainers that contained them might have been manufactured for the job, that her toes fitted neatly into the holes in the mesh, that she went up that fence like a — I was going to write 'monkey', but she was more like a very expert rock climber. All neat as could be. Must be the army training.

Hissing to her that she must be careful, I watched her flit across the grass, on to the concrete track that winds through the site, and approach the shed marked '10' on the diagram. A moment's pause, and there came the rumble of a door sliding. She was in!

I waited then, listening. And swearing at myself. I'm not *un*athletic: I can run and jump and climb reasonably well; but Jane's special in a lot of ways and that's one.

Turning, I stared at the black night into which the ribbon of road vanished. Still no light there. Across the bay in Albany almost all the houses were darkened now, though the lines of street lamps still burned yellow. Staring into the night, it was borne in on me just how isolated a place this was, and why Peterkin had chosen it, both to work at, and as a hiding place.

I wondered if Craig Brindell was in bed yet, and if so, whether he had the smallest inkling . . . In my mind's audio system the tape deck began to replay that familiar voice saying, 'Aw, yair, they usually had Cessnas. Different types, naturally, but always with those Continental engines. Aw, they're good, reliable old engines, those Continentals, and the service manual's just a piece of duff. Course, when they got the twin, there was twice as much work. That was a Cessna, too – last plane they had over there, for the whale-spotting. Aw, she was the best of 'em, too, with the two engines. Under no stress, you see. Anyway, it's not sensible being out over water single-engined. Nah – truth is, you have to be bloody mad going over water with just one mill. But the old 337 Mixmaster, well, she could go all day on one, and the other up your sleeve if you needed it.

'Mind, that's true of most twins, but if you've got one port and one starboard and one of them's lost, well, you're always gonna be a bit unstable. But with the Mixmaster they're in line, you see: two engines in line, and there's one pushing and there's one pulling, so it's dead stable . . .'

Jane had got there first while I was still drawing breath, and she said, with a kind of genteel surprise, 'Did you say one pushes and one pulls?' I'm sure she *thought* she said it quietly, but her voice throbbed like a saxophone in a thirties love song, and old Craig said patiently, 'Aw, they ain't in her now, of course. The old Mixmaster's up on blocks in the spotter hangar and the engines are valuable, so they were sold, I think. Dunno who bought them. Yair, they called her the old push-pull –'

I said, 'Would Peterkin have known that?'

He thought about it for only a moment. 'Aw, yair. He'd help me when I winched an engine out, and I always called it that. Yair, he'd know.' And Craig grinned then, and said, 'But I wonder why *you* wonder, young Close, and you ain't gonna tell me, are you?'

It was then that we exited, Jane and I, with great clumsiness and very little decorum, and almost no manners.

As I waited there in the black night for her to reappear, I kept turning this way and that, scanning the land- and seascapes that were all around. The night was very dark. The thin, new moon was lost behind thick cloud banked up from the

191

south-west, and the water looked as dark as the land, though across the ebony black of its surface something seemed to cut a faint faraway line. Shark? I wondered. Whale? But it was too dark to tell.

But where was Jane – and what was she doing? I could make out the shape of the steel hangar, just, could picture in my mind the scene inside, with the harpoon display in front, and, behind it, raised for a good view, the old aircraft, which I now knew to be the Mixmaster. Correction: Cessna 337 Skymaster. Jane would be scrambling over her now, doing what I ought to be doing, damn it, crawling along the wings, probing the corners of the fuselage, feeling over the roots of the wing stays. All with nothing to help her but the penlight; switching on lights would be risky; it wasn't impossible a night watchman was on duty, or a custodian of some sort could even live on the premises. I ached to be in there with her, beyond the fence, searching the plane myself, or even just holding the penlight. But the truth was, and I recognized it, that we were best disposed as we were, with one inside looking for whatever it was, and one outside on guard.

Stillness and silence. Nothing but thoughts. The steel walls of the hangar allowed no light out, the land was dark, the sea black, the very air seemed opaque. 'Come on,' I muttered to myself. 'Come *on*!'

Suddenly she was there. No door rumbling this time; just the silent flit across the concrete on to the grass and Jane whispering, 'Hey, sleepyhead.'

I went to the wire. She stood on the other side, holding something. 'You all right?'

She hissed, triumphantly, 'Got it!' and held something up.

'What is it?'

'Guess.'

'We'll play the guessing games this side,' I said. 'Come on over, quick!'

Quick was the word. She climbed, then dropped to the ground, darted across to the Land Rover, and got in. When I climbed into the driving seat, illumination from the courtesy light was already falling on the thing she held.

'Another bloody leaf!' I almost groaned with disappointment.

She said, 'Hold on – look,' and turned the leaf over. As before, words had been inscribed into the wet clay before firing.

'Mean anything to you?' Jane said, looking at me.

I read the words. I tilted the leaf in case light falling on it at a new angle might reveal something additional to the three words. But there was just the plain pale surface, and –

'VELL INTO NNOSE,' Jane said. 'Do you understand what he means?'

I was powerfully tempted, sitting there, full to choking of disappointment that Peterkin's bloody trail still hadn't ended, tempted to say, 'No, it's meaningless.' I stared at the words, with the picture of that awful place welling up in my brain. Yes, I thought, that's what I'd do.

'It's meaningless,' I said. 'To me, anyway.'

'Vell into Nnose.' Jane spoke the words slowly, encouragingly. 'It must mean *something* – it's a message left specifically for you!'

'No,' I said. The whole thing had gone on far too long. In the cause of Peterkin and his eternal, infernal secret, I'd been spun about like concrete in a mixer, I'd been chased, captured, escaped again, been in danger for weeks because that fool of a man had decided I was his cat's-paw! Well, I'd had enough. I wasn't going to spend the rest of my life obediently following the long, long trail he'd left for me. 'No,' I repeated. 'It means nothing to me.'

She just stared at me. After a bit she said, 'Look me in the eye and say it again.'

I turned and looked at her. Jane has good eyes, clear and brimming with health. Also honest. I didn't want to look deep into them, but I found myself doing so, and the eyes seemed somehow to compel – like a hypnotist's. I muttered, 'Nothing.' The eyelids came down.

'You, John Close, are a lousy liar!' Jane said. 'In both senses. In *every* bloody sense!'

193

I shrugged.

'But we've got this far. We might as well see it through, don't you think?'

'Oh, God – it never ends!'

'Listen, laddie,' she said in a low rasp that came direct from some barrack square, 'and listen carefully. It might be said by some, and you're among them, and so am I, that we two have an understanding. You've said will you and I haven't said no. Sitrep as of now. But we'll have no pikers and no backsliders in anything involving me. And I, in any case, have the right to the yes or the no. Not you. *I* have it. Now – let's start again! You understand!'

I nodded.

'And you understand the words on Peterkin's leaf, don't you!'

I nodded again, dumb and obedient.

'So, what do they indicate – where and what is Vell into Nnose?'

I muttered, 'It's where. *Where's* the nose?'

Jane nodded encouragingly. 'Go on.'

'South-west of here. Couple of miles.'

'And it's what?'

'A chunk of rock.'

She reached across me and turned the ignition key. As the engine started, Jane said, 'The nose, please, driver. And hurry!'

Major Jane Strutt sat there calmly in the passenger seat, Peterkin's leaf in her hands, turning it interestedly this way and that. I just wanted to be sick. After a minute she said, 'Why is nose spelled with two n's?'

I thought about it. 'Because,' I said, resentfully, 'he was a silly, illiterate old fool, and he thought he was being bloody smart, thought it was a code.'

'Well, I don't understand it.'

'Only because the three words are written underneath each other.'

'Oh – yes, I see.'

'Say it,' I said.

'Vellinton nose.'

'You understand now?'

Jane asked, 'This the same Vellinton who had the boots?'

'The very one.'

'Old Nosey?'

'That's him.'

'He's buried in London,' she said. 'St Paul's – I've seen the tomb. What's his nose doing out here?'

So I explained. Well, not explained, exactly. Told her something that had always puzzled me. 'Western Australia wasn't even founded till 1826 – that's eleven years after the Battle of Waterloo. Perth was even later. But all over the state you'll find the man's name. One of Perth's main streets is Wellington Street. Do you remember Bunbury?'

'Yes.'

'Picton Crescent's in Bunbury.'

'Who's he – this Picton?'

'I'm surprised at you – and you a soldier! Sir Thomas. His division turned the battle at Badajoz.'

'Military historian are you?'

I said, 'All I'm trying to say is that there's no escaping Wellington here in Australia.'

'There's such a street in Albany?'

'Aw, yair. Not just the Iron Duke, either, there's half his staff; and if it's not him, it's Nelson.'

'Tell me about Wellington's Nose.'

I waited a moment before answering. I'd already made the necessary turn left. In silence now, we crept along the little road built for tourists, and turned into the tarmac flatness of a car park.

'In a minute,' I said as I cut the engine, 'you can see for yourself.'

'Can I – in the dark?'

I said, 'Flying spray gives quite enough phosphorescence.'

20

We sat in the darkness for a minute or two. The Land Rover's lights were out and we were quiet. Dawn seemed hours off; there was nothing to be done except to show patience. Lots of patience. Like the ocean.

Patience is not my long suit though, and isn't Jane's, either. We'd only been there perhaps ten minutes, when she suddenly said, 'Okay, that'll do,' swung open the door, and hopped out.

'What'll do?' I demanded.

'My brain's humming like a motor. I can't relax. I'm going for a run.'

'A *run*?' I repeated, gaping at her. 'It's one in the morning!'

'Perfect,' Jane said shortly.

'But I don't want to go jogg–'

'So sit there like a pudden. I'll be back. Get some sleep.'

Suddenly there was no Jane. For a while I felt bereft. But the Land Rover had big, squashy seats – Aussie doctors value their comfort – and I was tired. I wriggled deep into the padding, thinking about Jane as a wife: a wife who goes jogging in the small hours, who is at least twenty-five per cent sergeant major, who can beat me at just about anything. Engineer, rifle shot, toughie. A wife like that? Yes, please. My head rested comfortably now on the dark blue velvet as I daydreamed. Correction: nightdreamed.

When the door opened, the night wind flooded instantly into the Land Rover, cold and startling. I shivered and blinked in the pool of light from the roof and muttered, 'Jane – you back?'

It wasn't Jane, though. I blinked again, and was rubbing

my eyes when a voice – female, but very certainly *not* Jane's – said, 'Out.'

I stared out of my lighted cabin into the dark outside, and saw people shapes, dimly illuminated. Misted-up windows hid the rest, but framed in the doorway in reefer jacket and navy-blue bonnet, Elin Gundarsson's perfect features were unmistakeable.

'Out,' she said again.

I leaned obediently against the Land Rover while somebody searched me – not Elin – and found nothing. She, meanwhile, was inside the vehicle, looking for, and finding, the leaf. She got out, stared at me coldly, then turned to examine the pottery leaf by the interior light. She held it in her left hand, looking at it carefully, finally turning it over. Her right hand held a pistol.

She hefted the gun, and said informatively, 'Nine-millimetre Makarov. Clip-fed. Double action. Tell me about this leaf.'

'Not mine,' I said. 'The car's borrowed. I've been wondering myself.'

She gave a little nod of the head, and I got a little knock on the right kidney that had my knees buckling, and left behind it a deep, hard, aching pain. She said, 'What do these words mean?' She peered at the lettering. 'Vell into Nnose.'

I said, 'I don't know. Really I don't.' I was flinching as I spoke, away from the anticipated kidney blow. It didn't come. I was wondering frantically where Jane was. Had she run straight into this bunch? Had they got her held somewhere, or was she free? I said, 'I can't even guess at the language. "Into" is an English word, but "vell" isn't, or not as far as I know, and the other one, "nose" with two n's, is incomprehensible.

Elin looked at me speculatively. 'You may very well be a fool. Certainly you behave with consistent foolishness. But I find it very hard to believe you cannot read this message.'

'Well, I can't. Always been a bit thick, you know. Since I was –'

'I can,' Elin said. 'It is – though there are two misspellings – the two words "Wellington's Nose".'

'Could be, I suppose,' I said. 'Yair. Vell into Nnose. Yair, could be.'

'What does it mean to you?'

'Not much. Wellington had a big nose, didn't he? They used to call him Old Nosey. But he's been dead two hundred years. I've seen his tomb.'

'One hundred and fifty years,' Elin said. 'Not that it matters, I suspect.' She paused. 'It seems to me, if one applies a little logic to the situation, that we have the following: you are here, Mr Close. Also here is a pottery leaf on which are inscribed the words "Wellington's Nose". Also here is a big cliff and rock formation shown on the British Admiralty charts as the Gap and the Natural Bridge. It seems likely to me that some part of this rock formation may have been named – perhaps by a climber – after Wellington. How do you feel about that?'

The first glimmer of dawn, the merest trace of light, now caught her face. Perfect those features undoubtedly were – pale and sculptured and with those great lambent eyes – but it was a face hard as marble and the eyes had turned fierce.

'You were born here,' she said. 'Were a boy here. Grew up here. Yes?'

'No,' I said.

'I think yes. There is excellent research. I have your house and its number, the street, the date of your birth, your school in Spencer Park. From there you went to the University of Western Australia in Perth to study law. You have something valuable to me – you possess local knowledge.' She paused. 'How is your kidney?'

'I can feel it,' I said.

'I shall ask you again. Where is Wellington's Nose?'

'Dunno. Never heard anything about it.' I was tensed for the blow. The kidneys are unprotected: it was going to be painful, and for a long time.

Elin Gundarsson said contemptuously, 'Heroics will do you no good. We have your girl.'

'Jane!' She must have run straight into them.

'So you will tell me, if you value this woman who is a spy. Where is Wellington's Nose?'

I can only say you'd need to stand in that place to understand. This is the southern tip of the continent: big and wild and hard. The cliffs are granite, gales blow brutal and chill from the south-west; the Southern Ocean has twenty-foot swells on a calm day. I doubt if there's another place on earth that can convince you so instantly that life is very fragile. Just a small push, it would take, no more, and then no more Jane!

So that made it the end of the trail. Not with a bang but with a whimper, that was how the world was ending. Hollow man, indeed. I said, 'Hold it, maybe it's the bit they call Porker Rock. I seem to have heard *that* called the Nose.'

'Show me.' No change of expression.

'It's a walk.'

'Then walk.' The Makarov clip-fed, double-action gun gave a little jerk to encourage me, and I began to lead the way along the cliff-top paths, with the wind buffeting and the ocean crashing eighty feet below. We passed a warning sign. I didn't read it because I knew what it said, and what it said was, watch out for the wind, because it hits the cliffs and bounces back, hard enough to toss you lightly over the edge. Elin Gundarsson didn't read it either, which seemed a bit foolish of her, because in a place like that it's best to be informed.

We made a little crocodile, five or six of us. Four were Elin Gundarsson's goons: broad, silent anonymous men who would do exactly as ordered, and who now walked quietly in my footsteps as I picked my way along.

'How'd you get here?' I asked her conversationally.

'Boat,' she said briefly.

'You'll let Jane go,' I said, 'if I help?'

'Perhaps. If you help sufficiently.'

I took them to the Gap first; there's a kind of steel balcony concreted into the granite that gives a really good view if your pleasure lies in watching white water rushing up at you every few seconds. It's a place where the heart beats faster, that one is, and I looked at their faces as they stood there, and saw Adam's apples bobbing as the men swallowed. Elin Gundarsson's face looked tighter, too, I thought, even limned as it now was in the blue-gold light of the southern dawn.

'The Nose is here?' she asked crisply, and below us a giant swell smashed into the Gap. Just a fifty-yard gap cut into the cliffs, that's all it is, but the foaming water came tearing up at us like an express train. Everybody, including me, took a smart step back. And felt the lashing spray.

As the great chunk of ocean fell back, hissing and roaring, down deep into the rock cleft, I said, 'No. Bit further on.'

Another twitch of the Makarov. 'Be quick!'

So now I led them to the other local phenomenon. It's called the Natural Bridge, and that's as perfect a description as you'll find. At some long-ago time, the ocean found a weakness in the granite, and pounded and pounded for a few thousand years, undermining the cliff, until bits of it fell away. But not all; it's hard stuff that southern granite, and while the base of the cliff tumbled into the water, what remained formed a vast natural arch, thirty metres up in the air, a hundred metres long, making a span beneath which the ocean boils viciously twenty-four hours in every day. If anything on this earth can be described as awe-inspiring, that scene can. You look at it and wonder which firm of consulting engineers God must have employed, because they were good, whoever they were, all the stresses precisely calculated. 'I want the bridge to endure ten million years.' 'Yes, O Lord. I'll get busy on the calculations.'

It even impressed the hard beauty beside me. I heard her breath make a noise that sounded like 'Phew!' Then she said, 'Which is the Nose?'

'Well,' I said. 'I haven't been here for a while –'

At that point she pulled out of her pocket a white plastic box, from which she slid an aerial. She muttered a few words into it, presumably in Russian, listened to some acknowledgement, then clipped the box to her coat.

I was looking across frightening space at the enormous stone arch. The Porker was a creature of light and angle: look from the wrong place and there's nothing but grey rock; viewed from the right spot in the right light, old Porker is unmistakeable, and Porker's nose is Wellington's nose, too. The lines that draw the creature so clearly in the grey rock are cracks and fissures in the giant granite blocks of which God built the Bridge.

'Show me.'

I nodded and pointed, thinking of Jane. And of Peterkin, too. He'd started it, she'd joined in, I was ending it, hoping, in doing so, to save her. 'There,' I said. 'You see the hind legs, do you?'

Elin Gundarsson shook her head. 'No.'

I could only just make out old Porker myself. The granite cracks were anything but clear, the light still dim.

'Group of three big loose boulders up on top,' I said, pointing. 'You see those?'

'I see them.'

'Fix your eyes on the front one, the smallest of the three.' Smallest, yet huge, the size of a bus.

'Yes.'

'Run your eyes down from it in a vertical line, then stare for a moment.'

'I still do not see . . .'

'Right down – down to the edge of the span!'

I watched her, beautiful and intent, trying hard to make it all out. It's one of those strange optical things: you don't see it for a while, but when you *do* see it, you see nothing else.

She said, 'No . . . no . . . no . . . point it out ag . . . *yes!* She was grinning suddenly. 'Now I see this pig, *there!*'

'Yes,' I said. 'There.'

'I see his nose.'

'Good.'

'It's amazing.' Briefly this tough, dangerous, lovely woman was like a small child. 'It is perfectly like a pig!'

'Perfectly,' I said. 'His nose is Wellington's Nose, too.'

She turned to look at me. 'This is certain?'

'Well, it's all I know about it.'

'Very strange,' Elin Gundarsson said. 'I do not understand. Wellington was a great man, yet here he is just part of a pig. We would never do that.'

'Called the Tall Poppy Syndrome,' I said. 'Well-known

Australian approach. Bloke rises above the rest, gets too big for his britches, your Aussie wants him back down to size.'

She nodded, snapped a word over her shoulder and was handed binoculars. Wellington's Nose and the Porker were carefully studied. 'I see nothing.'

'No,' I said.

'But the cracks in the rock are deep. It must be hidden in there.'

'What exactly are you looking for?'

'The same as you,' Elin Gundarsson said.

'Well – I don't *know* what it is. Believe me or don't believe me, I really and truly don't know.'

She gave a little jerk of that fair head, and a jerk to go with it of the Makarov 9mm and we set off, up a rock slope towards the span. Ten minutes' scrambling later, we were standing beside the giant boulders in the middle of the Natural Bridge's massive single span. Below us, out of sight now from where we stood, the Nose was rootling in eternal space. Standing there felt, and was, very precarious; with the wind buffeting around us we were all of us compelled to adjust our stances from moment to moment.

I thought: okay, Elin Gundarsson, you're one of nature's leaders. It's time to decide. She was looking downward, at a long slope of granite, damp in the morning air, that led down to Porker and his many cracks and recesses, and, beyond Porker, to a lot of fresh air and a long, long drop on to granite. No chance of tumbling off the old Natural Bridge and talking about it in the pub later. Drop down there and the waves wash you off the rocks as if you were plum jam. I'd never stood there before in my life. I'd always been too scared, and with good reason, and as I stood there now, with my feet tending to slip on wet rock, I thought of Scott's diary at the South Pole, and what he'd written: 'Great God, this is an awful place.'

Then Elin Gundarsson said, 'We will go down there on ropes.'

'We?'

'You,' she said, 'and me. And the Makarov.'

202

21

The party Elin Gundarsson had brought ashore was certainly well equipped: booted and spurred, wrapped against the wind, coiled round with ropes. I just wondered why they'd brought the ropes. When they'd landed, the possibility of climbing cliffs could hardly have occurred to them. Also, Elin's boots were strong, modern, moulded-sole affairs; I wore trainers, and protested they were no use. She looked at me, and then at the white trainers, implacably. Meanwhile a line was being knotted on to and around me by a big, reefer-jacketed, bearded man with bad breath. It didn't take him long.

So now we were ready, and she said, 'Backwards, you understand. Abseil backwards. They will take your weight. You are quite safe. We go side by side.' She turned and without hesitation began walking backwards down the wet granite virtually directly into space, paying out rope through her hands as she went. I wondered what her thoughts might be. Was she trembling, thinking of danger, wrestling with fears of her own? I was. But she seemed composed and competent, in this as in all things; she moved easily and without hesitation. I tried for a similar approach because it seemed safer.

We both leaned forward, at first, the wind striking our backs, but after not too many paces the moment came to lean back into space, terrifying as it was. I'd abseiled only once, years before, in the Porongorup Ranges, not far from Albany, but I'd been a boy then, and under the control of a Kiwi schoolmaster, an expert from the Southern Alps. This was something else, and in case I forgot that, Elin Gundarsson now said, 'You are expendable. Do not forget it. Do not take risks with your life and the woman's.'

'Right,' I said, and leaned back, paused for a moment, got

my legs flexed and my body to the proper forty-five-degree angle, and gave a little push-off. I went down the rock-face a good inch that time. It needs confidence, and I wasn't brimming with confidence that morning. A yard away, Elin Gundarsson bounced lithely out and back again, a yard or more at a time. Another Jane, I thought. Jane would abseil like a top-class Alpinist, I'd put money on that. But this Russian woman beside me on the rock, perhaps more formally beautiful, was no Jane. Courage and skill, yes; humanity not in abundance.

Her boots struck the granite again, and she was well below me, calling, 'Quickly! Be confident. They will not let you fall.'

I bounced outward and then bounced again. It was a damned long way down and abseiling doesn't allow you the chance to shelter in a crack. Here I was out on the exposed rock, feeling the southwesterly tugging at me, threatening to turn me and bash me against the granite at every step.

Down we went, Elin Gundarsson always ahead of me. I did ponder just for a moment whether it might be on to disarm her and try to escape somehow, but the briefest reflection said: no chance at all. The men of her crew were up on top. There was only space and hard rock and death below me. There was also the matter of Jane. Elin Gundarsson was safe, from me at least, for the moment.

We were now over the corner on vertical granite, she on one side, I the other, of a deep cleft in the rock that anatomically separated the Porker's gammons from his fore-hands. She had waited for me to catch up and now ordered briefly, 'Go inside, tell me what you see.'

I looked at her. 'How do you know I'll tell you?'

She hung there in space, lithe and blonde, as at home on the swaying line as an ape on a creeper. She said, 'Because you are already dead, my friend, and your woman also. And now you have the chance to earn your life and hers. Climb in.'

I scrambled eight or ten lateral feet across the granite until, with my feet braced, I could look into the crack. In terms of a real porker, these would be the soft underbits, but there was nothing soft at all, not here, not for a long way, and certainly not Elin Gundarsson. She said it again. 'Climb in!'

Nothing for it but obedience. She was muttering Russian into her walkie-talkie as I manoeuvred my bottom on to the tip of a little rock pinnacle, dangled my legs into the cleft and looked down into the depths.

It's hard to describe. At this point a vast, roughly triangular slab of rock had come loose at some time in the last zillion years, and dropped. But it had slipped only a few feet before it jammed into a new position, and there it had settled for eternity. But in the fall a space had been created, and into this hell-hole I now stared.

Down at the bottom of the twenty-foot cleft I could see daylight and the white of pounding water. Taking a deep breath, I began to ease myself down inside, trying to move steadily because sudden jerks on ropes in that kind of circumstance are not a good idea.

'One moment!'

I paused and she said, 'You will be the only one who knows – you realize that.'

I said, 'Okay,' thinking about it. If, as was likely given all I knew about Peterkin, the keys to the Kremlin lay somewhere in the rock cleft beneath my feet, then I was about to swap places with Peterkin. The old man had spent a lifetime on the run; he'd been the only one who knew, and been desperate not to pass the secret to his daughter. But, I thought grimly as the granite edge I sat on ground at my buttocks, it wasn't even necessary actually to *possess* the deadly knowledge. If it was thought you had it, then it was quite as deadly.

'Now go,' Elin Gundarsson ordered, and I began obediently to lower myself into the cleft once again, and to look round for hiding places. Peterkin had undoubtedly chosen well: nobody would shin down here and stumble over his secret in the course of a Sunday stroll . . . The rock was mainly smooth. This one piece had broken off from the main body of granite and slipped a bit, that was all. But there had been very little weathering and there were few cracks and therefore precious little to hold on to: I was reliant on the rope and such grip as my trainers gave on the angled granite.

As I moved tentatively downward, I realized that I was in a kind of funnel in the rock, a natural tube, wider at the top, narrowing as it descended, and open at the bottom. I looked up at the rope that held me, in sudden fear that it might be fraying on a granite edge, knowing that if the rope broke I'd drop unhindered straight down the funnel and straight out at the bottom. But it was holding. And would hold, I insisted to myself, as I looked for Peterkin's packet or parcel, his leaf or his leavings. I must be somewhere near it now. And find it or not, I'd be the only one who knew. The only one. Even if I knew nothing!

I eased myself down, jamming myself into the edge of the crack. There was light, but not much, and it was gloomy and in shade. If I were Peterkin, where . . . ?

White. Something white? It was wedged into the crack where the rock walls joined, almost gleaming in the gloom. Stretching, I failed to reach it. I rearranged my legs and stretched again, and slipped, and ended up dangling with my heart thumping as my feet lost purchase. But my fingers were still too far away to grip the thing. If I made myself swing on the rope, would I reach it then? Or knock myself unconscious on the rock? No point in debating, I thought. To swing was the only way.

I swung – and swung short; and tried again, gaining distance like a child on a garden swing, but awkwardly. Four, five, six times, forward and backwards like a pendulum, left arm reaching and reaching, I swung towards that little piece of whiteness. Finally my fingers touched it, just, and though the touch was very brief there was something strange about it. Not cold – that was the strangeness. Here in the heart of millions of tons of granite, everything was cold: the air, the rock itself. I gritted my teeth and swung again, pushing off with flexed knees, praying as I shoved myself towards that little flash of whiteness.

And grabbed it.

Triumph!

Except . . . what lay in my hand as I dangled there, swinging in the chill funnel between sky and foaming ocean, was the cracked remnant of a styrofoam cup!

I gave three tugs on the line, to tell them to pull me up. And up I went, towards the fair blonde head of Elin Gundarsson, peering down towards me, her body crouched on the funnel's edge. As I came near she said, 'What have you found?' I waited until it was possible to emerge on to the rock myself, then handed it to her.

She grabbed, frowned, scowled. 'This is *all*?'

'All I can see.'

'Did Kinsky put it there?'

I shrugged. How could I know? Peterkin might have had a flask and a cup with him on his solo descent into Porker's depths, but I doubted it. Not one for the comforts, old Peterkin. Careful preparation, yes; flasks of coffee, no.

'How did it get there?' She was turning the broken styrofoam carefully round in her hands, as though there might be a message on it.

'Somebody on top dropped it,' I said. 'Or maybe a king wave washed it up there and it stuck.'

She shook her head.

'Or even,' I said, 'the wind put it there. Serious gales here blow people into the air, let alone old plastic . . .' My voice died away. Over Elin Gundarsson's shoulder I could see a boat emerging from behind Green Island, a mile or two away, a boat that I knew – as I realized after a moment: *Abrolhos Lady*. There'd be Alex and Joe Hag aboard her. How could I get to her? If I . . .

But there was no hope. She demonstrated that. I was staring. She saw it, and spoke into her walkie-talkie. Moments later, just beyond *Abrolhos Lady*, a black mass appeared in the water, that turned swiftly into the sail of a submarine. Abruptly Alex's boat lay trapped now between submarine and shore.

'There is no hope for you there,' Elin Gundarsson said. She stuffed the remains of the cup into the pocket of her reefer jacket and produced a hand torch. 'This time we both go in.'

Two jerks on the ropes to go lower, three to be hauled up.

I plucked my rope twice, saw it slacken, and began to ease myself downward. She did likewise. As we went she was playing the torch beam on the rock. We went down, and then down again. She was no more than a foot or two away from me, and, what with the rope and the torch, busy. What if I grabbed her? The Makarov 9mm was tucked away, and I was the stronger. Probably I could overpower, or even kill, her. Yes, I thought bitterly – but then what? I was down a hole on the end of a rope: if I killed her and tried to escape downward, I would go to certain death; try to escape upward, to climb the rope, and I became the perfect target. Worst of all, the men up on top could simply abandon the rope, leave it unsecured with me on the end of it. No way out then: just stay here and die.

So, first aim: *survival*, as the management men always say, and humbly and obediently I went further down the funnel, following the playing beam of Elin Gundarsson's torch, peering into corners, sticking my fingers into the occasional crevice, finding nothing. After a while she tapped my shoulder with the toe of her boot: not a kick exactly, but no doubt at all where authority lay. I glanced up.

'Not here, is it?'

I said, 'Not that I can see.'

'But this is Wellington's Nose!'

'One side of it,' I said. 'There's another rock cleft further over.'

She looked at me, her lips thin with frustration. 'Then we go there. Here is nothing.'

So that's what we did. Except . . .

It was all accidental. We'd been hauled up into the open, blinking in the sudden bright sunlight. Glancing round me I saw one of Elin Gundarsson's crew at a vantage point a couple of hundred yards away, to the side of the bridge. He'd a rifle in his hands. Out to sea, *Abrolhos Lady* rose and fell in the ocean swell, neatly held between the sail of the sub and the rock shore. Above us, the ropes lay taut on the rock. We'd have to cross-traverse about ten feet, twelve maybe, over Wellington's Nose to reach the other cleft. It happened that my position on the rock was slightly above hers, therefore her traverse was a little below mine. Held by the two ropes, neither of us was wholly dependent on finding footholds, and we could move separately, she first.

I followed with fearful care. Rope or no rope, there was a lot of empty space around and below me, and granite death at the end of any fall. I concentrated on clinging to the rock. Out of the corner of my eye I saw Elin Gundarsson reach the target cleft and begin to scramble neatly inside. I was clinging to a small lateral crack, that was either the Porker's neck or the bridge of Wellington's Nose, depending upon your choice of nomenclature; my eyes were only a few inches from the rock, certainly too close to focus. I'd tilted my neck back for a better view, when suddenly something in the grey of the rock seemed different: another grey, a different texture . . . I stared. This was concrete! Peterkin must have come down here with a plastic bag of wet concrete to secure his message in position! What a man: hanging in space, all alone, no help, concreting something into the rock. What an *idiot*!

Should I now tell Elin Gundarsson? If I did, she might release Jane. My mind teemed with different possibilities. That was an ocean-going submarine out there, probably the one I'd already been aboard. And *that* time I'd been threatened with transshipment to Vladivostok! What was different now? Nothing would be simpler than to take us aboard, Jane and me, and take us north. And kill us? That was a possibility. Miss Elin, with her *Vogue*-model looks and her hard eyes and thin, determined lips, was not the kind to err in the direction of mercy.

No, I thought. Keep the secret – for the time being, anyway. It had been there for a few years: leave it where it was.

She was calling to me to hurry, and I obeyed as best I could, scrambling across till my hands could hook over the edge of the rock cleft and hold me securely.

'You must go down there again,' the Russian woman said. She was looking downward, and I did the same. This crack was different, roughly triangular as it descended, except that one side didn't exist. One side was open to the air. Make a mistake down there and I'd be in trouble! Elin Gundarsson's perch was a bit precarious, too, and I said so.

She said thinly, 'Worry about yourself, Mr Close. And move.'

I moved, lowering myself down the side of Old Nosey's left nostril under the Russian woman's wary watch, pretending careful scrutiny of the rock surfaces around me; not searching because I knew now where Peterkin's message lay.

'Deeper!' she called down to me. 'Into the far crack!' I moved across, looking – and listening, too, for this place was full of sound. As I swung down there, a tiny human creature on the end of his thin line, I could hear the crash and roar of the waves, and the wind blowing hard and tunelessly on some rocky whistle, and the voice of Elin Gundarsson at her hissing walkie-talkie. I looked up at her, crouched like a monkey beside Wellington's nostril, and in the moment I did so, heard acutely one sound among all the others, a sound impossible to describe, a sound I hadn't heard since boyhood, a sound utterly impossible to forget. I looked up again, debating it all in a fraction of a second. But I couldn't. I yelled up at her, 'Swing inside here. King wave! Quick!' and saw her head turn swiftly from side to side as the welling, surging noise increased. 'Jump!' I shouted. 'Jump, jump!'

She looked swiftly down at me, plainly suspicious, hesitated, and almost left it too late. What she saw that convinced her I will never know, but suddenly Elin Gundarsson was hurtling down on the end of her rope, hurtling down as, from far beneath, the ocean's power rose towards us in a vast, white, hissing, surging column like a massive watery piston.

I cringed back into the crack, clinging to my holds as the ocean roared upward at us. She jerked to a stop with a snap at the end of her rope, one arm flung out towards me, and I grabbed for it as the thousands of tons of rampaging water rode up at us like an express lift. My hand touched her sleeve, and gripped briefly for half a second or so before the ocean actually boiled right over us, up there, thirty yards in the air! And went on up.

I tried to hold on, but couldn't. In an instant, her sleeve was gone from my grasp. Desperately, for my own sake, I tried to cling on in the angled corner of the cleft as the vast column of water swept upward. There was nothing else in the world then, except the sheer, awful power of it: no sound, no sight, no hearing, no sense of where I was, up or down, right way up or not. I clung, tried to wedge myself into my corner, knowing what was coming was deadlier still, that the roaring water sweeping up did not enlist in its aid the power of gravity's force. But when it *fell* . . .

There was an instant's pause, the merest fraction of a second as the king wave reached the zenith of its surge, expended the last of the strength of its unbelievably violent upward reach. Then the water began to fall back and, unless I was very lucky, it would take me with it, snapping my nylon rope like gossamer, hurling me to death far below. I tried to force myself in deeper, to cling, to merge with the rock, to stay out of the main downward pull. *That* would dump like Niagara Falls. I was as good as dead, and I knew it, and the water began to hurtle downward past me, dragging at every part of me, seeking, as it dropped, to pluck me from my hidey-hole and sweep me along with it to the seething cauldron way below. I clung, mouth, ears, eyes swept by the raging water. Clothes being pulled at by a powerful grip, I was exerting with desperation every bit of strength in me. It was lasting an eternity. I couldn't possibly hold on!

It lasted two seconds and I held on. Then it was gone. The ocean is an efficient general who can advance overwhelming force in an instant, withdraw it equally overwhelmingly in another, leaving behind a bare battlefield, swept clean of the living enemy, only the dead and injured remaining.

She dangled. Her rope had held! Elin Gundarsson lay horizontally in the air, swinging gently on the line knotted round her waist and hips. I dashed water from my eyes and blinked a few times, and began to reach for her. Blood flowed down the side of her face from a cut where her bonnet had been, and one arm and one leg hung unnaturally. Dead? It was at least a possibility, more than a possibility. As she pivoted I caught a handful of reefer jacket, pulled her towards me, and put my hand on her throat. But I'm no doctor: I couldn't even find the pulse. Maybe that was because the wave *had* killed her. I looked at that beautiful, perfect face, pale now as ivory, framed in bedraggled golden hair, and thought life had gone.

But then one finely chiselled nostril moved. She was breathing.

I felt a brief rush of disappointment, even of anger. If the ocean had killed her, I could have left her there. Now . . .

It was a struggle to get to my feet, to take hold of her loose body with its flopping broken limbs, to draw our two ropes together and pull on them three times for the signal. Would anybody be there still, up on top of the Natural Bridge, to pull on the ropes? King waves will take people from anywhere. You're barely safe from them on the moon, my father used to say.

No response. If those men of hers had been washed away, then we were finished. No way up that overhang without help. I tugged again, realizing as I did so that at least the ropes were secured. It dawned on me, as I waited to learn our fate, that she had a walkie-talkie somewhere, if the king wave hadn't taken it. I looked. Not clipped to her jacket; though the Makarov pistol was there and I took it. I reached awkwardly over towards the left pocket and must have hurt her, unconscious as she was, for she gave a grunt of pain. But the white handset *was* there in the pocket. I clipped it to my soaking sweater and a moment later we began to rise and all my attention and strength began to be needed to guide her limp body away from further injury, for the men above were hauling away with a will, and progress was by a series of jerks, which jarred me and hurt her. As we reached the entrance to the crack, I moved the walkie-talkie switch, and heard with relief the crackle as it came to life, and I said, 'Slowly, for God's sake! She's injured!'

In return I got a grunt. No spikka da Inglski. I tried classroom German, '*Langsam, langsam.*' Same grunt. Meagre French was the last shot in my locker. '*Lentement,*' I said, '*lentement.*'

Nothing happened then, for a bit, except that there was no more movement, and we remained on the lip of the cleft. I was alert as a cat for anything that might happen: for another king wave, even, though it's unusual for two to strike in a brief period. I tried the handset again, got the crackle, got the grunt, and nothing else. But then there was

212

a scraping noise from above, and, as I looked up, a boot appeared, followed by a man's leg and then the rest of him, abseiling neatly down the Porker's rear end.

He was no linguist, but he was nimble and competent; above all, he was another pair of hands. From that moment it was relatively simple. Elin Gundarsson's arms were strapped to her sides, her legs fastened together, and we eased her upward, very still on the end of the line.

If I'd done nothing else, I thought, I'd earned myself and Jane a few Brownie points. By now I was back on top of the Natural Bridge, watching water dry in the sunlight, for the king wave had indeed reached the top surface. I was being ignored for the moment as a blond-bearded man talked into a handset, presumably to the submarine, from which a rubber inflatable was being launched. Ignored, that is, except for the far-off rifleman, who still sat patiently in his position of vantage.

Suddenly a Russian stood in front of me making gestures; he was turning an imaginary steering wheel, and then turning an equally imaginary ignition key. I understood. Land Rover needed to take Elin Gundarsson to the boat. Simple enough. The keys were in my pocket: no point in pretending not to have them, because a search would find the gun. Anyway, they couldn't take the Land Rover aboard the sub, so I'd get it back.

Meanwhile, I was looking carefully round for Jane. She had to be here somewhere, but there seemed no sign of her anywhere in that wide landscape. What there *was* was an air of urgency, of packing up. Elin Gundarsson's plight was plainly both serious and important, and they were intent upon moving her fast. I heard the roar and rev of the Land Rover's engine from the car park, glimpsed its roof as it moved off.

I was left strictly alone. Elin Gundarsson lay on the granite, still unconscious, with one man's coat over her and a sweater under her head. She was almost as white as paper, her skin virtually transparent. Concussion, or worse, I thought: that bash on the head as the king wave swirled about her.

We waited, and I glanced at my (still working!) watch. It was not yet 7.30 A.M. The sun shone brightly, the ocean was blue, even up here the breeze was gentle. But no Jane.

A few minutes later, ten or twelve, no more, I could hear the Land Rover returning, and then men came at a run, one of them plainly a doctor, another carrying an aluminium stretcher. Elin Gundarsson was examined, carefully but with urgency: eyes, ears, gentle fingers on her skull. Inflatable splints were then placed over her broken limbs and swiftly inflated from a gas bottle. Then she was lifted on to the stretcher, and two men began to carry her towards the car park, the doctor walking anxiously beside them.

I just stood there. Nobody spoke to me. *Their* priority was quite plain and it was the swift evacuation of Elin Gundarsson. Okay by me, except . . . where the hell was *my* woman, where was Jane? Possibly they'd taken her aboard the sub. Yes, it *was* possible, but unlikely, considering the sequence of actions. They'd landed from the sub hours ago. I kept remembering that faint line on the water I'd seen while I waited for Jane outside Whaleworld. I'd thought it a whale or a shark. It *must* have been this party coming ashore! They'd seen us, or seen the Land Rover anyway, and followed us *on foot* because they'd no other means to do so. Four miles? An hour or so of brisk walking. On that walk they'd encountered Jane on her run, and taken her prisoner. Would they then have detached two of their party to take her to the sub? Somehow *that* seemed doubtful. So she was probably held in open country, somewhere between here and Whaleworld.

While ropes were being coiled by the two remaining men, I set off quietly after the stretcher party. The rifleman, two hundred yards away, was also moving off. Still no one spoke, or signalled to me. I hurried along the pathway across the granite rocks and reached the otherwise deserted car park, just as one of the Land Rover's back seats was being lowered to admit the stretcher.

The doctor was closing the door, nodding briskly, anxious to be off. I rushed now straight to him, and said, 'You took a woman prisoner. Where is she?'

He turned and looked at me uncomprehendingly. Blond-beard, who seemed to be in charge now, climbed out of the driving seat, stood in front of me, and said, 'Go, or we kill.'

I grabbed him by the shoulder. 'I saved her bloody life!' I said. 'You've got *your* woman. Where's *mine*?'

Total lack of communication. Clearly he'd already expended his entire English vocabulary. He shrugged me away, powerfully. Tried, anyway. I was clinging to his coat with no little desperation. Hands grabbed me. I was flung to the ground and then they were all piling into the Land Rover. Fumbling in my pocket as I lay there, I pulled out the Makarov 9mm. There was a way to hold them up. I applied the muzzle to the nearside rear tyre and pulled the trigger, and listened to the bang and the hiss.

I was scrambling to my feet as they all poured out of the vehicle. 'Where is she?' I shouted, waving the Makarov. 'What have you done with her?'

Blond-beard swore. He swore in Russian, but I know a curse when I hear it. Then he barked an order and one of them reached inside the Land Rover and brought out a rifle. He raised it, levelled it at me. I could see the black little eye at the end of the barrel, could see the tightening index finger of his right hand on the trigger. About a square foot of the man was visible, the rest hidden by the Land Rover. I fired a hopeless shot at him, and missed, of course, and then another, and that missed, too.

Or had they missed? Because something strange seemed to be happening now. The rifleman's elbow had rested on the car bonnet. Now he rose to his feet, standing tall for a moment, then toppled slowly to the side. The rifle clattered down, and as he fell there seemed to be some kind of pole attached to him.

And then it dawned on me quite quickly that, however briefly, the Makarov gave me command of the whole situation. Normally I think more slowly than that. This must have been adrenaline caused by unexpected survival. I had to get the rifle, though. I dodged quickly round the bonnet. The rifle was trapped beneath the body of the man who'd held it, and two other people were competing to wrestle it free. One was blond-beard.

The other was Jane!

It was a lot to take in in one instant, as the men straightened and their hands were raised in the air on my order. Jane was wide-eyed, and tense, and then suddenly she was smiling a little, and then smiling a lot, and I saw what the pole was that protruded from the dead rifleman's back: it was a whaleman's harpoon!

'You?' I said.

'Lots of skill,' Jane said.

22

If, in the end, we were quite unnecessarily chivalrous, Jane's generosity of spirit was responsible. I could cheerfully have turned the rifle on the lot of them, but she took it from my hands, only saying musingly, 'AVS 36 Simonava. That's unusual,' as her hands moved on knowledgeably, and there were little clicking noises as bullets slid into breeches and it became ready to fire. No resistance from anyone. Her competence was clear.

Jane now walked around to the rear and pointed to the spare wheel. She didn't speak Russian, or need to; they understood and the wheel was briskly changed.

To me she said, 'Either we let 'em go or we have a major international incident. Think about it: Soviet sub in Australian waters, gunfire from naval party ashore. Russian sailor killed by harpoon. Don't think we want all that, do you?'

I looked at her. 'When you say "we"?'

'Australia,' Jane said.

'Not to mention the British, eh?'

'I didn't mention them, did I?'

'So off they go, is that it? And nobody any the wiser?'

'That's what I think. What about you?'

'I'm none the wiser,' I said.

'But you are. I can see it in your eyes.'

'Later, Jane.'

We left it at that. Later it was. In the meantime the Russians did their own spring-clean. Everything was loaded, ropes, men, including the dead man, and the Land Rover drove off.

'We walk, do we?'

'Nice morning for a bit of exercise,' Jane said, smiling at

me. 'We can walk, and we can talk a bit, get things clear in our minds. Does it appeal?'

'Yair. Appeals a lot.' I held out my hand and she took it, and we set off like that, towards the Gap. From the iron balcony there, we watched a few minutes later as the big inflatable, loaded to the gunwales, emerged from the direction of Frenchman Bay and began to make for the submarine. Soon everything was loaded aboard and it began to submerge and soon after that there was nothing. The ocean shows no scars. 'I reckon they've gone for good,' Jane said. She tossed the automatic rifle down into the Gap with a laugh. 'Give me a kiss,' she said. So I did.

We met pretty well everybody in the course of the next hour or two. With the sub gone, Alex and Joe Hag had brought *Abrolhos Lady* in to Whaleworld at Cheynes Beach and we could smell cooking bacon at about half a mile. They spotted us walking down the road and came ashore to say hello, and look for news. I told them everything, with one little exception: I didn't mention Peterkin's concreting work on the Porker, not to them, not even to Jane, not to anybody. I'd now taken Peterkin's place as custodian of the secret, the only difference being that it didn't seem to be so dangerous a secret any more, if only because nobody knew there was a secret except me.

So when, eventually, on the way back to Albany from Whaleworld in the good doctor's Land Rover, we encountered the American man and woman who'd chased me all over Bradford weeks earlier, we simply stopped politely, told them everybody, including the Russians, and including us, had given up the hunt because the trail had run out, and apparently we convinced them, too. It must have been our light-heartedness that did it. We were happy, we must have looked happy, even to them, who probably didn't encounter much in the way of happiness, ever. They simply shrugged, turned their hired Ford around, and went away. It was all very easy. Strangely easy. I had offered to show them the leaves and perhaps that offer was itself what convinced them, because they didn't take it up.

I was thrilled and delighted by my own juvenile cunning. It was over now, the great adventure. Everybody was dispersing. Jane intended to stay in Australia for a few days, but she'd turn back into Major Strutt pretty soon, and hurry off home to serve Her Majesty once more on the far side of the world. That was why I hadn't told her about Peterkin's sand-and-cement legacy, his hard-core secret. Because it concreted her to me. I only had to whistle . . .

It was a bit more than a whistle, to be truthful. There were steps to be retraced, *my* steps, and before I could retrace them, I had to work up enough nerve and get the help of somebody I could trust – Bob Collis to be exact – and let a few weeks go by, in case my innocence was not as widely accepted as I imagined. I passed the time playing fair, sending the remainder of Peterkin's money and the golden leaves back to Alex, and so on.

Late March, when everything that had happened seemed well behind us, so far back as to be almost unreal, I flew to meet Jane at Whistler Mountain, British Columbia. It's a nice half-way house between Perth and London, and there's first-class skiing. It seemed like a good idea, and only three hours from there to Las Vegas if anybody should suddenly decide to get married. I had it worked out: dinner *après ski*, candlelit, romantic etc, etc. Let a couple of happy days pass by first, then the close, as the salesmen say.

I never got the chance. Second afternoon, just at the top of the ski lift, I was putting my skis on my shoulder when a cultivated English voice murmured something in my ear, and I turned my head to see who'd spoken, and there stood Sergei in bilious mixed colours and a woolly green ski cap with two purple bobbles on it.

'You said something?'

'What I said was, it's not a coincidence.'

Jane had looked around by this time, smiling. He gave her a little bow and wiped the smile off her face at the same time. 'Ah, the good major,' he said.

'What do *you* want?' Jane's tone was the crisp one.

'Your time. I'm at Chateau Whistler like you. Come round at six, I'll have a pitcher of very cold, very dry Martinis making little clinking noises. Room 237.'

I said, 'I don't think so.'

'A drink?' Sergei looked me in the eye. 'What's it cost you?'

'There's no such thing,' I parroted sententiously, 'as a free Martini.'

Left to myself, I wouldn't have gone near him, not with a thirty-foot pole in one hand and a lion tamer's chair in the other, but Jane didn't see it like that. Jane Strutt, pretty girl on ski trip, had now vaporized and in her place stood the holder of Her Majesty's commission, observing that you never knew, a thing like this could be important, if not to Britain then to Canada, her friend and ally, and, 'I am, in any case, an officer serving in Intelligence.' So that was that. Hers is not a mind one changes readily. At six o'clock, because Jane is also prompt, we were knocking on the door of 237.

To me it all seemed crazy: standing there a minute later in a comfortable hotel room being handed evening drinks by a polite gent who just happened to be a Russian spy. 'Pretzels?' says he after a moment. 'Cashew nuts?'

'For God's sake, Sergei!'

'Well,' he said, shrugging, 'might as well be comfortable. You've been reading the papers, I imagine.'

'Just the cricket scores,' I said.

'Things have changed. Quite a bit as a matter of fact.'

'Well, they laid the new wicket at the WACA,' I said, 'and it's pretty fast and bouncy.'

'But not changed as much,' Sergei ploughed on, 'as you might imagine.'

'Poms get no better, that's the trouble. It's their batting –'

'What is it,' Jane broke in, her voice even, 'that hasn't changed as much as we might think?'

'The entire enchilada,' Sergei said. 'You want to hear a little about it? You should.'

'Go on. Tell me.'

He sat, settled himself, took a pull at the Martini. 'Well, for a start, the KGB isn't what it seems . . .'

And so it went on. Nothing was what it seemed, not populist politicians with silver hair and prodigious thirsts (Stalin in an Italian suit), nor military withdrawal from Eastern Europe (tanks go fast and jet aeroplanes a lot faster, and rockets faster still), nor electoral processes (you can get a PhD in electoral *management*). This wasn't Sergei at all. The incisive, persuasive, suave Sergei was all at once rambling, discursive.

I broke in rudely, 'What do you want?'

He looked at me steadily for a moment. What he was thinking, I didn't know till he spoke. Then he said, 'Out! I want out!'

Jane was brisk. 'If that's the case, then I'm quite sure you must have better contacts than us.'

He nodded.

'But?' she said.

'Resettlement is inconvenient. One has to leave things behind, move into new surroundings, make new friends. It's also expensive, if you wish to be comfortable. Personally, I have no wish to be, for instance, an ageing postman in a place like Yellowknife.'

'Money?' Jane said.

'Money.'

'Have you anything to sell?'

Sergei grinned. 'Just my country.'

'That market's in a slump,' Jane said, 'and continuing on down.'

'Well, yes. But there's always some information that's more valuable than the rest and in addition, and much more relevant, is – well – the Kremlin.' He looked at me as he spoke, just a flick of the eyes, but I felt it strike me somewhere in the chest. I swallowed. The reflex was audible and he grinned again.

'What *about* the Kremlin?' Jane asked in innocence.

Sergei crossed his feet and looked at the shiny toecaps of his shoes. 'There are many things,' he said, 'but two are especially relevant to us.'

'Us?' she said. 'What do you mean – us?'

'Well, I don't mean the intelligence community, such as it is, or may be.'

'What *do* you mean, then?'

'You and me and him, is what I mean.'

I could see it coming; Jane couldn't. But then I hadn't told her yet.

'I've done a little more digging,' Sergei said. 'Know more about you than I once did. A very general picture shows he' – pointing a steady finger at me – 'is a youngish lawyer on the make. *You*' – pointing accusingly at Jane – 'are fairly rich, and you're a career girl, God help you. I am a weary spy with a few thousand dollars in the bank in Geneva and a wish – and, oh, it's a profound wish – to retire from the fray. Champagne taste, Coca-Cola pocket, that's me.' Sergei looked at us. '*He* wants to marry you. *You* make the mistake of believing the parade ground is more important than he is. *He* can't afford you. *I* can't afford to retire. Which brings us, in a straight logical line,' Sergei said, 'to the Kremlin. The Kremlin as palace. Money.'

Jane said, 'But I don't see –'

Sergei looked over at me. 'Been keeping your little secret, have you? Close by name, close by nature, that's you, eh? Tell her.'

Looking into Jane's eyes at that moment was like looking into the business end of a double-barrelled shotgun. They had swung around on to target and widened slightly.

'Tell her, John.'

I said to Jane, 'I was saving it.' Sounded lame, even as I spoke the words.

'Key to the Kremlin door,' Sergei said. 'One of the world's great treasure houses, and guess who holds the key?'

I don't believe I've blushed, really gone crimson, since puberty, but I was beyond crimson then; I was puce or vermilion, one of those extreme shades; Jane continued giving me her look.

Sergei said cheerfully, 'He went back there afterwards, to pick the Duke's Nose, or rummage round the Porker's hindquarters, or whatever, and he got it. Didn't you, John?'

222

No need to answer in words. Jane can read my soul without trying.

'Private entrance, it is,' Sergei continued. 'You can just go in, help yourself, and come out again. Not even any danger, except from accumulated cobwebs, if my conclusions are accurate. And they are.'

Jane stopped looking at me and looked instead at Sergei. I love that girl, but she's formidable. When she gives you that look something passes along it: nerve gas, gamma rays, high tension power, something that pins you down. Sergei was pinned, too, if only for a moment.

'I went to see Kinsky's daughter,' Sergei said, recovering after a moment. 'The little cray-boat one, Alex, and she showed me those leaves, once she was quite sure I'd been sent by the Prime Minister's office in Canberra.' He grinned, rose, and picked up the pitcher. 'Ice is melting. Martinis, anyone?'

'Thank you. I think we prefer,' Jane said, 'to remain sober. Cold sober.'

'As you wish. Personally I feel the need.' With a refilled glass, he sat down. 'Joe Stalin's own,' Sergei said. 'Sounds like a regiment in the British Army, doesn't it? May be one for all I know, but when I say Joe Stalin's own, I'm referring to the treasure.'

I intervened. 'I've been reading up on Stalin. He doesn't seem to have been much interested in private possessions. Held a hundred jobs, apparently, and got a wage packet for every one of them once a week, and never opened any of them.'

'Propaganda,' Sergei said. 'Pyotr Kinsky, whom you call Peterkin, stole gold, didn't he? Well, I can tell you, from long experience, that the man who collects a little gold unfailingly wishes to collect a lot of gold. And what Stalin wished, Stalin could do. Ergo . . . as we used to say at The Queen's College. It was a little fashion in my time,' he added apologetically, 'one of those silly undergraduate fads. Soon faded. Ergo.'

Jane said to me, 'It's fantasy. Come on,' and rose.

I stood obediently. Sergei didn't. He took a packet from

the inside pocket of his jacket and held it out towards her. 'Look at these.'

'No, thanks.'

'Oh, but I would if I were you. They're photographs. Not the usual kind of compromising KGB photographs, of course, but compromising none the less.'

I said, 'What are they?'

'Can't bear to look, eh? Oh, they're innocent enough just to *look* at. It's when the people are identified, when the captions are stuck on the back, you know, that they could be troublesome. Major Strutt in the company of, well, there's me. Then there's – what *did* she call herself? – oh, yes, Elin Gundarsson. Both of us known hoods from Moscow. Phoney name she carried about with her; you should have known that, both of you, and so should the lady. If she *had* been Icelandic, it would have been Gundarsdottir. Gundarsson is a masculine form and Elin didn't *have* a masculine form, not if memory serves.'

I looked from him to Jane and back again. Sergei was cool now, and Jane pale. Initiative seemed to have passed. She said after a moment, in great surprise, 'You're blackmailing me!'

'True.'

'It won't work! I can explain.'

'Possibly. Your department may even believe you in the finish. But in future they'll trust you a good deal less. Let an old spy tell you a great truth. Even if you put in a full, detailed report months ago – and maybe you did – even *then*, and even if they believed every word of it, it's different when they see the pictures. Seen it happen many times. "Look," they say, "there's the major with the Russians. Hobnobbing. Yes, of course we did know, but . . . well, I mean . . . have you seen the expression on her face? The look in her eyes. Not sure she's altogether . . . er . . . are you, old boy, I mean *really*?"'

Even to my Australian ears it sounded like Truth with an initial large T.

'So you badly need *something*,' Sergei went on. 'You see that, don't you, my dear? Have to give the slavering dogs at home a juicy big bone. Which brings us immediately back to the Kremlin, which has more juicy bones than a butcher's shop – especially a Russian butcher's shop.' He gave a merry little smile. 'Then there's murder by harpoon, theft of harpoon from museum, and so on. As for *him*' – this with a mildly deprecatory wave in my direction – 'I don't think he's transgressed the law very far. I mean, he's not a big-time criminal like you, Major. I can't actually coerce him into anything – not by blackmailing him directly. But among his weaknesses, and there are several, the big weakness is you. He'd do anything for you, John Close would.' He looked from Jane to me and back again, smiling a little. 'And he *will!*'

We wriggled a lot for several days, but Sergei had the hooks in and the landing net waiting and he pulled us in like fat trout.

He took photographs of us, there and then, before wishing us good night and *bon appétit*. Two days later there came a little packet, addressed to me, at Chateau Whistler, with a Victoria BC postmark.

I looked at it carefully. Jane and I at this point were like a couple of nervous horses who'd been tricked into harness by a cunning horse-coper, and were about to be paraded in the ring: we were ready to bolt at the first opportunity, but opportunity never came, and meanwhile we felt the harness straps biting deeper all the time.

'Who do you know in Victoria?' Jane asked.

'Nobody,' I said glumly.

'I'll bet it's Sergei, damn the man!'

It was. And he must have had resources in the provincial capital. Two passports: red-plastic-covered EC passports. We were Irish, it seemed, Jane born in Killarney, me somewhere called Kenmare, which the library atlas later showed to be a few miles away.

We kept looking at those passports. It's a terrifying thing to find you are suddenly somebody else, no option, your own identity gone; more frightening yet when you add *that* to the realization that you're under *control*; and the fears were piling up on each other. We were actually going into *Russia!*

225

An article in *Time* magazine that week reported the Gulag still existed: unknown tens or even hundreds of thousands still suffered in Arctic detention camps. Russia might *seem* to be breaking apart, might *seem* to be poor and half-starved, and becoming more liberal by the minute, but they kept popping satellites into orbit and stamping with heavy and bloody boots on certain protest activities within her borders. However fast life was changing, there was still enough violence around – and there would certainly be enough members of the old guard left – to make our adventure very risky indeed.

I said often to Jane that Sergei was probably all bluff, that he couldn't do it. 'What would be the point,' I argued, 'of having you put in gaol in Australia? And, anyway, he couldn't *do* it. They took the body away with them, when they took Elin Gundarsson. There's no evidence at all. Even if the harpoon were known to be at the bottom of the Gap – and for Christ's sake who's going down *there* to look for it – it would either be washed clean or pounded to matchwood.'

Jane remained unconvinced. 'Sergei's very smart. He knows everything, either by finding out or by some process of understanding. There'll be evidence. There were certainly *witnesses*, weren't there? You know – you're *one!*'

'But I'd never –'

'Maybe not.'

'*Certainly* not!'

'Oh, John, he could actually end up killing us – both of us!' The strong, self-confident, stainless-steel Jane, unaccustomed to subservience, was beginning to come a bit unstitched under it as the days went by. She'd been in danger before; she'd been a prisoner before, but she'd never been in a situation like this in her life – free to walk, talk, ski, do anything, but held ready to jump into a very hot frying pan at Sergei's order.

Which came quickly. Tickets, instructions, details, delivered in another little packet, this time by one of those express parcel services, and from Manchester of all places. Jane opened it, since it was addressed to her, and began thumbing through the bits of paper.

'Balkan Air,' she muttered, 'to Varna – that's in Bulgaria, isn't it? One of those airline vouchers for two seats on three-day excursion to – oh, *John*!'

I hadn't seen Jane cry in earnest before. For that matter, I wouldn't see her cry again; now, travelling, she sat pale-faced and withdrawn for ten hours to Manchester, four more to Varna, six to Moscow. It was like travelling with a zombie. And Sheremetyevo Airport, when eventually we reached it, isn't a reassuring place. Fly into Perth or Vancouver, you sense sunshine and good humour, cheerful people enjoying themselves. In London or Rome what you sense is enormous prosperity. In the Moscow terminal the air itself seems weighed down with menace. Rigid shoulder boards of the waiting border-guards, an immigration officer in a cubicle so designed you can only see his eyes and nose, but he can see all of you. And he stares flatly for endless long seconds and you wonder what to do with your eyes and your hands. Not a word spoken. Entry visa stapled to the passport, it's handed back. No smile, no word of welcome. Just the eyes. Suitcase searched: everything out, everything looked at, replace it yourself. I remembered Sergei's comment that things in Russia had changed quite a bit, but not as much as we might imagine.

We got to the Hotel Rossiya in a cab, queued to register, were stared at wordlessly, resentfully. The feeling of threat persisted everywhere: in the lift; in the corridors, presided over by tough-looking old women with faces of stone. Subjective maybe, but *there*.

'I have to get *out*!' Jane said, rather desperately. 'I *have* to!'

We left our bags and just went.

Red Square draws like a magnet. We left the Rossiya Hotel by a side entrance, but in the street everything flowed in one direction, traffic, people – it was like a river. I didn't want to go into Red Square, but there was simply no alternative. A parade of kids was to take place next day, and the Square had been decorated and readied.

It was smaller than I'd imagined. You tend to think of it

in terms of huge columns of tanks and armies of marching men, but that's distortion by camera: Red Square is not exactly intimate, but it's on a human scale. Willy-nilly that night, Jane and I shuffled along with the crowd. In other cities, it would have been cheerful. Here it was sombre: expressionless faces, mumbled talk. We didn't talk much either; we hadn't talked much for days. Jane hung on to my arm, an action miles out of character, and wore worry-lines at her eyes. I remember only one decent human moment, when an American lady, one of a group, suddenly tapped Jane's shoulder, and said, 'Haven't you a map? You must have a map. We have several. Here, take this!' Having spoken, she simply went back to her friends. Nice.

I said to Jane, 'Bet she's Sergei in drag,' but didn't raise a smile and didn't feel like smiling myself because we were now approaching the Kremlin wall close to the Saviour Tower. We turned right now, still in the grip of crowded humanity, on a pavement that would take us between the red lump of Lenin's Tomb, and the immensely solid strength of the high wall that guarded the vast fortress itself.

I hadn't intended it. We were just there, carried along by the pressure of people. Ahead a row of statues was coming into view under the fir trees, and Peterkin's instructions were running through my mind . . .

Bob Collis and I had each secured a rope, then we'd each checked that the other had done the job properly. We were up on top of the Natural Bridge in the deserted early morning of what was clearly to be a beautiful day. I wore a climbing belt, with hammer and stone chisel in it, and proper boots with moulded gripping soles. And when all was done, and there was no remaining excuse for delay, I had to abseil down there again, to the Iron Duke's left nostril. I didn't want to, but Peterkin's shade kept turning up in my mind, urging me to do it. So eventually I did it. Twenty minutes later, I was back on top, panting with relief, and clutching the small torn plastic bag which Peterkin had cemented into the rock. Hands trembling a bit, I ripped it open.

23

We would encounter Sergei somewhere that night, we thought. His instructions had been explicit, and been followed; our rooms were the ones he'd reserved for us, the date was the date specified.

No Sergei.

We walked, expecting him to appear any moment, to be suddenly there, in the way Sergei had, murmuring in our ears.

He didn't appear and we walked on, past the statues behind Lenin's Mausoleum, past the graves in the Kremlin wall, the great names of the Soviet Revolution, Kirov and Kalinin, Dzerzhinski, chief of secret police, Vishinsky the prosecutor – names to make anybody's blood run cold, even if they're all long-dead. Lastly, Stalin himself, lying right there, the greatest mass-murderer in world history, a title contested only by Mao Tse Tung. We paused a moment, looked briefly at that moustachioed face with its marble eyes, and moved on. Lenin might be discredited, but the queue to enter his tomb stretched out into Red Square sixty or seventy metres, then ran diagonally across to the St Nicholas Tower, well marshalled by guards, and left well alone by the mooching crowds.

High above, one on each of the Kremlin's main towers, there still glowed the bright red stars of Communism, brilliant against the dark night sky. 'The colour of blood,' Jane muttered with a shudder.

On we went, map in hand, towards the looming shape of the State Historical Museum, then down the remarkably steep little hill to the Corner Arsenal Tower, and still the queue to see Lenin stretched ahead of us. Round the corner, now, and here, surprisingly, were gardens. The guide map

229

named them. These were Alexandrovskii Gardens and ahead of us across our path two towers linked by a bridge: the left one the enormous Trinity Tower.

As indicated by Peterkin.

And our target. But not tonight, it seemed. All the same, walking by I could see the patch of black shadow. I said so. Jane wasn't interested.

I increased the pace, hoping exercise would stimulate something in her. She kept up effortlessly, but remained quiet and withdrawn as we walked the whole way round the Kremlin Fortress. I found myself wondering what dark cell I would find myself in next night. What Jane was thinking – well, I had no way of knowing.

We returned, by way of a long, chilly walk along the bank of the Moskva River, to the unmistakeable domes of St Basil's Cathedral, then Red Square, and the hotel.

Still no Sergei. Nor any message.

Next morning, Jane was still in her strange, silent mood, offering nothing in the way of talk. She ordered her food, and ate it, with every appearance of normality but that was all.

I didn't dare ask at reception if there was a message for us, for fear of alerting attention. Sergei would contact us. He'd said so, and would have to do it, though I was beginning to nurture a hope, as the morning went by, that something might have happened to Sergei – accident, injury, arrest – and that when our flight left Moscow tomorrow evening, we would *still* be innocent Irish tourists, resuming a holiday.

Meanwhile, we went to the Park of Culture and Rest, the Space Museum, and to a long lunch – long because the service was unbelievably slow.

Jane remained in her almost trance-like state. And still no Sergei.

In the middle of the afternoon, I took out my wallet to pay for two ice creams, and found a cigarette tucked into the fold. Since I don't smoke, never have, and don't carry cigarettes to hand out to others, it was pretty noticeable. Furthermore it was a Russian cigarette, hollow cardboard tube and all.

In the tube was a piece of paper, a Western-type cigarette paper, and on it the words *Ordzhonikidze, 8 P.M.* Sergei was evidently skilled in pickpocketry. I said, 'Who, where or what is this Ordzhonikidze?'

'Friend of Stalin. He had him murdered.'

We killed time. Had some food early, then went out, Jane doing everything dully, as she had for days now. What her heart was doing I don't know; mine was thumping and my hands trembled; I was sweating. It seemed unbelievable, but was nevertheless stark fact: *we were going to break into the Kremlin!* As human activities go, you'd be hard pressed to find one less likely! Or more hazardous.

Neither Jane nor I read Russian, and the names on the statues were in Cyrillic. Sergei plainly had thought of that: Kirov was a short name; Ordzhonikidze was the longest name in the line of statues. We stopped to look. No Sergei. But then it was only two minutes to eight.

At eight precisely he strolled by, not looking at us. He was whistling as he walked, and the tune, trust Sergei, was 'Advance Australia Fair'!

Peterkin's instructions, characteristically obscure, now hung around my neck on a gold chain. I'd dug from the cement on my second trip down the side of the Natural Bridge a two-ounce bar of gold. Pure gold: the Perth Mint's chop stamped into one side of the bar proved it. When I turned the heavy little thing over in my fingers, there was a crude drawing scratched into the blank, flat surface.

We followed Sergei obediently into the Alexandrovskii Gardens. Beside the Tomb of the Unknown Soldier he paused and took off his hat respectfully, standing until we came level, then walking beside us. 'The next one is Middle Arsenal Tower,' he said. 'Trinity is the big one with the red star.' The colour of blood again, I thought, praying the blood would not be mine.

There were few people about now, the roadway largely deserted. I said, fear rusting my voice, 'At least it's quiet.'

'Be not deceived,' Sergei said. 'This is Moscow. Move slowly into the trees. We're out for an aimless walk.'

We found a wooden park bench and sat while Sergei smoked a cigarette, then we rose and moved on. 'There are guards,' he said, 'on all the towers and at all the entrances. You two are lovers, behave like lovers.' So, arms around each other's waists, we went through the arch of Trinity Bridge. I pulled Jane into the shadows on the other side and kissed her. With Jane in her strange mental state, though, this time once was enough. Over her shoulder I saw Sergei jerk his head, and move to his right. We followed softly. This was the period of maximum danger. In front of us now was the great Kremlin wall, lighted and guarded along its entire length. But close to us was a freak of lighting, a patch of shadow that must have been designed and put there on Stalin's personal order. We stepped into the shadow like a courting pair, with Sergei playing gooseberry.

I looked for Peterkin's indicated rectangle, and sure enough there it was, a darker patch in the shadow. Now the leaf! I ran my eye along the courses of ancient bricks, wondering what the leaf would be made of: steel, or some other metal, pottery, what? Whatever it was, I couldn't see it. The faces of the bricks just seemed to meld indistinctly into one another, none clear. I was looking at head-and-shoulder height, looking carefully at each brick in the rows. But nothing showed. Until . . . again it was a trick of the light – an angle changed and there it was, perfectly clear, and no more than a slight colour variation in a single brick. But there was no doubt – it was the outline of a leaf.

I swallowed. Up until this moment there had been a possibility that we had been living a fantasy of Peterkin's, made up of elements of his strange life. Even the golden leaves could have been a part of it: Peterkin had moulded gold before.

But now . . . I looked at Sergei. His face was set and his eyes glittered; no trace of his lazy grin now. Jane's face was pale, almost inanimate. 'Righto,' I said, and pushed at the brick. It didn't move. I pushed it to the left, to the right, downward. 'Nothing,' I said.

'Try up,' Sergei said. 'Stalin was a small man.'

I pushed upward with my fingers at the face of the brick, and felt movement. Not much, a few millimetres, no more. But then in the patch of shadow, a deeper darkness showed itself. Behind me I heard Sergei exclaim, and said, 'What is it?'

'The lights are out.' I glanced along the wall. It was true. 'Quick,' I said. 'There's a door!'

We were through it in a second, like bunnies into a burrow. The door must have had some timing mechanism built in, because no sooner were we through than it was closing automatically behind us, a movement of such strength and power that it shoved Sergei sideways. For a moment we stood in total darkness, there within the great wall itself, fear coursing through us. It flashed across my mind that we were now literally walled in, as per the horror stories. Then there was a whisper of sound, and lights came on along the walls beside us.

I looked thankfully up at those lights, covered as they were in the dust of forty years: they had once shone down on Stalin and on Peterkin, and probably on nobody else at all except the doomed German engineers who put them there.

Sergei, ever-practical, said, 'Steps up. Steps down. You go up. I'll go down.'

For once I was assertive. 'We stay together,' I said. 'And upstairs must have been his bedroom. Peterkin described going downstairs when he made his escape. That brought him down here, to the door.'

So we went down.

It was a dusty, cobwebby world. Where we'd come through the door, the structure had been, if not exactly new, at least not worn. Recent construction. On these stairs we were in an altogether older world, steps and walls of stone. 'One of the secret passages,' Sergei whispered. 'Napoleon got out via one of them.'

'This one?'

'Rumour says there are several. Some very ancient.'

We went on down. At the foot of the stairs, a heavy wooden door faced us. I put my hand on the handle and turned. It opened freely. 'No lock, no key,' Sergei said. 'Hardly believable given the old bastard's character.'

The room was primarily an office. Comfortable, leather chairs, a big, pleasant desk. Maybe study would be a better word.

I said, 'Better have a look round, hadn't you, for all the treasure that'll make you rich?'

'Patience, think about booby-traps. Remember this was Stalin's. Anything we touch is likely to blow up in our faces!'

I stood still, watched him and put my arm round Jane's shoulders. She wasn't trembling, as I was; she wasn't anything, except still. I tried to make her sit on the edge of a cabinet, but she resisted.

Sergei, meanwhile, was opening the drawers of the desk.

I looked carefully round the room, my mind full of the terrifying, cruel tyrant who had occupied it, and knowing something about him by now. There are many biographies, and I'd read a few, read of the paranoia, readiness to have people arrested, tortured, murdered, but never face to face. The 'Wonderful Georgian' who destroyed all but a few of his friends and comrades out of pathological suspicion. Yet a man of fairly simple personal habit. Here in this room was no great ostentation or luxury. The place was at best comfortable.

'Bit like a London club, isn't it?' Sergei was straightening, holding something in his hand.

'What have you found?'

'A key. Question is, what does it fit?'

There was a door in the wall behind the desk. Opened, it revealed a bathroom and lavatory, which Sergei looked at and said, 'Vacuum flush, you see. Imported from America.' There was an old, cracked bar of soap, some towels, a shaving brush and a cut-throat razor. Nothing else. The toilet paper was American too!

Back in the study, I looked at the dark side table that ran the length of one wall, much of its surface full of filing trays with envelopes in them. I picked one envelope up: coarse, brown paper, sealed and heavy. There was paper inside, too, and coins. Plainly a wage packet. But whose? I opened it.

Notes, coins. A name was printed on it. CTAVNH. I said, 'Does that say Stalin?'

Sergei nodded. 'What is it?'

'Wages. Stalin's. The story must be true. There are thousands of these envelopes.'

He nodded. 'You told me before. He had a lot of different jobs and got his pay packet for every one of them. You're not always wrong, are you?'

'Well, he didn't spend it.'

Sergei said, 'He didn't need to. When you're Stalin, everything's free.' Then he grinned. 'Except the people. This door, now . . .'

There were three doors in Stalin's study. The one by which we had entered, the one to his bathroom, and this. Sergei put his hand to the doorknob and turned, and it opened. I don't know what I'd expected, but it wasn't unlocked doors. Sergei's sudden breath showed his relief. 'Like a refrigerator,' he said. 'Open the door, on goes the light!'

There were three steps leading downward inside the doorway. Sergei walked inside. Before following him, I turned to look at Jane. She was still standing with her back to the wall of the room, just inside the entrance. 'All right, Jane?' I said, though clearly she wasn't.

But she nodded. 'You go ahead, John.' Her voice was little more than a whisper.

I hated to leave her just standing there as she was. Though nothing was evident, the whole stuffy place reeked of some nameless menace, a lingering atmospheric trace of the Great Terror.

'Go on,' she insisted, with the first faint animation I'd seen in days. I glanced at her once more, but the little spark had already faded. Reluctant, but fascinated now, I followed Sergei into the lower room.

The first thing to see was a cell door: steel bars, floor to ceiling, blocking off an area about eight feet by eight. Sergei stood in front of it, staring in.

'Bones,' he muttered. 'Look.'

It wasn't *just* bones, not a skeleton as one thinks of a skeleton; it was a body, its flesh dried to husk, and lying on the concrete floor. It had been there a long, long time.

'Who is it?'

'Nice question,' Sergei said. 'Somebody he didn't like.' Nobody could have recognized the body, I thought. The skin had dried to a taut paper-like appearance, stretched over skull and ribs. I looked past the body. The cell contained only a concrete shelf raised on bricks – presumably a bed – and a small chamber pot, which could be removed though a gap in the bars.

Sergei said, 'Raises questions, doesn't it? Like who emptied the pot? Stalin himself, was it? Or did somebody else come down here? And then food's involved, and water.'

'Water'd be from the bathroom,' I said. 'Easy. Food from tins, maybe.'

'I don't see any empty tins, do you?'

'He could have died, whoever he is, before Stalin did.'

'Millions of people went missing. No knowing who this one could be. It's not,' Sergei said, 'as though Uncle Joe was here every day. He'd go weeks, even months, without entering the Kremlin at all.'

I said, 'Then this bloke lived a lovely life.'

'Makes you shudder,' said Sergei, not one of nature's shudderers.

I'd been looking at the walls of the cell. 'No name scratched anywhere I can see.'

'You can't make scratches in concrete with fingernails,' he replied grimly. 'Well-known fact in prison circles. Certainly known to Stalin.'

I turned away, to look at the other end of the room. Overall the room was long and narrow, perhaps twenty-five feet by eight, and another strong grille like the cell door stretched across it. Inside, floor to ceiling, were steel filing cabinets painted dark green. There was only one break in the wall of green they formed, and there a picture in a faded gold frame was fixed to the wall.

'Ikon,' Sergei said. 'Virgin and child.'

'Funny thing to find here. Maybe it's a relic of his days in the seminary, training to be a priest.'

'His mother insisted on the priesthood: but all he learned

there was how to play politics.' Sergei was trying the key in the lock, fitting it with extreme care. 'Could blow up in our faces,' he muttered.

But the key turned smoothly and at Sergei's push the door swung open. As we stepped inside, I glanced again at the ikon, over which a lamp now glowed. Something strange . . . I stepped nearer and saw the big X made by two slashes which ran corner to corner of the ikon. 'Would he have done that? If so – why?'

'Capable of anything at all,' Sergei said. He was leaning close, inspecting the little painting. 'Doubt if this ever had any value; it's crudely done and the frame's just painted, it's not gold leaf.'

'So why's it here?'

'At a guess, it belonged to somebody he hated. But then he hated just about everybody. Leave it, I want to look in the cabinets.'

He began at once, sliding open the drawers in the first cabinet in the left-hand corner of the room. Looking over his shoulder, I could see it was full of files, each with its identifying tab. Sergei raised one, apparently at random, looked at the tab, and said disgustedly, 'Georgian.'

'So?'

'It's another language altogether. Obscure. I haven't a word of it, and hardly anyone else has except another Georgian. Effectively it's a secret code.' He opened the file and riffled quickly through the contents, until he found a photograph. 'Molotov and his wife,' Sergei said, looking up. 'Stalin had her arrested and sent to a camp. Molotov carried on as foreign minister. They lived in an unusual sort of world, eh?' He replaced the file and closed the drawer. 'Historians would kill for this stuff,' he said, opening the next drawer down. More papers. There were four drawers to each cabinet. The third was also full of files. The fourth rattled as it slid out, and contained jars and bottles, most of them empty. Sergei picked up a bottle, looked at it with a judicious eye, and said, 'Local brandy, but what's this?' holding up a jar. It had a cover of paper, bound tight with fine string. He smiled. 'Walnuts. It's walnut preserve.'

I'd read about this. 'His mother used to make it and sent it to him. Dictator's favourite food.'

Sergei gave me a sceptical look. 'Sounds a bit sentimental for Uncle Joe.'

'But true, apparently.'

'We've read different books.' He was closing the bottom drawer, moving on to the next cabinet; its four drawers detained him only moments, full as they were of card files and papers. The third was the same, everything in it perfectly neat and labelled in Georgian. He started on the fourth of the five cabinets that lined the left wall: papers in the top, and in the second, and in the third. He barely glanced at that one, sliding the drawer out quickly, and then in again, but something had caught his eye, and he re-opened it in a hurry. These cabinets were standard filing equipment, made in America: each drawer eighteen inches wide by two feet deep, and in this third drawer files occupied the front foot. Behind them was a parcel wrapped in yellow oilcloth.

'The question is' – Sergei turned to me – 'is it a bomb? Or something equally horrible?' He lifted it carefully, and unwrapped the cloth. Inside lay a book, bound in padded black leather that was worn and torn. 'Georgian, too,' he said.

'Looks like a Bible.'

'It *is* a Bible. Whose, why, and what's it doing here?' Sergei opened the front cover. 'Ah – I can read this much. Keke. That's his mother's name. Must be hers.'

'I thought the Bible was a banned book.'

'It was. But he did as he liked.' He wrapped the oilcloth round it again, and, replacing it in the third drawer, opened the bottom one. This was a repeat of the one above, files at the front, a parcel behind. 'Books again, eh?' Sergei grumbled, picking the parcel out. Heavy enough, anyway. He put it on the flat top of the cabinet, and unwrapped the cloth.

Suddenly, as the covering came away, the thing was gleaming and glowing and glittering in the light: a kind of crown, gold and jewels and velvet. I said, 'Bloody hell!' Then I said, 'Whose, the Tsar's?'

Sergei didn't know and neither did I, and this wasn't a

238

place where you start on the reference books. What *he* did was open all the drawers in even more of a hurry. Speed did no good; he came to the end of the row of cabinets without any other significant find.

That left only the wall cabinets which rested on top, and he began on those. Nothing was to be found there, either, and after a few minutes he swore in disgust.

I said, 'That crown will keep you in comfort.'

'I don't *want* comfort,' Sergei said savagely. 'I want genuine luxury, and a lot of it!'

'There's another apartment up the stairs.'

We went there, and the study/bedroom was almost identical, almost a repeat of the room below: more trays of wage packets, a bottle of iodine on the desk, another blotter on which he had doodled drawings of wolves. What there wasn't was another prison cell, another corpse, another set of private files. Sergei searched where he could: in drawers in the desk and side table; he examined the two pictures on the wall, neither especially good or likely to be of value.

Then there was nothing more. Sergei swore, and I said, 'The crown's not exactly *nothing*!'

He was angry. 'There *was* gold – Kinsky found some. Where?'

I shook my head. 'Must have been here.'

He blinked, obviously thinking. 'Either there's a safe we haven't found yet, or – there's something in the cell where that body's lying!'

'Cell's bare, just brick and concrete and bars.'

'No,' said Sergei. 'The concrete slab rests on a small wall of bricks. It makes a box. Let's go look.' He froze. 'Is that your girl?' I heard a scuffed step on the stairs.

'I expect so.'

It was *not* Jane! A man walked in through the doorway. He had a thin, hard face and determined eyes, and he carried a gun built on a substantial scale. He spoke sharply in Russian. Sergei raised his hands. After a moment, I did the same, and then Elin Gundarsson came through the door. She was equally well-armed, and her face, like the man's, was set hard. She gestured with her machine pistol for us to move into a corner. The man, meanwhile, was looking carefully around the room. In a moment he went back to the door by which we and he had entered – it still stood open – and closed it. When he did so, the door simply disappeared and became part of the wall; the side of the door on the inside of the room was of bookshelves, perfectly matched to those on the wall itself. He stepped close and tapped at it with his knuckles, then with the pistol butt, listening. There was no hollow noise that I could hear. He said something to the girl.

Sergei said to him, in English, 'Yes, that's how they got out.'

'They?' Elin said.

'Kinsky when he escaped. Joseph Vissarionovich on his evening strolls.' He turned to me. 'The woman you know. The man is Yuri Anastasovich Gusenko, joint deputy chairman of the Komitet –'

'Be quiet.' The man Gusenko spoke for the first time. He continued looking round him, a man in at least his middle sixties, seventy even, but fit and well. His hard face wore a strange expression of mixed anger and disappointment and it wasn't hard for me to read his thoughts. All these years – nearly fifty – he'd sought to answer the puzzle of his partner Pyotr Kinsky's disappearance from this place. And had never solved it. In Gusenko's mind it must by now have turned into something almost mystical.

Now at last he knew the answer, and that answer was, to him, mundane: a mere secret passage in an ancient wall.

'Didn't you look for this passage?' Sergei asked Gusenko.

'We looked.' Gusenko spoke to Elin in Russian.

'Says it's like an airlock,' Sergei translated for me. 'Indistinguishable. Sealed completely. Paranoia, he says. Well, we all knew that.' He remained relaxed as he always did; though like me he must have been acutely aware how easily we could all die in here, with nobody any the wiser, like the corpse in the office below.

And as if that thought of mine had been a cue, Gusenko said to me, in accented English, 'How did he leave Soviet Union?'

'Kinsky?'

Gusenko nodded.

I gave him the summary: 'Skis, out of the city,' I said, 'then a train. He just kept going. In the finish, he walked over the mountains into India.'

'Impossible!'

I said, 'He fought a bear on the way, once. And won. He ate it!'

Sergei said, 'Always wondered, haven't you, Yuri Anasta-sovich? And now you know. Now we *all* know. So what next?'

'You were looking for things to loot,' Gusenko said con-temptuously.

'Yes, and there isn't much.' Sergei's tone was defiant, even humorously resentful. 'You'll have an enjoyable month or two reading, *if* you read Georgian, and you're still out of gaol, but that's all.'

'Where?' The question was snapped.

'Chamber below. Haven't you seen it? Like this one. Exact copy –'

Elin Gundarsson glanced a question at Gusenko and when he nodded, crossed to the door. She couldn't open it. Nor, when he tried, could Gusenko. The door's edge couldn't even be discerned, so perfectly did it fit into the surrounding shelves. Meanwhile Sergei and I stood hands-up. Finally, as my arms began to ache, Gusenko turned and said, 'How?'

I had no idea, and told him so. We'd opened the door from outside, from the stairs.

'How did Kinsky open it – he must have told you?'

'No,' I said. 'When he got out of here, Stalin himself had left the door open. But I expect *you* can get out into the Kremlin the other way.'

Gusenko said, 'I can, yes. And Major Gundarsson. But you'd be killed on sight –'

'Unless you vouched for us,' Sergei offered.

Gusenko smiled, not prettily, and shrugged.

I said, 'Let me look at the door,' and when they didn't demur, I walked across the room and began to look at the books – at their spines anyway.

I saw it almost at once, at chest height, a black book with

a gold leaf embossed on its spine. No certainty that it was the key to the door, but it might help to know and not mention it. 'Cleverly camouflaged,' I said. 'Done by the German engineers, that's what Peterkin said.' I turned to Gusenko. 'What happens now?'

'You go to prison,' he said, 'to a camp.'

I said, 'I thought the camps were closed, now.'

He smiled again, and shook his head. 'Some are all closed. There are enough still. For you, one in the arctic Kamchatka, perhaps.'

I felt the shudder run through me. Until this moment it had all been a bit like acting in a play – unreal, feigned, false; it had felt impossible that Johnny Close from Perth could be *in actuality* in the Kremlin itself, about to be sent into the Gulag! The man who stood opposite me now actually *was* one of the great butchers of the Red Terror. There was much to shudder about!

And Jane. *Where* was Jane? God, was she gone already?

I said angrily, 'Where have you taken Jane Strutt?'

They looked at one another, and it was perfectly clear from their expressions that in the movement of events, they had forgotten her.

'Where is she?' Gusenko snapped.

'Other side of the door,' I said. 'Where you can't get at her.'

Elin gave me a pitying look. 'There's no such place – no place where Yuri Anastasovich cannot reach. Even in Russia as it is now, there is still need for a KGB.'

Gusenko, as she spoke, had turned again to the bookshelves that concealed the door and was systematically moving each book in turn, lifting and twisting. I pointed at him. 'Portrait of a man of power,' I said sarcastically. 'Can't even open a bloody door.'

He turned, furious. 'I'll have *you* behind a door that will *never* be opened,' he said slowly.

I thought of Jane two floors down, and wondered what she might be doing, but it was impossible to guess. With the old Jane it would have been easy; she'd be already on the other side of the door, armed in some way, prepared to act. But the old Jane was not a presence; now she was lethargic and dull. She might still be leaning against the wall of the office two floors below, staring at nothing.

Gusenko still pulled at books, working his way along each shelf, systematically and vigorously. And now, suddenly, there was a click and the door swung open, outward into the stairway. He gestured with the hand cannon he carried, and said, 'Down.'

Sergei went first, then Elin with her pistol dug into his back, then me, and Gusenko behind me. There must have been fifty steps between Stalin's two rooms, with the small landing halfway down where the outside door led into the shadows beside Trinity Tower.

There was still no Jane, nor any sign of her on the stairs, not on the landing, not even when our little armed convoy got to the bottom and filed through the doorway into Stalin's secret office-cum-bedroom where Gusenko, now speaking in English, presumably for our benefit, said to Elin, 'Keep them here. Any trouble – shoot them.' She nodded, and Gusenko went alone through the door into the file room. He left the stout door open and we could hear sounds as he moved about, searching: a key turning, the drawers of filing cabinets sliding in and out, his footsteps on the floor.

Then his head appeared in the doorway and he spoke, in Russian this time, to Elin. Sergei translated for me: 'He recognizes the body. It's Vlasik.'

'Who he?' I said.

'Shut up!' This from Elin.

'Stalin's butler,' Sergei went on as though she hadn't spoken. 'Evil brute. Must have crossed the boss in some minor way.'

'I will shoot at the next word from either of you,' Elin Gundarsson said, meaning it. She really was astonishingly beautiful, and equally astonishingly chilling, the perfect features cold and hard as stone.

So we stood there in our little triangle, listening to the sounds Gusenko was making beyond the door and worrying, in my case, about where Jane might be. There seemed only two possibilities: she was either in Stalin's private bathroom, or she had stepped out, through the Kremlin wall, back into the shadows and the Alexandrovskii Gardens . . .

We must have been standing there ten minutes or more when there was a sudden sliding sound, followed by a single metallic bang that seemed to echo on almost musically, and then Gusenko called something to Elin and she frowned.

'He's raised the cell bars,' Sergei muttered, and translated again as she turned her head to call back, 'What cell bars?'

'Come on, move.' Elin's pistol waved to us to back against the wall further away from where she now stood, in the doorway. A moment later, satisfied with our position, she turned her head, watched Gusenko, and gave a sudden exclamation.

'She said, "Be careful, Father,"' Sergei murmured.

I said, 'So he's –'

'It would seem so, yes.'

She kept giving us quick little glances of warning, but it was plain enough her attention was focused on Gusenko, not us. I did wonder briefly if a quick dash might succeed in disarming her, but Sergei was policing my thoughts. 'Don't be a fool!' said he.

And then came the yell and – no, that's *not* right! What came, all together more or less, was a new metallic sliding noise, and a bang, also metallic and echoing, but louder than the one we'd heard earlier, and all this was *accompanied* by the yell which, in truth, was half yell, half groan. And all of it despairing.

'*Nyet, nyet!*' Elin cried, and, ignoring us, dashed through to the long, narrow room, where her father was.

'The old bastard left something behind, bet your best boots,' Sergei said. 'That was a nasty noise.'

'Let's go see,' I said.

'What, unarmed?'

'But you're not unarmed,' a reasonable voice behind us said. A female voice! Jane's –! She said, 'Here,' and handed Sergei an automatic pistol. He worked the slide familiarly as I said, 'Where?' and Jane said, 'I had a good look round while you were up there.'

'You all right?'

She smiled and said, 'Perfectly, thank you.'

Gusenko was yelling now, his shouts louder and full of fear, and as I crossed the room I heard Elin's voice.

Sergei had reached the doorway first, and now he stepped down into the room. As I followed, the yelling changed in its very nature, became a low, gut-wrenching, despairful moan.

24

What it could all mean beyond the simple fact of obvious, stark terror, I had no idea, until I'd descended two steps and could see into the room. The sound then became understandable, for now two men were behind the cell bars; the long-dead Vlasik had been joined by Yuri Anastasovich Gusenko, and it was from deep in Gusenko's belly that the groans of despair were coming.

Inside the cell he was gripping the bars on his side and striving to lift the whole steel grille. Elin Gundarsson was doing the same on her side, both of them straining with effort. The combined strength moved it not a millimetre.

Elin turned her head. 'You – and you, take hold and lift,' she said. 'Use all your strength. All of it. We must raise the bars!'

'What happened?' I asked. 'How did he –?'

'Disappeared upward,' Gusenko said, grunting. 'The whole grille went into the roof.'

'Something triggered it,' Sergei offered. 'What was it?'

'I moved the ikon to the side,' Gusenko said. 'Then the bars rose up and I came in and raised the slab there, the one on the bed.'

'And down it came, eh?' Sergei said.

Gusenko shook his head rapidly from side to side. 'No, no. In the bottom' – he gestured at the bed, its lid down now – 'in the bottom there's gold – a bar of gold. When I bent to pick it up, the whole grille crashed down.'

'So there's a mechanism,' Sergei said. He turned to me. 'Go move the ikon over there.'

'Not me,' I said. 'There's another grille over there. You do it.'

'Nor me,' Sergei shook his head.

'You *men*!' Elin turned, enraged. 'You're cowards. He could die!' She stamped angrily across the floor into the file room. Then, after hesitating briefly, reached up to touch the gold-painted frame of the ikon. Nothing happened, except that Gusenko called, 'Push to the right.' Now Elin did so, and then leapt back out of the file room, for another sliding sound now began. As we watched, almost in disbelief, a two-slab section of the floor slid to one side, right where I stood, and I damn near fell into the hole! Not that there'd have been any room for me – for that space beneath the stone floor was full. I know my jaw fell open, because I felt it drop. The hole was full of treasures! I don't know, really, whether that word should be singular or plural. Treasure implies lots of things jumbled together, doesn't it? Well, these were treasures – objects of great value, one beside the other, packed into the six-foot by two-foot space. Even as my eyes ran over them and my mind struggled to absorb what was happening, I recognized two objects: one was a Tsar's crown; and there was another I had been reading about quite recently. It was the golden headdress from the treasure of Troy: the one Heinrich Schliemann had put upon his wife's head, and photographed her wearing!

But behind us a voice was shouting, 'Leave that, leave that! Lift the grille! The grille!'

I looked at Sergei. Sergei looked at me. He said, 'Like all of them, wouldn't you say – good at dishing it out, not so good at taking it.'

Elin jammed her pistol at his head, and screamed at him. Then she screamed at me. Then she laid the pistol on the floor and seized the grille herself. It remained immoveable. Gusenko was chanting, 'One, two, three, lift!'

It did no good at all.

Then Elin did the obvious thing. She said, 'I'll get help.' She was turning towards the door when there was yet another yell from her father. We'd all had our eyes on Elin; now we turned back to Gusenko. He was holding out his hand, staring incredulously at something in his palm: a few fine grains of something golden.

247

His head tilted back and he stared upward at the ceiling high above him, and he yelled a word.

'Sand?' Sergei said. 'Why sand?'

But sand it was, dropping in a thin stream from up above, a stream not much bigger than the one you'd see in an egg-timer. But as we watched, it thickened. First the stream was merely the thickness of a needle, then of a pencil; soon it was the thickness of a cricket stump, a golden, falling, hissing rain of sand that was now beginning to spread across the floor. Suddenly Gusenko jumped back, staring at the floor, leaving behind him two footprints in the sand. They were filled even as we watched.

'I'll go!' Elin turned again to the door. But now there was another stream of sand, falling at the rear of the cell. The soft, almost silent whisper of the falling, myriad grains was enormously loud, because all of us were silent and appalled. We knew what it was we were seeing. This was Gusenko's death: the cruel death planned for a man imprisoned to be buried alive; but more – this was Stalin's vengeance from beyond the grave; this was the punishment for fracturing the dictator's privacy, even forty years after his death.

We all stood rooted now, looking up at the holes in the ceiling from which the sand was coming. Soon it was falling from a dozen of them, and when I glanced at Yuri Anastaso-vich Gusenko, joint deputy chairman of the KGB, he was gripping the bars of his cell and the sand came up nearly to the top of his soft leather boots. Now, all through the long, narrow room, piles of sand were growing on the floor, separate for the moment, but soon they would join, and the level would rise and submerge everything within its space.

Beside me Sergei muttered something I didn't catch. 'What did you say?'

He gave a brief, chilling grin, and jerked his chin towards the doomed Gusenko. 'Never knew Stalin believed in justice,' Sergei said. 'Listen, we'd better be getting out!'

He turned to the hole in the floor. Then began to look around him. 'A bag,' he said. 'I need a bag.'

But there wasn't a bag. Nor was there a sheet on Stalin's bed, and certainly no time to try to find one. For the streams of sand were yet thicker now and it was pouring in among the treasures in the floor. Sergei dropped to his knees and began scrabbling with his hands, pulling things out of the sand, handing them to me, then digging again, like a terrier trying desperately to find things before everything was buried.

Elin, meanwhile, hadn't moved. It must have been as plain to her as it was to me that there was no chance at all of saving her father. Gusenko would be covered within a few minutes, and there could be no hope of bringing help in time, even if help could achieve anything. And that was unlikely, for Stalin had chosen the ancient, the *certain* way of defending his secrets; the way the Pharaohs had defended their tombs, with sand running the moment a thing was moved, and blocks of stone moving as their sandy supports disappeared.

Christ! I thought, and looked up. Before my astonished eyes, part of the wall was sliding inward, quite slowly, but unmistakeably.

'Out!' I shouted. 'Everybody out! We'll all be buried!' I pointed at the moving block, not stone, but concrete, the modern material just as lethal as the one the Pharaohs had trusted.

'Here, take this!' Sergei said, handing me a piece of chain-like jewellery that flapped as I took it. The Trojan headdress! I shoved it inside my shirt, then moved to the door, still burdened with six items from Sergei's sandy excavations. He was beside me at once.

'Go!' he said. 'The whole place may be coming down.'

I turned for a final look. The sand, entering faster within the cell where it had first begun to fall, was up to Gusenko's waist. He was already firm in the grip of death. And in front of him Elin stood, a yard or so away, with sand flooding through the bars and settling around her, already up beyond her knees.

How could we leave her?

Sergei, the thought policeman, read my mind once again. 'Impossible,' he said. 'She says she won't leave him.' She was gripping her father's hands on the bars, repeating like a mantra, a simple phrase over and over. 'Together for ever, that's what she says,' said Sergei.

Then, as I watched, I was shoved to one side, violently, and somebody went by me – Jane. Sinking almost to her knees with every step she took, she came up behind Elin Gundarsson, put her thumbs hard and certainly on the pressure points in Elin's neck and, as she collapsed, began dragging her bodily towards the door.

'Going to leave her, were you?' she demanded of me, looking contemptuously at the treasure piled precariously in my hands. 'Prefer all that, eh? Now, help me. One arm each!'

I don't know quite where women get their moral authority, but there's no question they have it, or that it works. Sergei and I obediently took one of Elin's arms apiece and pulled. Jane, on her knees in the sand, dug Elin's legs loose again, and we got her to the door. I took one last look back. The sand, now flooding in in great golden streams from a dozen points in the ceiling, was beyond Gusenko's waist, and he had stopped screaming and raging, was no longer hysterical. He stood now, straight and still, and above the whispering of the falling sand, called 'English woman!'

Jane turned.

'Thank you for my daughter,' said Yuri Anastasovich Gusenko, and saluted.

Beside me Sergei was now digging again, scrabbling for the treasures Jane had made him drop. But by then it was almost too late. We got out, but the door was now impossible to close, for despite the steps sand was spilling outward already into Stalin's office. Jane had Elin over her shoulder in a fireman's lift and was holding her hand out to me as she struggled to wade through the rising sand. I seized and pulled and called, 'Sergei!' and he seized and pulled too, and slowly, gradually, we dragged them through the door.

Now sand was falling into this room, too, already ten or twelve inches deep, with the streams thickening. I tried to take Elin, but Jane wouldn't release her. We hurried across to the door – still open, thank God! I'd been terrified some other cunning mechanism would have walled all of us in here. Through it, then, to the stairway leading up: and no falling sand here, thank God! But it was on and in our shoes and our clothes. Every step we took was to the crunch of sand that fell from our clothes. Behind us though there was only silence, for the dry, falling grains made insufficient sound even to carry the few feet we had travelled.

As we raced up that long stairway, I tried again to take the unconscious Elin from Jane and was again rebuffed. A man, and therefore not to be trusted, that's what Jane's bitter glance told me. She didn't speak – hadn't the breath; carrying another human being up a long flight of steps is killing work; even when the burden is a beautiful eight-stone girl, she still weighs a hundredweight.

So Jane was labouring. I was beside her, wanting to help. Sergei was striding energetically ahead, two steps at a time. He reached the landing while we were only halfway up and turned to watch us, and I could see in his hands a regal crown and a long, dangling necklace of diamonds and rubies that flickered and glowed with brilliant shafts of light refracted from the overhead bulbs on the landing.

Yes, he turned. And until the day I die, I shall remember the look of astonishment on Sergei's face, and hear his shout. It made me turn my own head, and I saw that behind and above us the great concrete slab that made a roof for the lower half of the stairway, was sliding downward, lowering itself, and none too slowly, to a position where it would cover the entire flight of steps.

We had only seconds! 'Quick!' I shouted.

I literally grabbed Elin, forcing Jane to one side, and began to run. Jane stumbled, but bounced back to her feet, and ran beside me. Above us we could almost feel the pressure of the slowly lowering giant slab of concrete that would crush us within a few more seconds if we failed to reach the landing.

There were ten steps, then eight and six and four more, and then the thing actually touched my head! Its angle now made running impossible and I flung the limp body of Elin from my shoulder on to the landing where Sergei grabbed and broke her fall. Then I dived, literally dived like a free-style racer, for safety, and Jane dived beside me and we hit the hard floor and rolled and behind us, with a soft thud, tons

– dozens of tons – of concrete slipped neatly into position.

I got to my feet and looked. There was a line in the floor beneath my feet where the edge of one concrete slab met the edge of another, but that was all. Nothing whatever remained, apart from ourselves, to indicate the existence of the secret places far below. There would be no echoes to indicate hollow wells, for sand would fill the spaces. And Yuri Anastasovich Gusenko, servant of Stalin, murdered by the dead Stalin as he murdered so many servants and friends while he was alive, was buried eternally as any ancient Egyptian grave-robber trapped in the secret chambers of the Pyramids!

So we stood there. We were breathing hard, all of us, and stunned with a kind of disbelief that it could all have happened. For we stood now not on a landing, but in a corridor. There were no steps down; just an empty space between high walls.

And a door. I opened it cautiously and we stepped out into the fresh air. The lights on the Kremlin wall were out. As the door swung to behind us, they came on again, but we were still in our patch of darkness.

Elin was giving little groans. Sergei had picked her up and carried her through the door. Now she was coming round, he set her on her feet and she stretched and rolled her neck, and said something in Russian. Consciousness was back, and needed to be back, because moments later another, louder voice, also speaking in Russian, issued a harsh and peremptory challenge: not Who Goes There, but something along those lines, and she drew herself up and stared down her superb nose at an officer and four men of the Kremlin Guard and spoke her own name and that of her father, and they all snapped to attention. They examined her identity card, as they were entitled to do, I expect, but after that it was all salutes, and this way, please.

And that's the story really. Major Elin Gundarsson GRU, orphan and beauty, knowing that between us we had now saved her life twice, eased our journey out of Russia – Jane's and mine, that is. How Sergei got out I don't know, except that he did, because months afterwards, in faraway Perth, I got a picture postcard. On the picture side was The Queen's College, Oxford, and on the other my address and the words, 'moderate luxury'.

Jane and I flew back to Bulgaria as the Irish tourists we still pretended to be, and we had our holiday on the Black Sea beaches. As we left Moscow we didn't, thanks to Elin, have to pass customs, as everyone else does, and I still had Schliemann's Trojan headdress tucked into my shirt. Jane asked on the plane, what did I intend to do with it?

'Well,' I said, 'there's Christie's, and Sotheby's and I'm sure there are collectors all over the pl–'

And she said, 'It belongs to a German museum, John.'

So I bowed to the inevitable. Except that officialdom decided *they* rather than I should return it, and return it, furthermore, to officials on the other side of the North Sea. In return for official favours, of course, and they're still in negotiation about those.

But one day soon you'll see it in the papers: just a bald story about the Trojan headdress being back in the Museum of Pre and Proto History. But they'll certainly leave out all the interesting details.